A MILITARY EXPERIMENT GONE WRONG

She glanced toward Osten's left arm where the symbiont was attached, but as she did so, its length unfurled toward her, and its coils wrapped around her throat. She instantly tightened her neck muscles before it could squeeze too hard, yanked her boot free from Osten's hand, and spun around, intending to bring her sword up and strike at the aberration.

A PROUD SOLDIER TAINTED BY CORRUPTION.

But before she could do so, she watched in horror as the tentacle whip's mouth detached from Osten's arm, anchor tendrils tearing free from his flesh with tiny sprays of blood. Then, using its grip in her neck for leverage, the whip flexed, bringing its mouth-end swinging toward Lirra's left arm.

A WARRIOR BECOMES A LIVING WEAPON.

It happened so swiftly that she had no time to react, and then the beaked mouth bit into the inner flesh of her forearm and its anchor tendrils burrowed into her skin, seeking purchase in the muscle beneath.

Lirra screamed.

AND THE BATTLE FOR LIRRA'S SOUL BEGINS.

THE ABYSSAL PLAGUE

From the darkness of a ruined universe comes
the source of a new evil . . .

Follow the story from its very beginning with
The Gates of Madness, a five-part novella prequel
by James Wyatt

Part one is included in
FORGOTTEN REALMS®
The Ghost King by R.A. Salvatore.

Part two is included in
DUNGEONS & DRAGONS®
The Mark of Nerath by Bill Slavicsek

Part three is included in
DARK SUN®
City Under the Sand by Jeff Mariotte

Part four is included in
FORGOTTEN REALMS
Whisper of Venom by Richard Lee Beyers

Part five is included in
EBERRON®
Lady Ruin by Tim Waggoner

Bear witness to the worlds-spanning DUNGEONS & DRAGONS
event beginning in March 2011 with
DUNGEONS & DRAGONS
The Temple of Yellow Skulls by Don Bassingthwaite

EBERRON

TIM WAGGONER

Lady RUIN

LADY RUIN

©2010 Wizards of the Coast LLC

Published by Wizards of the Coast LLC

EBERRON, DARK SUN, FORGOTTEN REALMS, DUNGEONS & DRAGONS, WIZARDS OF THE COAST, and their respective logos are trademarks of Wizards of the Coast LLC in the U.S.A. and other countries.

Printed in the U.S.A.

Cover art by Erik M. Gist
Map by Robert Lazzaretti

First Printing: December 2010

9 8 7 6 5 4 3 2 1

ISBN: 978-0-7869-5625-8
ISBN: 978-0-7869-5810-8 (e-book)
620-24744000-001-EN

U.S., CANADA,
ASIA, PACIFIC, & LATIN AMERICA
Wizards of the Coast LLC
P.O. Box 707
Renton, WA 98057-0707
+1-800-324-6496

EUROPEAN HEADQUARTERS
Hasbro UK Ltd
Caswell Way
Newport, Gwent NP9 0YH
GREAT BRITAIN
Save this address for your records.

Visit our web site at www.wizards.com

For generations, all the world of Eberron knew was war. The five nations—Aundair, Cyre, Breland, Karrnath, and Thrane—clashed long after the warring heirs of Galifar had died, allying and attacking as the tides of battle shifted. Then the Mourning—an atrocity no nation claimed—wiped Cyre from the face of Eberron.

THE TREATY OF GALIFAR ENDED THE LAST WAR.

Though the war is over, the world abounds with reminders of a magical arms race, the spectacular technology born of magic and ambition. The influential dragonmarked houses ply their magical skills in trade instead of weapons. The warforged, a race of living constructs, strive to find a place in a world that resents them. The lightning rail and the elemental airships that once sped weapons across Khorvaire now haul goods and travelers.

THE TREATY OF GALIFAR REDREW BORDERS

Where once a sprawling empire claimed the continent, disparate nations now clutter the landscape. Only four of the Five Nations still stand. Warrior elves defend their ancestral lands in Valenar. Goblins and monsters have established kingdoms of their own and demand recognition. Rebels take old grievances to the streets, and the dragonmarked houses gather power in secret. And no one has forgotten the old hatreds.

THE TREATY OF GALIFAR SPURRED DIPLOMACY

In the shadows of the cities and on the frontiers of the fledgling nations, a new kind of hero arises. They are veterans of the Last War, looking for closure. They are spies tasked with protecting their realm from new threats and old. They are inquisitives investigating crimes, trying to make a living while avoiding the state's attention. They all want to forget the Last War . . .

BUT THE LAST WAR WON'T FORGET THEM.

THE NEXT WAR IS BREWING.

DEDICATION

For Mark Sehestedt and Erin Evans—one at the beginning, one at the end.

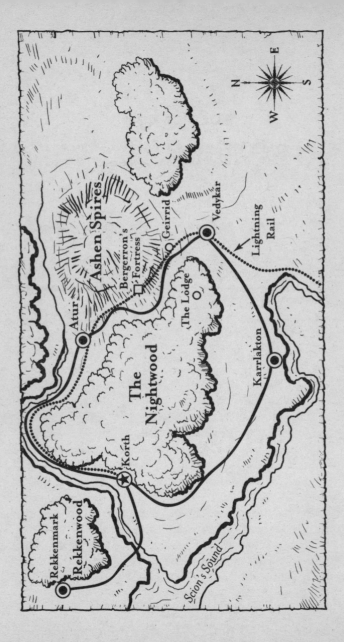

CHAPTER ONE

"Whenever you're ready, Osten," Captain Lirra Brochann said.

The man nodded, his brow furrowed in concentration. Coiled in his right hand, the tentacle whip pulsed softly as blood—a mixture of its own and that of its host—circulated through the symbiont's rubbery red flesh. The barb at its tip quivered slightly, as if it enjoyed the taste of Osten's blood and looked forward to sampling someone else's—namely, Lirra's.

Two men stood on opposite sides of the room, swords belted at their sides, hands resting on the pommels of their blades. One was a handsome man in his late twenties, close to Lirra's age, while the other was a white-haired lion of a man in his mid-fifties. General Vaddon Brochann, the older man and Lirra's father, wore full armor with a series of runes engraved upon the breast plate, while Rhedyn, the younger, wore only a mail shirt over a tunic and leggings. Despite the illumination of the everbright sconces set along the cold, gray walls, the younger man's features were indistinct. Still, Lirra didn't need to be able to see his face clearly to know that he—like Vaddon—watched the fight intently, ready to step in at the first sign that something was about to go wrong.

Osten's eyes narrowed in concentration and sweat beaded on his forehead. He was a boyish-looking man with a shock of midnight-black hair cut by a white streak on the left side.

1

While Osten was barely into adulthood, his broad shoulders and strong limbs hinted at the man he would one day become. Osten was serving two years in the Karrnathi military, as was mandatory for every citizen in the country—man and woman—and he had the makings of a fine soldier. At least physically, Lirra thought. Mentally . . . well, that's what they were here to find out.

Osten stepped forward, and as he did so his left eye twitched and his lips moved, almost as if he was talking to himself, but no sound came out. Though he was young and strong, his movements were stiff and awkward, as if he were having trouble controlling his limbs. Or as if he were *fighting* to maintain control, Lirra thought. A distant look came into his gaze, and she knew that his focus had turned inward.

"Hold," she ordered. If he didn't have full control . . . But it was too late. With a sudden motion, Osten extended his right hand and released the tentacle whip.

Lirra kept her gaze fixed on the barbed tip as the fleshy coils of the whip straightened and extended toward her. The barb streaked toward her right eye, and she could see a bead of poison glistening on the tip. A tentacle whip's range was roughly fifteen feet, and Lirra stood about that distance from Osten, but she wasn't about to take any chances. She drew her head back, leaned to the left, and brought her wooden sparring sword up to deflect the attack.

But at the last instant before it struck the sword, the barb angled sharply downward and shot toward the hilt—or more precisely, toward her hand. If the whip managed to pierce her flesh and inject even a low dose of its poison into her, she'd be incapacitated and completely at its mercy. And if it managed to get a full dose into her, only the blessings of the Sovereign Host would be able to save her life. She knew Osten wasn't trying to harm her—at least, she *hoped* he wasn't—but the tentacle whip had a mind of its own. She released her grip on the sword and yanked her hand away an instant before the whip-barb struck the weapon's leather-wrapped handle. The sword's wooden blade pitched toward Osten as the force of the whip's strike flipped the handle toward Lirra. Lirra was already in motion, though, and she caught hold of the sword in an overhand grip with her left hand and she managed to keep her weapon from falling. Then with a flip of her wrist she swung the sword in a downward arc and struck the tentacle whip. The symbiont recoiled from the blow and retracted toward its host, giving Lirra time to shift her wooden sword back to her right hand.

She retreated several steps and regarded Osten. Sweat ran freely down the man's face, despite the fact that he'd put forward little physical effort so far. The tentacle whip undulated in the air, like a sea plant moving to the rhythm of an underwater current. Lirra had the impression from the easy, almost lazy confidence of its movements that, whatever effort Osten was putting into their internal struggle, the tentacle whip was winning.

"Osten," she said, "stand down."

The man's head jerked slightly when she spoke his name, but otherwise he didn't reply, didn't even acknowledge her existence. His gaze remained clouded, unfocused, and his lips continued to move as he whispered silently to himself. Lirra could just make out the shape of a single word, repeated over and over: *No. No, no, no, no, no . . .*

Without taking her eyes off Osten, she gestured with her left hand, a signal to Vaddon and Rhedyn to make ready. She then lowered her wooden sword to her side and started walking slowly to Osten, speaking in calm, even tones.

"I think you've made a good start, Osten. That initial strike was clever. Even if for some reason you didn't manage to inject poison into the hand, the blow itself could cause someone to lose hold of their weapon. The precision with which your

3

symbiont can strike is one of its greatest assets, as you've amply demonstrated today. What I think we need to do now is continue to devise ways to best use that precision in battle. I have a few ideas . . ."

Lirra came within striking distance of Osten while talking, raised her sword, and swung it toward Osten's left temple, aiming for the white streak in his hair and—

The tentacle whip lunged toward the practice sword, wrapped around the wooden blade, and with a single, savage yank tore the weapon free from her hand. She caught a momentary glance of Osten's face—eyes wild with dark joy, mouth stretched into a feral grin—before the symbiont brought the sword swinging back around toward her. Lirra managed to twist to the side and take the blow on her right shoulder, but the tentacle whip was far stronger than it looked, and the impact sent her flying.

Training took over and she rolled as she hit the floor, using her momentum to bring her back onto her feet. She remained upright only a split second before instinctively diving forward into a somersault. She felt more than heard the sound of the wooden sword slicing through the air where her head had been an instant ago. As she rolled into a standing position, she drew a dagger from inside her right boot and spun around to face Osten—or rather the symbiont, because that was her true opponent. Osten's personality was still there, somewhere inside his mind, but he was no longer in control of his actions, and that changed everything.

Osten's features were twisted into a mask of fury, his eyes bright with madness, and he moved toward her with a sinuous grace that contrasted sharply with the awkwardness he'd displayed only moments before. The tentacle whip hurled the practice sword aside—directly at Vaddon, as it turned out, who was approaching Osten from behind, sword in one hand,

dagger in the other. A single slice from
was enough to cut the wooden blade in
rate halves clattering to the stone floor.

Not for the first time since joining th
marveled at a symbiont's ability to percei
ings despite an apparent lack of sensory orga   ..en's back
might be to Vaddon, but the tentacle whip still knew the
general was approaching.

Lirra risked a quick glance to Rhedyn. He moved more
swiftly than her father, and it appeared he was within a half-
dozen yards of reaching Osten. But a shadowy skein rippled
across his body, making it difficult for Lirra's eyes to focus on
him clearly. He might've been closer than that, or perhaps farther away. Rhedyn had drawn his sword and held it gripped
tight in his right hand, and he stretched his left hand out as if it
were a weapon in and of itself. Vaddon continued approaching
Osten as well, features set in an expression of grim determination, but he was farther away than Rhedyn. Not that it made
much difference how close either of them were, Lirra thought.
Neither could reach Osten before his—or the symbiont's—
next strike. The wisest thing for her to do would be to put
as much distance between herself and Osten as she could, to
give herself the few extra moments necessary for Vaddon and
Rhedyn to move in close enough to help her.

But she remembered something one of her teachers at the
Rekkenmark Academy had once told her: *You can run from
danger, but you can't run from yourself.*

She grinned. She'd never been one for making the safe choice.

Rhedyn shouted for her to stop as she ran toward Osten, but
she ignored it. Lirra had fought enough battles to narrow the
focus of her attention to a single objective. In this case, getting
close enough to Osten to slam the handle of her dagger into the
side of his head and render him unconscious. The man wasn't in

his own actions right then, and she'd spare his life if ...ɔle. But Osten had known the risks when he'd accepted the symbiont, and if she had to slay him, she would.

Osten's left arm flexed upward, and the tentacle whip coiled back into his waiting hand. He then swung his arm around and released the whip again, its length unfurling toward Lirra as she ran to him. She dodged to the left and the barbed tip of the tentacle shot past her, but a half second later she realized her mistake; the whip hadn't intended to strike her directly. The end of the whip curled down, approached her from behind, and wrapped around her right ankle. Osten yanked his left arm back, and Lirra's leg was pulled out from beneath her. She fell onto her left side and hit the stone floor hard enough to force the air from her lungs. Sharp pain stabbed into her side, and she thought she might've broken a rib or two. She still had hold of her dagger—a Karrnathi soldier didn't release her weapon until she was dead, and maybe not even then—but stunned as she was, the blade did her little good at the moment.

The tentacle whip coiled loosely around her right wrist and its barbed tip continued slithering through the air toward her face. She feared that the whip intended to inject her with poison, but instead it wrapped around her neck. Then the coils around both her wrist and her neck tightened, preventing her from wielding her dagger while at the same time cutting off her breath.

She reached up with her left hand and clawed at the coils around her throat, but her fingers could find no purchase on the symbiont's rubbery flesh. The coils constricting her neck were tight as iron bands, and they were growing tighter by the second. Gray began nibbling at the edges of her vision, and flashes of light sparked behind her eyes. A deep lethargy swept through her, and she knew she had only seconds of consciousness remaining. She focused the last remnants of her rapidly fading strength and continued tearing at the coils around her throat. She knew it was hopeless, but she would keep fighting until she could fight no longer.

Everything went black for an instant, but then she felt a shudder pass through the coils around her throat, and the pressure eased enough for her to draw in a gasping breath. Before her vision could clear, she grabbed hold of the coils and began yanking them off of her. As Lirra struggled to sit up, she saw a blurry outline of a shadowy figure standing between her and Osten, with the midsection of the tentacle whip gripped in one hand.

She understood what had happened. Rhedyn had used the corrupting touch imbued by his own symbiont to stun Osten's tentacle whip, thereby saving her life. She unwrapped the last of the limp coils, careful to keep the barbed tip away from her skin. Osten stood staring at Rheydn's shadow-shrouded form, as if he were having trouble seeing it—or perhaps he saw it, but in his weakened state of mind he didn't understand what he was looking at. All signs of the fury that had gripped him were gone, leaving only confusion in their wake.

"What . . . happened?" he whispered.

Osten didn't see Vaddon coming up behind him, and Lirra's father couldn't see the expression on the other man's face. Lirra tried to call out a warning, to tell her father that Osten was no longer under the influence of the symbiont, but her voice refused to work, and all that came out of her mouth was a soft croak. The general's own features were horribly calm as he stepped up to Osten, raised his sword and brought it slicing down onto the man's arm where the symbiont was attached.

Osten screamed, and Lirra's fragile hold on consciousness evaporated.

CHAPTER TWO

Warm healing energy spread through Lirra's side like liquid sunlight, suffusing skin, muscle, and bone, washing away pain as it mended. The sensation was so soothing that Lirra found herself drowsing, and she nearly started when a soft feminine voice spoke a single word.

"Better?"

Lirra opened her eyes and looked up at the speaker, a lithe middle-aged woman with large green eyes and pointed ears whose blonde hair held only a few strands of gray. "Much. Thank you, Ksana."

The half-elf smiled. "You're most welcome." The cleric removed her hand from Lirra's side, and the warmth dissipated. Lirra started to sit up, but the half-elf gently yet firmly pushed her back down onto the cot.

"Best to lie still for a few moments longer," Ksana said. "A bit of rest will do you good."

The bedroom window was open and the curtains drawn back, allowing the late afternoon sunlight to filter into the infirmary, along with a pleasantly cool breeze. The wind felt soothing on Lirra's skin, but she was especially grateful for the sunshine. Summers in southern Karrnath were cloudy more often than not, and sun was always a welcome sight.

Lirra looked at the cot where Osten lay, eyes closed,

hands—both of them; Ksana had managed to save his arm, she noted with relief—folded on his stomach. The tentacle whip was gone and he was alive, but despite Ksana's attentions, the young soldier's skin was pale and his breathing shallow. His clothes had been exchanged for a simple white robe—a good thing, considering how much blood had been on them. At first Lirra had no idea if the man was conscious, but then she noted the way his eyes moved erratically beneath his closed lids, saw his facial muscles jerk and spasm. He was sleeping then, but from the look of it, not sleeping peacefully.

"Will Osten recover?" Lirra asked.

Ksana's expression grew more serious. "Yes . . . despite your father's best efforts to kill him." She shook her head, though Lirra couldn't tell whether she did so in frustration, admiration, or a combination of the two.

"He was just trying to protect me."

"Of course he was," Ksana said. "Vaddon is never more dangerous than when he thinks you're in trouble."

Lirra started to reply, but she bit back her words. She knew Ksana wasn't mocking her father. Ksana had served with Vaddon on numerous campaigns, and she'd been around so often while Lirra had been growing up that she was like a member of the family. When Lirra's mother Mafalda had been killed during the Battle of Jaythen's Pass when Lirra was just a child, it had been Ksana who'd helped Lirra through her grief. And the cleric had done the same a few years later when her brother Hallam fell at the Siege of Thiago. Ksana might tease on occasion, but she would never mock someone she cared for.

"The boy's strong, which is a damned good thing considering the state he was in when he was brought to me. After Osten lost control of his symbiont, your father ordered the creature be removed from his body. It wasn't an easy—or a neat—process with the boy unconscious, but your uncle and his"—her upper lip curled in disgust—*"assistant* helped, and in the end they managed to detach the tentacle whip. Unfortunately for Osten, his injuries were so severe that being weakened like that nearly killed him. If I hadn't been there to tend to him as soon as the symbiont was removed . . . Well, it was a close enough thing as it was, and let's just leave it at that. He will recover, though even after the blessings of Dol Arrah, it may yet be a couple days before he regains his full strength."

"Thank the Host," Lirra said.

Ksana smiled. "As always," she said, but her smile quickly fell away. "Would that I could heal his mind as easily as I mended his flesh. Being bonded with a symbiont can take a heavy toll on the host's mind and spirit. Vaddon told me what happened during Osten's test. I won't know for certain what sort of damage it might have done to his mind until he awakens." Ksana turned to regard Lirra.

"The situation got out of hand today," she said. "You're lucky you weren't injured more seriously than you were. Attempting to control symbionts is a chancy proposition under the best of conditions, but Osten—"

"Nothing personal," Lirra interrupted, "but I'm bound to get a lecture from my father about what happened today. I don't need one from you too."

The cleric scowled and was about to reply when the infirmary door opened and Rhedyn stepped into the room. His shadowy aspect wasn't drawn so tightly around him at the moment, and his features were clear—handsome face, chestnut-colored hair brushing his shoulders, neatly trimmed beard, and piercing blue eyes—though even with the sunlight from the open window, he still appeared partially cloaked in shade. He smiled as he walked over to the two women.

"Good afternoon, Ksana. I see you've managed to keep our Lirra alive for yet another day."

"That's *Captain* Lirra, to you," Lirra said in a mock-stern voice.

Rhedyn smiled as he executed a half bow. "Of course. My apologies." As he straightened, he glanced over at Osten and his expression became grim. "I suppose he'll recover as well."

Ksana gave Lirra a last look before turning to Rhedyn. "You don't sound too happy about the prospect."

"Osten failed to maintain control of his symbiont, and in so doing, he placed Lirra in great danger *and* forced the general to nearly take his life."

"Try not to judge Osten so harshly," Lirra said. "It's not an easy task to resist a symbiont. You know that better than most."

The shadowy sheen surrounding Rhedyn's body darkened slightly, and the effect caused his blue eyes to appear dark gray. "It's precisely because I know what that struggle is like that I *can* judge him. Osten didn't merely hesitate due to the symbiont's influence, nor did he simply fail to make it obey his commands. The tentacle whip took him over completely, both body and mind. Osten was the puppet, and the symbiont was the one pulling the strings."

Rhedyn was a few years older than Lirra, close to thirty, and like her, he'd been trained at the Rekkenmark Academy. He was a nephew of Veit Bergerron and, since the warlord had produced no children of his own, that made him a potential heir to Bergerron's lands. Despite his noble upbringing, Rhedyn didn't act as if he were better than any other soldier, and he was as skilled as any warrior she'd ever served with.

She admired how well Rhedyn controlled his own symbiont—a shadow sibling—although she had to admit that she found herself at times uncomfortable around him since he'd joined with the creature.

"Osten's failure is as much my fault as his," Lirra said. "I'm the one that recommended he be considered for a symbiont."

She looked over at the young man once more, self-conscious to be talking about him as if he weren't there. But Osten was still sleeping soundly.

"He was a good choice," Ksana said. "He's young and strong, and don't forget, he volunteered willingly. *And* your uncle interviewed him thoroughly before approving him."

"And it wasn't as if he received just any symbiont," Rhedyn added. "That tentacle whip is particularly strong and willful. It will make a powerful weapon . . . assuming a suitable host can be found."

"I suppose you're right," Lirra conceded. "Thanks for stepping in to help. If you hadn't stunned the tentacle whip . . ."

"I could hardly stand by and allow my captain to be killed, could I?" Rhedyn smiled. He started to reach out to touch her hand, but then paused, as if thinking better of it. Before he could withdraw his hand, she reached up and clasped it. His flesh felt cool and too smooth, like a serpent's, and she had to force herself to keep holding on.

Rhedyn smiled gratefully and gave her hand a gentle squeeze before releasing it.

"What happened to the whip?" Lirra asked. "Was it damaged?"

"Not permanently. After I stunned it, your father's sword blow weakened Osten to the point where the whip could fight no more on its own, and your uncle was able to detach it from Osten's body. Elidyr and Sinnoch are making sure that the symbiont is returned to its cage as we speak."

Lirra remembered capturing this particular aberration. She often led the hunting parties that journeyed into the Nightwood in search of symbionts. Osten's tentacle whip had a presence that was stronger than most. It radiated a sly, baleful intelligence that Lirra found daunting, and in retrospect, she wasn't all that surprised that the creature had proved too much for Osten to handle. She wasn't certain Rhedyn would've been able to master it, and he had already proven that he could serve as a host to a symbiont without having his personality overwhelmed.

"I hate to do this to you," Rhedyn said, "but the general sent me to bring you to the den. He wants to, and I quote, 'Have a few words with that rock-headed daughter of mine.'" He turned to Ksana. "He'd like you to come too, cleric—and he's summoned Elidyr as well. Not Sinnoch though. I don't think your father cares for the dolgaunt."

That was understatement. Vaddon absolutely loathed the creature.

Ksana glanced at Osten, who still slumbered fitfully.

"I'd prefer not to leave Osten's side," she said.

"The general was most insistent," Rhedyn said.

Ksana sighed. "What else is new?"

"Osten's well liked among the Outguard," Lirra said. "I won't have any trouble finding a volunteer to sit with him so you can attend the meeting."

Lirra sat up and swung her legs over the side of the cot. The movement made her feel a touch lightheaded, but the sensation soon passed and she was able to stand without difficulty.

Her father had summoned them all. She knew it had to have something to do with the reason why he'd insisted on being present during Osten's test, but she couldn't imagine what it might be, and there was no way to guess. Her father was a man of many moods, and she'd never been able to predict them with any degree of accuracy. One thing was certain though. Whatever Vaddon wanted, Lirra doubted she was going to like it.

"Gently now. I don't want this one hurt."

Elidyr stood watching while a pair of soldiers attempted to wrestle the tentacle whip into its cage. The soldiers—one man, one woman—wore full armor, including helms and visors, that had enchantments embedded in the metal by Elidyr to repel a symbiont attack. Even with the armor, there was still a risk that a symbiont might be able to attach to the wearer, especially if the symbiont was strong and determined. But it helped to cut down on the danger.

Neither of the soldiers showed any sign of having heard the artificer's words of caution as they continued fighting the thrashing, writhing symbiont. Though the tentacle whip made no sound—indeed, it possessed no capability of doing so—the air in the chamber was charged with tension, and the other captive symbionts moved about restlessly in their cages. The soldiers wielded devices Elidyr had specially designed for handling symbionts—metal poles with retractable cable nooses. Both ends of the tentacle whip—the barbed tip and the mouth—were held tight by the nooses, allowing the Karrns to drag the symbiont across the stone floor to its cage. Though someone unfamiliar with symbionts would've thought the whip fought fiercely, Elidyr knew the whip was putting up only a token fight, weakened as it was by Rhedyn's attack and the forced removal from its host. Still, its struggles were strong enough that it might injure itself if its handlers weren't cautious.

The hooded brown-robed figure standing beside Elidyr sniffed in derision.

"It seems the reputation you Karrns have for bravery is somewhat exaggerated. Not only do your people need to wear armor to handle one symbiont, they also need *enchanted* armor." The dolgaunt spoke in a phlemgy, whispery rattle, his voice a sickening parody of human speech.

"I'd speak more softly if I were you, Sinnoch. Your presence in the lodge is tolerated only because I've interceded with my brother on your behalf. But his sufferance is not without limit, and if he heard you speaking of soldiers in his command like that, he'd run you through without a moment's hesitation."

Sinnoch sniffed again, but he said nothing more. Sinnoch's robe was large on his almost skeletal frame, the voluminous hood and long sleeves concealing the dolgaunt's inhuman features. There was movement beneath the cloth over Sinnoch's shoulder blades, sinuous and serpentlike, indicating Sinnoch's true nature. Elidyr didn't know if the movement of the shoulder tentacles was an unconscious gesture on the creature's part, or if he did it on purpose to remind all within eyeshot that he wasn't human. Given the chaotic thought patterns of Sinnoch's kind, it was impossible to know for sure, perhaps even for Sinnoch himself.

Elidyr Brochann was a middle-aged man with an unruly mass of white hair badly in need of trimming. Elidyr was reed thin—almost as thin as the dolgaunt. The artificer had a tendency to remain motionless until such time as movement was required, and even then he moved with a deliberate precision and economy of motion that said he was a man who despised waste of any sort. He wore a leather apron over a plain white shirt, gray trousers, and black boots. Bloodstains covered the apron, remnants from the rushed and none-too-gentle removal of the tentacle whip from Osten. The blood didn't bother Elidyr. After all, it was something of an occupational hazard for him these days.

Finally, the two soldiers managed to get the symbiont inside its cage, loosen the cables binding it, and withdraw the poles. After that they swiftly closed the door, visibly relaxing once it was locked. The symbiont cages had been fashioned from spell-reinforced steel built to Elidyr's precise specifications by artisans of House Kundarak, and in addition, Elidyr had added an enchantment to the cages to keep the symbionts sedate. Once the tentacle whip was inside, the spell went to work, and the creature curled up and became still.

The soldiers stepped away from the cage and lifted their visors as they approached Elidyr. The man kept his gaze fastened on Elidyr, but the woman looked at Sinnoch with undisguised disgust. The tentacles on the dolgaunt's back writhed more noticeably beneath his robe, and the woman quickly looked away. Sinnoch let out a soft, hissing laugh.

Before either of the soldiers could speak, Elidyr said, "Thank you. That will be all."

They nodded, both looking grateful to be excused, and departed the chamber. Elidyr walked over to the tentacle whip's cage and Sinnoch followed, the dolgaunt moving with silent, inhuman grace. Elidyr gazed upon the quiescent symbiont for a time before speaking.

"This is the most magnificent specimen Lirra has ever brought back for us. So strong, so willful . . . to think my brother wanted to destroy it." He shook his head.

"You made a mistake in allowing Osten to serve as the whip's host," Sinnoch said. "He was too weak." He glanced sideways at Elidyr. "You are all too weak."

Elidyr refused to rise to the bait, but privately he admitted the dolgaunt was right. The whole point of this project was to find the perfect marriage of host and symbiont, and Osten had been completely overmatched by the tentacle whip. The boy was strong in body, but his mind and spirit simply weren't enough to stand up to the symbiont's corrupting influence. The whip would make a wonderful weapon—provided they could find the right person to wield it.

"I have to go," Elidyr said. "My brother has summoned me to a meeting."

"I take it I'm not invited," Sinnoch said. He reached up with clawed hands and lowered his hood to reveal a pale inhuman face with empty eye sockets. His skin was covered in a layer of writhing cilia, and a mane of longer tendrils surrounded his head. "Too bad. I do *so* love to visit Vaddon and bask in his utter loathing of me." He grinned, displaying a mouthful of discolored fangs. "Go. I'll stay here a bit longer to make certain our friend suffered no ill effects from its less-than-tender treatment at the hands of your oh-so-valiant countrymen."

Elidyr scowled at the dolgaunt, and handed his gore-smeared leather apron to Sinnoch. "Take care of this for me, would you?"

"With pleasure."

The dolgaunt snatched the bloody garment from Elidyr and held it up to his nose. He inhaled the blood scent, the mane of tentacles surrounding his head quivering with excitement. Elidyr then turned and walked away as the dolgaunt began licking the apron clean with eager strokes of its grotesquely long tongue.

CHAPTER THREE

Vaddon Brochann's office was located in the den, one of the most impressive rooms in the entire lodge: stone fireplace, oak-paneled walls draped with tapestries depicting hunting scenes, leather-upholstered furniture, and—incongruously—an obscenely expensive chandelier hanging from the ceiling with everbright crystals in place of candles.

Vaddon stood in front of the fireplace, hands clasped behind his back, when Lirra, Rhedyn, and Ksana entered. Vaddon had discarded his protective armor in favor of the basic Outguard uniform: green leather armor vest over a white shirt, black leather gauntlets, black pants, and black boots. Warlord Bergerron's crest was emblazoned on the left side of the vest, with a sigil representing the Outguard branded onto the right. Whenever Vaddon was in the lodge, he went without the silver helm and crimson cape that designated his rank, and Lirra didn't blame him. She thought they looked silly.

Despite the absence of flames—or perhaps because of them—Vaddon stared into the fireplace as if he were searching for something within it. He didn't turn to greet Lirra and the others as they entered, and she took that as a bad sign. Vaddon wasn't a man given to deep contemplation, and when he was lost in thought, it usually didn't bode well.

"How fares Osten?" He spoke without turning to face them, his voice soft.

"His wound is healed," Ksana said. "He's resting now."

"I'm glad. Osten's a brave lad, and I'd hate to lose him."

Lirra noted that Ksana refrained from mentioning her concerns about the state of Osten's mind, most likely because she didn't wish to say anything to Vaddon until Osten woke and she'd had a chance to examine him more thoroughly. Ksana and Vaddon had been friends for many years, and while the cleric didn't keep information from the general, she often delivered it at a time of her own choosing—especially if she thought it was information that would only worry Vaddon unnecessarily.

The general glanced over his shoulder at them. "Sit down, please. I don't want to begin until my brother—"

As if Vaddon's words had summoned him, the door opened and Elidyr walked into the den.

"Sorry to keep you all waiting, but I had to make sure Osten's symbiont was returned safely to its cage." He paused. "Well, to be technical, I suppose it isn't Osten's anymore, is it? Still, you'll all be happy to know that the tentacle whip sustained no serious injury as a result of today's test."

Vaddon turned away from the fireplace and faced them, as if goaded by his brother's words. "I'm sure Osten will take that as a great comfort."

"Perhaps," Elidyr replied, "but I doubt it will be as much of a comfort to him as knowing that he's going to get to keep the arm you tried to lop off."

Vaddon scowled, but otherwise didn't respond.

Every time Lirra saw her father and uncle together, she was struck by the stark differences in their appearance. They were clearly brothers—same thick hair, blue eyes, and sturdy chin, and their voices sounded so similar that if you closed your eyes, you might have trouble telling which one spoke at any given moment. But Elidyr's body was scarecrow slender, in contrast to Vaddon's more muscular frame, and while Vaddon's mien was normally serious to the point of being dour, Elidyr smiled often. In terms of temperament, they couldn't have been more different. Vaddon was a soldier through and through, and he lived his life by core principles of honor, duty, and sacrifice. Orders were given, and orders should be carried out. End of discussion. But despite serving his mandatory two years in Karrnath's military, Elidyr was a scholar who'd studied the craft of artificing at Morgrave University in Sharn, and he believed that everything should be questioned—authority included—otherwise, how could true learning take place?

Needless to say, the two didn't always see eye to eye.

"So why did you summon the four of us, Brother?" Elidyr said. "I'm sure you have an extremely good reason for pulling us away from our work."

Vaddon walked toward a large cherrywood desk in the corner of the den, picked up a document from its otherwise empty surface and carried it over to Elidyr.

"This arrived this morning, carried by a rider from the garrison at Geirrid," Vaddon said. "It's from Bergerron. He had it delivered to the garrison from his keep by an Orien courier."

Lirra was surprised. Delivering a message using a teleporter from House Orien was an extravagant expense, especially considering that Bergerron couldn't have the courier teleport directly to the lodge, given the secretive nature of the work taking place there. Though Bergerron was their patron and funded their experiments, the warlord left them alone to do their work as they saw fit. He hadn't contacted them once during the months the lodge had been operating. So why start now, Lirra wondered, and why pay so much money to have a message delivered so swiftly? It had to be bad news.

Vaddon handed the letter to Lirra, and she immediately began reading the missive.

"What does my uncle have to say?" Rhedyn asked.

Lirra looked up from the letter and looked at Rhedyn with a mixture of anger and disbelief. "Basically, he says, 'Stop.' Bergerron wants us to shut down the project, erase all signs of its existence, and depart the lodge within a day. See for yourself."

Lirra gave the letter to Rhedyn who quickly scanned it.

"Bergerron can't do this!" Elidyr said. "He's supported us from the beginning."

The Last War might have been over, but not everyone in Khorvaire was optimistic enough to believe it truly would be the last. The cessation of hostilities in Khorvaire was due in no small part to the nation's ruler, Kaius ir'Wynarn III, who pressed for peace toward the end of the Last War and helped establish the Treaty of Thronehold. At the time, many of the Karrnathi warlords believed their king mad, but the nobles had since come to believe that Kaius's desire for peace was a ruse, that the king truly wished for hostilities to cease only long enough so that Karrnath might rebuild its strength and once again seek an advantage against the other nations. But some warlords—Bergerron among them—believed Kaius was soft, and they viewed the Treaty of Thronehold as a symbol of his weakness. Refusing to support a weak king, these warlords began seeking ways to return Karrnath to its former glory. To that end, the rebel warlords had set a number of schemes in motion, and one of Bergerron's was the Outguard's experimentation with symbionts.

"Bergerron is a warlord," Lirra said, "which means at heart he's as much politician as soldier. My guess is some other warlord has gotten wind of our project—perhaps someone loyal to Kaius—and Bergerron wants to erase all signs of our work as swiftly as possible, before the king is informed and sends someone to investigate."

"Those were my thoughts as well," Vaddon said.

"It *would* explain my uncle's haste to get the message to us," Rhedyn said.

"Whatever his reason, the man's a fool," Elidyr said, voice tight with barely controlled fury.

"Perhaps the truth of the matter is entirely opposite," Ksana said, "and Bergerron has found a measure of wisdom."

Elidyr turned to glare at the half-elf. "What do you mean by that, cleric?" he snapped.

Lirra knew her uncle could be sharp-tongued at times, especially when he was dealing with people he viewed as his intellectual inferiors, but she'd never known him to get this upset before. She understood why he was so passionate about the project though. Exploring the use of symbionts as potential weapons of warfare had been Elidyr's idea originally. As a scholar, he'd always believed that knowledge was a far greater weapon than any object forged of steel, no matter how sharp its edge. During the course of his studies, he'd become fascinated with Xoriat and the daelkyr, and he'd learned about those called impure princes, warriors who chose to accept the corrupting embrace of a symbiont in order to use its power to hunt down and destroy the aberrations of the world. Fight kind for kind, blow for blow, was an old saying in Karrnath, and it seemed a philosophy well suited for impure princes. But Elidyr had realized that symbionts could be used for purposes other than fighting those malformed monstrosities created by the daelkyr and loosed upon the world; they could serve as weapons of war.

And—thanks to Vaddon's efforts to persuade him— Bergerron had come to believe that too. At least, that's what the warlord *had* believed. It seemed he'd had a change of heart.

Ksana arched an eyebrow in surprise at Elidyr's tone, but her own voice remained calm as she answered, "Perhaps Bergerron has finally come to realize that not only are the creatures we've been working with unnatural, they are ultimately uncontrollable as well."

"Ridiculous," Elidyr spat. "*Everything* can be controlled. It's simply a matter of discovering the most effective way to do it."

Lirra had a sudden realization, and she turned to her father. "This is the reason you attended Osten's test today. You were hoping to witness a success that you could report to Bergerron, something that might give you the leverage to argue that the project should be allowed to continue."

Vaddon sighed as he nodded. "In the months since this project began, we've had numerous failures and precious few successes. You being a prime example of the latter, Rhedyn." He paused. "Our only example, really. Of the four soldiers who managed to bond with a symbiont and not be immediately dominated by the creature's corrupting influence—including Osten—only you have remained free of the creature's taint."

Rhedyn inclined his head to acknowledge the general's recognition of his accomplishment.

Like Osten, the other two soldiers eventually had needed to have their symbionts forcibly removed, and one had died in the process. Not exactly a stellar record in anyone's book, Lirra thought.

"Whatever pressures Bergerron may or may not be feeling to end our work here, I'd hoped that if we had some small measure of success to show him, that he might reconsider and allow our efforts to continue," Vaddon said. "Unfortunately, not only wasn't Osten's test successful, he came very close to killing you, Lirra."

"As second in command and the one who recommended

Osten in the first place, I take full responsibility for how his test turned out," Lirra said.

Vaddon waved her words away with a gesture. "It's not your fault. The foundation for these experiments is fundamentally flawed." He gave Elidyr a look. "Symbionts simply cannot be controlled."

Elidyr walked over to Vaddon and stopped less than a foot away from his brother. "When I first came to you with the idea of using symbionts as living weapons for Karrnathi soldiers, I told you that it would take some time. *You* stressed this point when you presented the idea to Bergerron. Or was the warlord too addled by one too many blows to the head during his fighting days?"

"Calm yourself, Brother." Vaddon said. "Bergerron has given us ample time to test your theories regarding the use of symbionts in warfare, and he's been more than generous when it came to funding. I remember something you told me once, back when I was in command of a regiment of undead. Since the dead do not tire, it occurred to me to try using them to perform menial duties as well as martial ones: setting up camp, digging latrines, preparing meals, doing laundry. . . . And while they could perform all these tasks to a certain degree of effectiveness—though I admit using them as cooks was a bad idea all the way around—they proved too slow and their attention to detail was sorely lacking. They were really only good for one thing: killing the enemy. During one of your visits home from the university, I told you of my experiment. Do you remember what you said to me?"

Elidyr glared at Vaddon and didn't answer, so Vaddon went on.

"You told me that the majority of experiments end in failure, that the more times we're wrong, the closer we come to being right. Our experiment here is a failure, Brother. Accept it."

Elidyr continued to glare at Vaddon for a long moment, and then he slowly smiled, but there was no mirth in the expression. "How clever of you to use my own words against me. I didn't know you were that smart."

"There's no point in arguing," Lirra said before Vaddon could reply. "The simple fact remains that Bergerron has ordered us to shut down the project and vacate the lodge, and no amount of bickering will change that."

The two brothers continued glaring at each other, and Lirra thought neither would give in, but finally Vaddon sighed and nodded.

Lirra looked at Elidyr. "Our duty is clear, and that's what we should be focusing on, whether we like it or not. Don't you agree, Uncle?"

"I suppose," he muttered. He paused then, looking suddenly thoughtful. "You say that bickering won't change Bergerron's mind about shutting down our project, but I just thought of something that *might* do the job—if you're all willing to hear me out."

"Bergerron has made his wishes quite clear," Vaddon said, exasperation creeping into his voice. "I doubt there's anything—"

"What harm is there in listening, Father?" Lirra said. "Remember what you taught me: 'Good ideas win battles as often as sharp steel.'"

Vaddon frowned at her, but one corner of his mouth lifted in a half smile. "I hate it when you quote me like that." He turned to Elidyr. "Very well. Let's hear what you have to say, Brother."

CHAPTER FOUR

Lirra made her way to the great room of the lodge. A good-sized fire blazed in the large stone fireplace, as the dreary cool summer set in, and the cheery warmth of a fire was always welcome. Thick wooden beams crossed the length of the high-ceilinged room, and the walls were adorned with the stuffed, mounted heads of beasts that Bergerron and his ancestors had run to ground and killed: stags with huge antlers, fierce dire wolves, massive bears, razor-tusked boar, and sleek forest panthers.

Located in the hills on the southeastern edge of the Nightwood, the lodge was well away from main routes of travel but still close enough to the town of Geirrid, where the lightning rail could easily bring supplies. Plus Geirrid had its own garrison, which Bergerron made certain was well funded and well staffed, just in case he should have need of a military force when in residence at the lodge. And while the lodge's hidden levels had proven perfect for the symbiont experiments, the creature comforts of its aboveground levels had made it a most pleasant place to bunk during the Outguard's time there.

Chief among those comforts was the great room. Men and women sat in chairs or reclined on couches, talking and laughing while sharing after-dinner ale or playing a game of Conqueror. Over in a far corner of the room, a soldier with a bit of musical talent—a very *small* bit, judging by his playing—strummed a lute and led a merry group in song. Despite the would-be musician's meager skills, his friends received his playing with happy enthusiasm, clapping along in time to the tune.

Tonight Lirra had come in search of one soldier in particular, and she spotted him resting on a couch by the fireplace. She walked over to Osten and sat in the empty chair next to him. The others in the great room grew quiet and looked in their direction, more than a little curious. A quick glance from Lirra reminded them to mind their own business, and they resumed their conversations and merrymaking, though perhaps at a softer volume than before.

"Hello, Osten," she said.

He lay propped up on the couch, a blanket over his legs drawn up to his waist, two pillows supporting his back. He stared into the fire, its flickering orange-yellow light reflected in his brown eyes. At first he didn't react. She was about to repeat the greeting when he finally spoke.

"Hello, Captain." His voice was soft, the tone almost completely devoid of emotion. Lirra didn't like the sound of it.

"Ksana tells me you're going to make a full recovery," she said.

"I'm sorry I let you down today, Captain. Sorry that I . . ." He paused, swallowed, and when he resumed his voice held an undercurrent of sorrow. "That I hurt you."

"Don't worry about it. I took far rougher hits than anything you can dish out when my father first taught me how to handle a sword."

Osten's lips formed a small smile, but he didn't take his gaze from the flames. "Knowing the general, I can believe it." His smile vanished then. He took in a deep breath, let it out. "It's a lot harder than I thought."

"What is?"

"Bonding with a symbiont. Your uncle tried to prepare me, as did Ksana. I practiced the meditation techniques the cleric taught me, ran their advice over and over in my mind. And when the day arrived, I thought I was ready."

A bitter chuckle escaped his lips. "I was a fool. Nothing can prepare for you for the reality of the experience. Even before the symbiont latches on to you and pierces your flesh, you can feel it beginning to assault your mind. There's a . . . a pressure, as if phantom hands have gripped your skull and are squeezing it. And then there's a whispering in your ears. No, deeper than that. Inside your mind. Words spoken in a soft, sly voice—words that always seem just on the verge of being understandable, but no matter how closely you listen, you can't make them out. It's maddening. And then, when the symbiont actually bonds with your flesh . . ."

He trailed off and shuddered from head to toe. After a moment, he continued speaking, his voice so soft she could barely hear it over the gentle pop and crackle of the fire.

"The whispering in your mind becomes shouting loud as thunder, but you still can't understand what's being said. The ghost hands gripping your head squeeze so tight you feel your skull will shatter and collapse inward like a rotten melon. Your blood seems to boil in your veins, and if you could, you'd grab a dagger and slice open your wrists to drain the molten fire out of you, but you can't move. You can't even draw in a breath. The symbiont is on the verge of claiming your body as its own and you have to fight, and fight hard, or be lost. It was a near thing for me, Captain, my fight to retain control of my own body, and to be honest, I feared I would lose. But in the end I won. Or at least, I thought I had."

Osten tore his gaze from the fire and turned to her with a look of haunted desperation in his eyes.

"They're intelligent. And if they don't manage to gain control of your body when you first bond, they bide their time and wait for another opportunity. See, they *never* stop trying to take you over. Never! The voice quiets after a time, the pressure lessens, and the fire in your blood cools somewhat, but the sensations are always there. Sometimes worse than others, but you're never free of them. It . . . it wears you down. I thought I was strong. I grew up on a dairy farm not far from Geirrid, the youngest of seven children. Not only did I work hard at my chores, I had to be tough to hold my own against my brothers and sisters when we played, and we played *rough*. When it came time for me to serve in the military, I chose to apply to the garrison at Geirrid. It was close to home, and my parents were getting older and . . ."

His gaze went blank and he frowned, as if he were in danger of losing his line of thinking.

"You joined the garrison," Lirra prompted.

His gaze sharpened once more and he continued. "Anyway, my point is that I believed myself strong in both body and mind. I thought I could do anything, *endure* anything, to serve Karrnath. But I was wrong. I was overconfident today. I was determined to do well, to justify your faith in selecting me to receive a symbiont, Captain. And when I saw that the general himself was going to observe my test, I was doubly determined to acquit myself with honor. I was so concerned with impressing you both that I forgot about my symbiont, just for an instant. But that's all it took. If it had managed to kill you . . ."

"But I didn't die, Osten, and Ksana was able to heal the injuries I sustained. And while I'm sure the process wasn't pleasant for you, we were able to remove the symbiont. You're free now. And while the test may not have turned out the way you'd have wished, remember this: You resisted the symbiont's influence longer than most could have. You should be proud of yourself." But even as she said this, she wondered if she would feel proud if their roles had been reversed. Probably not, she decided.

"You're wrong, Captain." He turned his head so that he could gaze upon the fire once more. "About my being free, I mean. The symbiont is no longer attached to my body, and it's sealed up tight back in its cage. But I can still hear its whispering in my mind. I think perhaps I always will."

Lirra had to suppress a shudder at Osten's words. "Give it time. The whispering will fade."

"Perhaps." But Osten didn't sound as if he believed it. He changed the subject then. "Most of the others have been keeping their distance from me, but a few have come over to talk. They told me that Lord Bergerron has ordered the Outguard to cease our experiments and vacate the lodge. They also told me that your uncle has managed to convince the general to allow one last experiment to prove to Bergerron that our program has merit and should be allowed to continue. Are these things true?"

"More or less. The general has given the order for us to begin packing up our equipment in preparation for leaving. He wants us to be out of here before sunset tomorrow. My uncle has proposed a final experiment—one that he's been preparing for the last several weeks—but the general is still considering the matter and hasn't given his permission yet."

"But Elidyr prepares nevertheless," Osten said. It wasn't a question.

"Yes. Just in case."

"Do you think your father will approve the experiment?"

"I don't know. I hope so." She was of two minds about the matter. On the one hand, she'd devoted months of her life to this project—as had everyone else in the Outguard—and she wanted it to be a success. But on the other hand, she thought of what Ksana had said earlier in Vaddon's den, about how symbionts could never be controlled, certainly not reliably. Rhedyn may have succeeded, but he was the only success out of dozens of attempts. She was beginning to believe that the cleric was right, and the project had been a fool's dream from the start. Still, if there was a chance to salvage even a modest success from all their failures, she believed they should at least make the attempt.

"What sort of experiment?" Osten asked.

"Elidyr believes he has a way to artificially nullify a symbiont's ability to dominate its host. He'd hoped to have a few more weeks to work out the details before attempting the process, but he's almost finished with the construction of the apparatus needed for the experiment, and he believes he'll be ready to test it by tomorrow morning or afternoon at the latest." At least, that's what her uncle had promised Vaddon. She wondered if he'd be able to deliver on such short notice. Then again, Elidyr was a brilliant man. If anyone could accomplish the task, he could.

Neither of them spoke for several moments after that, and Osten appeared to be deep in thought. Finally, he said, "So if Elidyr gets the chance to test this new process tomorrow, he will need volunteers to help him."

Lirra understood where Osten was going with this, and she didn't like it.

"I know what you're getting at, and while I can sympathize with you wanting to make another attempt at mastering a symbiont, I can't—"

Osten interrupted her. "Hear me out, Captain. I'm not asking for a second chance simply to redeem myself." He paused. "Well, not *only* for that reason. Believe me, after what I've been through, I'd be only too happy never to hear the word *symbiont* again, let alone have one of the damned things attached to my body. But as you said earlier, I did manage to successfully bond with the tentacle whip, and I was able to maintain control for several days before it finally succeeded in dominating me. I know what it's like to resist a symbiont's influence. I've *done* it, even if for only a short time." He turned away from the fire to look at Lirra once more. "Besides, if Elidyr's process works, the whip won't be able to dominate me."

"And what if the experiment is a failure and the whip takes control of you once more?"

Osten shrugged. "Then you'll just have to cut the thing off of me again. Look, I know better than most just how powerful a weapon a symbiont can be. After all, I was bonded to one. Can you imagine the contribution a division of symbiont-enhanced warriors could make to Karrnath's defenses. Five divisions? Twenty? That's worth the risk to me."

Lirra understood how Osten felt. After all, it was the same vision that had motivated her to join the Outguard in the first place.

"Very well. I'll discuss the matter with the general—*if* he allows the experiment to go forward. All right?"

Osten gave her a smile—a real one, this time. "Thank you, Captain." He then turned back to face the fire once more.

Lirra sat with him in silence for a few more moments before taking her leave. Osten needed to rest . . . especially if he was going to attempt to bond with a symbiont again the next day.

She just hoped her uncle knew what he was doing.

"So now that I've promised my brother I'll work a miracle tomorrow, I need you to help me deliver, Sinnoch."

The dolgaunt made a liquid rattling in his throat, a sound Elidyr had learned was the equivalent of a sigh. "Ideally, we could use another two weeks to prepare, but I suppose we could be ready in three days if we pushed ourselves. But in less than twenty-four hours?" The creature shook his head, his mane of tentacles writhing slowly like a nest of half-asleep serpents. "I don't see how we can do it."

The two stood in Elidyr's workroom in one of the lodge's lower levels. Wooden tables lined the wall, their surfaces covered with books, scrolls, and bits of parchment arranged in seemingly haphazard piles. Everbright lanterns resting on the tables provided illumination, and while Elidyr appreciated the lanterns' convenience—unvarying light, no wick to burn down—he missed working by candlelight, as he had during his student days at Morgrave University. There was something romantic and mysterious about it, as if one were reading in some hidden chamber, delving into ancient and forbidden lore.

One table in the workroom was reserved for Elidyr's artificer's tools, devices both small and large, mundane and arcane, from simple hammers and screwdrivers to etheric energy aligners and thaumaturgic rebalancers. And in the middle of the table rested a square metal framework constructed from two-foot lengths of focusing steel, an extremely expensive material designed to collect and channel various types of energy. There were three flat panels inserted into the framework, and upon each was fastened a row of crystalline objects even more expensive than the focusing steel. Some were translucent with pulsating veins that made them seem almost alive, while some were a glowing blue and green.

"The dragonshards and psi-crystals are in their correct places," Elidyr said, sounding more defensive than he liked.

"But they haven't been properly attuned to one another," the dolgaunt pointed out. "If you tried to activate the device now, at best it wouldn't function, and at worst it would fail catastrophically and destroy half the lodge in the process." The creature's leathery lips stretched into a smile far wider than a human could manage. "Although now that I think of it, that could be amusing."

Elidyr knew the dolgaunt wasn't joking—he *would* find the devastation amusing—but the artificer chose to ignore the comment. Sinnoch's mind was sharper and more focused than others of his kind. That was the only reason Vaddon had agreed to allow the dolgaunt to assist with the Outguard's work. But in the end Sinnoch was still a creature of chaos, and thus periodically given to bizarre and unsettling turns of thought. However as long as the dolgaunt chose not to act on those thoughts, Elidyr didn't worry about them—much.

Elidyr had dubbed the device the Overmantle, a rather elegant name, he thought, for a somewhat unimpressive-appearing piece of equipment. But he'd always been more practical than artistic—the Karrn in him coming through, he thought with some amusement—and he really didn't care what the device looked like, as long as it worked. The Overmantle was designed to help humans bond with symbionts while leaving the hosts in complete control. The psi-crystals would form a psychic barrier in the hosts' minds to protect them from symbiont influence, while the dragonshards would open a miniature portal to Xoriat and channel a small measure of its chaos-based energies into the hosts in order to create a kind of "chaos inoculation" to help further shield them from the symbionts' psychic contamination. If the Overmantle worked as designed, hosts would have complete control over their symbionts and be able to use them as safely and effectively as any other weapon, without fear of succumbing to the aberrations' corruption.

"The basic attunement of the shards and crystals shouldn't take more than a few hours," Elidyr said. "My major concern is making certain the dragonshards we configured to open a portal to Xoriat will be able to do so safely."

The portal in question would be smaller than a pinprick, but that would still be large enough to draw the needed amount of the realm's energy into Eberron's plane to allow the Overmantle to complete its work. So far all their tests in this area had proven to be failures—sometimes quite spectacular ones. The last such had created a portal to Xoriat the size of a man's fist, and a slime-covered green tentacle had slithered through. There had been a tiny toothless mouth on the tentacle's tip resembling an infant's, and it crooned a wordless song in a woman's voice. Sinnoch had managed to close the portal, severing the tentacle, and Elidyr had hacked the still-writhing monstrosity to pieces with an axe he kept close at hand. Pieces which Sinnoch had disposed of by devouring them. Elidyr shuddered as he remembered the satisfied moaning sounds the dolgaunt had made as he'd feasted.

Needless to say, Elidyr had decided not to report the result of that particular test to his brother. But it pointed out the reason why they needed to proceed with extreme caution, and Elidyr had been determined to do so—until Bergerron's recent ultimatum that they shut down the project and vacate the lodge. But he couldn't do that without at least trying out the Overmantle, not when they were so close. . . .

Elidyr had first become fascinated with Xoriat during his early days at Morgrave University. His homeland had a long and proud history of military service, but at the beginning of the Last War the nation had become a military dictatorship, and still was. Martial law remained in force, and unlike the rest of Khorvaire, instead of following the Code of Galifar, Karrnath followed the more rigid Code of Kaius, a set of laws restricting many rights in the name of national defense. Men and women like his brother saw nothing wrong with this system, or if they did, they accepted it as a necessary evil for the protection of Karrnath and its people. But there were those like Elidyr—freethinkers who chafed under the Code of Kaius. And so even with the Last War still raging, Elidyr had left his homeland to study in Sharn. At Morgrave University he studied the craft of artificing, telling Vaddon that he planned to use the skills he gained in service to his country when he graduated. Which was true enough—though admittedly Elidyr hadn't been in any great hurry to graduate.

Elidyr had studied many subjects at the university, but he'd found himself most fascinated with the subject of Xoriat, the Realm of Madness. At the time Elidyr hadn't understood the strange attraction he'd felt toward Xoriat, but in the years since, he'd come to believe it had something to do with how different the dimension of madness was from Karrnath. While Karrnath was tightly structured—Elidyr often ironically used the word *regimented* to describe life there—Xoriat was the exact opposite: total freedom reigned in that realm . . . so much freedom that even the basic laws of nature held no meaning there. The very existence of Xoriat had posed a compelling question for the young scholar. Was there such a thing as too much freedom? Without some sort of structure to give it form, like water given shape by the cup that held it, could existence truly have purpose?

Elidyr read everything he could about Xoriat and its denizens, of the daelkyr, and of the aberrations they created to be their servants. He'd learned of how the daelkyr had once attempted to take over Eberron and, when they failed, how some had retreated with their servants to the subterranean realm of Khyber, where they were reputed to still live to that day. Elidyr had learned of a handful of explorers and adventurers who supposedly had traveled to Khyber and survived, and he sought them out, hoping to gain firsthand knowledge of the daelkyr and their aberrations, but while he'd tracked down a few adventurers, all he'd learned were a few scraps of information, little more than what his own studies had taught him. He'd eventually set out on expeditions of his own in search of aberrations to study firsthand. He began with symbionts, for as dangerous as they were, they were tame kittens in comparison to creatures such as mind flayers and their brethren. It was during one such journey into the Nightwood that Elidyr encountered Sinnoch.

He'd been in the forest for several days when he discovered a subterranean cave system that showed signs of symbiont habitation. He'd gone into the caves, which displayed a dismaying lack of aberrations, when the dolgaunt approached him. At first, Elidyr thought the creature intended to attack, and he prepared to defend himself using a rod he'd designed to collect energy from the sun and release it in a blast of light and heat. But when the dolgaunt made no move toward him, Elidyr had lowered his weapon and was surprised when the dolgaunt spoke.

"I've been watching you. You search for that which most humans fear and loathe. Why?"

They talked for hours after that. Elidyr was fascinated and thrilled by their conversation. Not only was this his first true encounter with an aberration, it was with one who could think and communicate. For his part, Sinnoch seemed intrigued to meet a human who did not revile him simply for being what he was. Sinnoch explained that he had stumbled through a naturally occurring but unstable portal from Xoriat some years previous and, unable to find his way back, he had lived in the cave system ever since. Elidyr learned much that day about Xoriat and Khyber and the nature of aberrations, and the young artificer stayed with Sinnoch for three more days before reluctantly heading back to the university.

Elidyr made several more trips to visit Sinnoch over the years, both before and after he graduated from Morgrave. And when he developed the idea of finding a safe way to employ symbionts as living weapons, he'd returned to the Nightwood and asked Sinnoch to help him. The dolgaunt was skeptical at first. Why should he wish to help humans when they despised his kind so much, when they took every opportunity to hunt aberrations down and destroy them?

"Because it'll be more interesting than sitting here alone in your cave," Elidyr had said.

Sinnoch thought over these words for a time before finally nodding.

The dolgaunt wasn't his friend—Elidyr had no illusions about that. But there was an understanding between them, a connection that Elidyr was hard-pressed to define but which was real nevertheless. Sinnoch's motivation for helping with the project was simple—he found the idea of an army of impure princes amusing, and he found the challenge of creating such an army intellectually stimulating. Nothing more. But it was enough to gain his assistance, and without his intimate knowledge of Xoriat's chaos energy, Elidyr would never have been able to construct the Overmantle. So what if the others didn't trust Sinnoch? Elidyr didn't blame them in the slightest. After all, he didn't fully trust the dolgaunt himself.

Sinnoch moved toward the Overmantle. One of his shoulder tentacles snaked out from under his robe and stretched toward the device. The tentacle tip began touching the crystals, seemingly at random.

"There are no guarantees, Elidyr, especially when dealing with the forces of chaos. You know this. We could perform a dozen successful tests of the Overmantle and still fail to safely open a portal to Xoriat the next time. The best we can do is to fine-tune the crystals and hope for the best."

Elidyr sighed. He knew the dolgaunt was right, but that didn't mean he had to like it.

"Then I suppose we should get to work." He reached for a thaumaturgic rebalancer and got started. He had a feeling it was going to be a long night.

CHAPTER FIVE

Lirra sat before her dresser mirror, staring at her reflection in the dim glow of the candlelight without really seeing it. She was thinking about what had occurred in the testing chamber that day . . . and what might occur there the next.

She'd changed out of her uniform and into a roomy white nightshirt that stretched down to her ankles. It wasn't the most flattering of outfits but it was comfortable and, more importantly, warm. Summer nights in Karrnath weren't nearly as cold as winter ones, but they could get chilly enough.

A soft knocking came at her door. She rose, crossed the small bedchamber, and quietly opened the door.

Rhedyn stood there, still dressed in his uniform.

"I couldn't sleep. Can I come in and talk for a while?"

"Of course."

Rhedyn entered, and she closed the door, once again careful to do so silently. Rhedyn stood in the middle of the bedchamber, looking around.

Without thinking, she said, "It's not as if you haven't been in here before, you know."

He looked at her and smiled sadly. "True, but it *has* been some time since my last visit."

Lirra instantly regretted her words, but she couldn't take them back, and she didn't know what to say to relieve their sting. A single candle resting on the nightstand illuminated her room, and in the soft light the shadowy cast that always covered Rhedyn's form appeared even darker. It was an eerie effect, made the more so because she knew he was minimizing it. If he wished, he could draw the darkness around him like a cloak and virtually vanish in the shadows.

"I wanted to talk with you about tomorrow," Rhedyn said. "About what it might mean for us."

Lirra frowned. "I don't understand."

Rhedyn took a step toward her, and without meaning to, Lirra took a step back. She regretted doing so, but she couldn't bring herself to move any closer to Rhedyn.

He gave her a sad smile. "I'm talking about what you just did. Things haven't been the same between us since I bonded with my shadow sibling. You have difficulty looking at me sometimes, and you can't bring yourself to touch me. Even being physically close to me makes you uncomfortable."

She opened her mouth, intending to tell Rhedyn it wasn't true, but she respected him too much to lie, so she remained silent.

Rhedyn continued. "I don't blame you. How can I, when I understand better than anyone the nature of the creature I've joined with? I knew when I volunteered to receive a symbiont that it might end our relationship, but I chose to go ahead anyway . . . chose to do my duty."

As his superior officer, Lirra knew she shouldn't ask this next question, but as his former lover, she couldn't stop herself. "Do you regret your choice?"

"As a soldier, no. But as a man . . ." He took another step toward her. "Very much so."

Lirra didn't move away this time. She gazed upon Rhedyn's features, and in the candlelight, the perpetual shadow that cloaked them didn't seem as unnatural. And if the candle was out, she thought, his shadowy aspect wouldn't be noticeable at all. She almost reached out to touch his hand, but the thought of the cold, oily way his flesh would feel stopped her.

"You said you wanted to talk about tomorrow," she reminded him. "What of it?"

"If Elidyr's experiment proves successful tomorrow, it will provide an opportunity for us."

Lirra frowned. She had no idea where this was leading.

"I cannot—will not—give up my shadow sibling. As an impure prince, I can serve Karrnath in ways others could never hope to. And as long as I remain bound to a symbiont, I will repulse you physically." He paused. "But if *you* were to accept a symbiont . . ."

Suddenly, she understood.

"You believe that if I was bound to a symbiont, I would no longer fear your touch, and we could be . . . close once more."

"Yes. At least, that is my hope. I would never ask you to attempt to bond with a symbiont naturally. The process is . . . difficult in ways that I cannot easily communicate."

Lirra thought of her earlier conversation with Osten in the lodge's great room and how he described being bonded with a symbiont. "I think I understand . . . at least a little."

"But if your uncle succeeds and we're able to control the bonding process so that the host remains dominant, then being bonded with a symbiont is no different than carrying any other weapon."

"Except a weapon isn't fused with one's flesh," Lirra pointed out.

Rhedyn ignored her comment. "I'm not suggesting you volunteer to join with a symbiont tomorrow. But if Elidyr's machine works . . ." He reached up and gently took hold of Lirra's arms.

She drew in a sharp intake of air at his cold, clammy touch, and despite herself, a look of revulsion passed across her face. Rhedyn held her for a second longer before letting her go.

"Just think about it. Please."

Then he moved past her, careful not to come too close, and departed the room, closing the door softly behind him.

～～～

Ksana stood outside Vaddon's bedchamber, hand raised to knock on the door. But she hesitated. Not because she felt uncomfortable disturbing him at that hour. It wasn't all that late, and despite a lifetime of military service that had trained him to rise with the day's first light, Vaddon was something of a night owl. No, the cleric hesitated because she wasn't sure if she should interfere. She'd been Vaddon's friend for several decades and had fought by his side on numerous occasions, and she knew that the general valued her counsel. But she was always careful not to force that counsel upon him too often. Still, Vaddon had been the one to request that she serve as healer for the Outguard, and he knew that Ksana wouldn't limit her contributions to simply repairing wounds and relieving illness. She smiled. So if what she had to say was going to make Vaddon angry, he was only getting what he'd asked for.

She knocked.

A moment later Vaddon opened the door. He was still fully dressed, and he gave her an amused smile.

"What took you so long?" He stepped aside so she could enter.

"Am I that predictable?" she said as she walked past him and into the room.

"Would it hurt your feelings if I said yes?" He closed the door and walked over to join her.

The room was lit by an everbright lantern sitting on the nightstand next to the bed, and an open book lay facedown on the slightly rumpled bedclothes.

Ksana nodded toward the book. "Another volume of history?"

"The Collected Letters of Galifar."

"This is, what? The third time you've read it?"

"The fourth." Vaddon smiled. "But who's counting? So . . . do you want to sit on the bed or the chair? Or is this something that can only be discussed while standing?"

Ksana walked over to the writing desk, pulled the chair out, and turned it to face the bed. She then sat. As much as Ksana admired Vaddon, there had never been any hint of romance between the two of them, and she felt perfectly comfortable being alone with him in his bedchamber at night. But even so, she felt a bit . . . awkward at the thought of sitting on his bed. Vaddon walked over to the bed, picked up his book, noted the page he'd been reading, then closed it and placed it on the nightstand next to the lantern. He then sat on the edge, facing Ksana.

"What's on your mind?" he asked.

"Have you decided to allow Elidyr to go through with his experiment tomorrow?"

He sighed. "Yes, though reluctantly so. We have some time before Bergerron wants us out of the lodge, and I see no reason why we shouldn't put it to good use. Elidyr can conduct his experiment while the rest of the Outguard are packing everything up in preparation of our leavetaking. And my brother made a good argument when he pointed out how much Bergerron has invested in our project—especially considering the cost of the dragonshards and psi-crystals Elidyr's built into this latest contraption of his . . ."

"He called it the Overmantle," Ksana said.

"I don't know if Elidyr will be able to get the device functional in time, but the man's brilliant—though if you ever tell him I said so, I'll deny it—and if anyone can get this Overmantle working, he can."

"You sound convinced to me. So why did you say your decision was made reluctantly?"

"For the same reason you've come here, I'm sure," Vaddon said. "I'm a soldier, not an expert in magic, but from the way Elidyr described the experiment, I have no doubt it would be dangerous under the best conditions. My brother may be a master artificer, but a rush job is still a rush job. How much more dangerous will his experiment be because the Overmantle was completed in haste?"

Ksana thought of her earlier hesitation to speak with Vaddon, and she couldn't help smiling. She should've known the man's thoughts would've been running parallel to her own. Although now came the moment for those lines of thought to diverge.

"I believe you should reconsider allowing the experiment to take place," she said. "I'll grant that Elidyr's reasons for why the experiment should be allowed to go forward were persuasive enough, at least on the surface, but in the end they all boil down to the same thing—Elidyr wants to prove that symbionts can be used successfully as weapons. You know better than I how obsessed he's been with Xoriat and its aberrations all these years. That obsession has blinded him to the risks involved with attempting to control symbionts. We all saw the results of those risks today, and it nearly cost Osten his life—Lirra too. They both might have died if things had gone differently. As you said, the Overmantle, assuming Elidyr can finish it in time, will be completed in haste. But even if it does function perfectly, do you really think it's wise to open a portal to Xoriat, regardless of how small that portal may be or how short a time it may be open? Who knows what sort of chaotic forces we may unleash and what sort of havoc they might wreak?"

"We are soldiers, Ksana," Vaddon said sternly. "Taking risks is our duty."

"Taking risks, yes. Taking *foolish* ones, no. A wise soldier plans before heading into battle. She knows the enemy's strengths and weaknesses as well as her own, knows the terrain upon which the battle will take place. And she knows when a battle simply isn't worth the cost. Over these last few months, I've come to see that Elidyr's view that symbionts can be used as weapons is based on a false premise. Symbionts are creatures of chaos, and chaos—by its very nature—*cannot* be controlled. And the more you attempt to control it, the more disastrous the outcome. Elidyr's experiment is doomed to failure. If not tomorrow, then later, when those soldiers who become bonded to symbionts are inevitably corrupted by them. Please, Vaddon. Do not allow Elidyr to test the Overmantle tomorrow."

Vaddon had listened to Ksana without expression, and when she finished speaking, he did not reply for several moments. When he did finally speak, his voice was calm, but firm.

"There's a line in one of Galifar's letters: 'Some see duty merely as a task to perform, while others see it for what it truly is—placing the good of one's people above one's own desires.' If there's even the slightest chance that Elidyr's right about using symbionts as weapons, then we have to give him one last try to prove it. It's our duty."

Ksana sighed and nodded. If Vaddon truly believed he was acting in the best interests of Karrnath, there was no use arguing with him further. She decided to change the subject.

"I checked on Osten before coming to see you. He told me he wished to volunteer for tomorrow's experiment and that Lirra was going to ask you to allow him to do so."

"Lirra came to see me earlier, and she did indeed tell me of Osten's desire to attempt bonding with a symbiont once more."

"You're going to let him, aren't you?"

"Yes, though I admit Lirra didn't have to work hard to convince me. In a way, Osten is the perfect subject for Vaddon's experiment. We know that he could not control a symbiont on his own, but if he can do so after having been exposed to the magic of the Overmantle, that will be proof the device works."

Ksana frowned. "You sound like Elidyr."

Vaddon chuckled. "Don't insult me."

Ksana wanted to argue with Vaddon, to try and convince him to deny Osten's request, but she knew it would be fruitless to do so at this point. After all his talk about risk and duty, Vaddon's mind was made up and there would be no changing it. The experiment would take place, Osten and a number of other soldiers would volunteer, and she'd be there to put them back together as best she could after everything went hideously wrong, as she feared it was bound to.

Sinnoch continued work on the Overmantle while Elidyr slept in a wooden chair, slumped over in a position that looked exceedingly uncomfortable to Sinnoch. Humans had so many frailties, the dolgaunt thought, the need for sleep chief among them. As soundly as Elidyr slumbered, anyone could sneak up on him and slit his throat before he had a chance to defend himself. As the dolgaunt worked, he amused himself by imagining the patterns the resultant blood spray would create in the air along with the desperate gurgling sounds Elidyr would make as his life rapidly bled out of him

Despite Sinnoch's earlier skepticism that the Overmantle would be ready in time, the work had gone rather well, and the device was almost finished. Actually, it was complete as far as Elidyr's design was concerned, but Sinnoch had a few touches of his own to add before tomorrow, so it was just as well that the artificer slept. Of course, it helped that an hour ago the dolgaunt had offered to fetch Elidyr a cup of water—*and* that the water had somehow managed to get a sleeping draught mixed into it before Sinnoch had served it to the human. The dolgaunt grinned. Life was funny that way sometimes.

Elidyr would doubtless give the device a thorough going-over before the experiment, but Sinnoch wasn't worried that the artificer would detect his tampering. The changes he was making consisted of subtle, but vital, alterations in various energy valences that, while innocuous enough in and of themselves, would produce quite a dramatic effect once the Overmantle was activated.

As he continued making adjustments, Sinnoch thought back to his first meeting with Elidyr. The man had been much younger then, though the dolgaunt had a difficult time judging the ages of other species by appearance.

When Elidyr the young scholar had first met Sinnoch, it had never occurred to him that the dolgaunt didn't make his home in the empty cave where they'd talked. Sinnoch's abode lay deeper in the earth, a cave filled with a collection of mystic artifacts he'd acquired since escaping Xoriat. Sinnoch had gathered these items, often pried from the rapidly cooling hands of their recently deceased owners, for a single purpose—he had once traveled from Xoriat to Eberron through a dimensional portal, and he hoped to discover a way to create a similar passage for his lord and master, the daelkyr Ysgithyrwyn, to step through. And when Sinnoch encountered Elidyr, he'd realized the brilliant young artificer might prove to be the perfect tool to help him achieve his goal.

At first, he'd merely encouraged Elidyr's interest in matters related to Xoriat and its denizens. But as time went on and the young artificer—who was no longer quite so young—continued his visits, Sinnoch began to pry information from him about spells designed to breach the dimensional barriers between planes. And then, one day, Elidyr, now a middle-aged man, had come to the cave and asked Sinnoch to help him with a very important project . . . Sinnoch wasn't certain how aiding the artificer in creating a battalion of impure princes would help him free his master, but he'd recognized the opportunity for what it was and agreed. And now, with the Overmantle nearly completed—and modified by Sinnoch—the day of Ysgithyrwyn's liberation was finally at hand.

Sinnoch turned his face toward Elidyr's sleeping form. Though the dolgaunt could not see by conventional means, his sensitive cilia allowed him to perceive the artificer's body.

Tomorrow you will learn more about Xoriat than you ever imagined, my friend, Sinnoch thought with amusement. You will make wonderful clay for my master to reshape. I cannot wait to see what dark wonder you will become beneath his hands.

Sinnoch was about to turn back to the Overmantle to make further adjustments when he sensed a presence outside the door. There was no sound, no knock. Nevertheless, the dolgaunt knew someone stood outside, waiting. More, he knew who—and what—it was. A creature of corruption himself, he could always recognize its presence in another. Though Elidyr had been drugged and was unlikely to wake even if someone were to sound a trumpet blast next to his ear, Sinnoch moved silently across the room. He opened the door quietly, glided into the hall, and closed the door behind him.

While most of the soldiers in the Outguard had quarters on the lower levels of the lodge, none of their rooms were near

Elidyr's work chamber. Even so, Sinnoch spoke softly as he addressed his visitor.

"How did it go?"

The visitor also spoke in hushed tones. "I do not believe she will ever choose to accept a symbiont."

The disappointment was clear in the other's voice, and Sinnoch couldn't help thinking how weak humans were made by their emotional needs. Then again, their emotions certainly made humans easier to manipulate.

The dolgaunt laid a lean-fingered clawed hand on the man's shoulder then smiled with his mouthful of sharp teeth.

"Fear not, Rhedyn. Tomorrow we both shall get what we want."

CHAPTER SIX

Lirra stood on the far side of the chamber where the symbionts were kept, Vaddon on her right, Rhedyn on her left, Ksana on the other side of her father. The general wore the protective armor that Elidyr had created to guard against a symbiont attack, but as during Osten's test yesterday, Lirra and Rhedyn wore their Outguard uniforms, and—despite her preference for comfortable clothing—Ksana also wore her uniform. In addition, she'd brought her halberd with her, and she held it in her right hand, the butt of the handle resting on the chamber's stone floor. Lirra, Vaddon, and Rhedyn were armed with swords, along with daggers for backup weapons. Standard precautions for any Outguard experiment, but that day their weaponry was even more important. Given how rushed Elidyr had been to complete the Overmantle, Lirra figured there was a good chance that the device could go wrong, and they needed to be ready for whatever might happen if it did.

Lirra thought the Overmantle was a bit on the disappointing side. Given what the device was supposed to do, she'd been expecting something more impressive than a box holding a handful of pretty stones. But her uncle was a skilled artificer, and if he thought his metal box could generate the magical energies necessary for the day's experiment, then she knew it would function as advertised, regardless of its unprepossessing appearance . . . hopefully.

The Overmantle rested atop a stone column that one of the soldiers had hauled into the chamber at Elidyr's request. Her uncle stood on one side of the device, while the dolgaunt stood on the other. Sinnoch wore the outsized robes which concealed his inhuman form with the hood up. Even so, Lirra could see slow, sinuous movement beneath the cloth of Sinnoch's robes which she knew came from his shoulder tentacles and, to a lesser degree, the cilia covering the rest of his body.

Four symbiont cages sat on the chamber floor—two on one side of the room, two on the other. The rest of the cages had been removed by soldiers earlier and hauled off to another chamber for temporary storage. Elidyr always insisted that an attempted bonding between symbiont and host take place in the chamber where the symbionts were normally kept. They were more comfortable there, he'd explained to her once, which helped them relax during the bonding process. Well, relax more than they might have otherwise. During an ordinary attempt at joining, the other symbionts remained in the chamber, but Elidyr had thought it best if only the symbionts that were going to be involved in the day's experiment were present, and Lirra thought it a wise move.

Soldiers wearing enchanted armor stood guard by each cage, keeping a close eye on the symbionts inside. Their soldiers' swords were sheathed for the time being, and instead they carried the metal rods Elidyr had designed for capturing and handling symbionts. A steel table was positioned in front of the cages, and upon each a volunteer lay prone. Affixed to the foot of each table was a single three-foot long crystalline rod, its milky-glassy surface gleaming in the illumination cast by the everbright lanterns stationed around the chamber. Each volunteer was an Outguard soldier, and they all wore their uniforms.

The volunteers lay still, features composed, though it was clear to anyone watching that they were working hard to project the appearance of calm, in defiance of how they really felt inside. Their hands were clenched into fists, their chests rose and fell in erratic patterns as they struggled to master their breathing, and they swallowed often. Lirra looked at Osten. Given the bad experience he'd endured yesterday, she wouldn't have blamed him for being a nervous wreck, but of the two men and two women who'd volunteered to receive a symbiont today, he looked the calmest. Out of the four, he was the only one who'd been bonded to a symbiont before, if only for a short time, and she figured that experience was helping him manage his anxiety.

Elidyr had chosen to use four different types of symbionts today: a tongueworm, a crawling gauntlet, a stormstalk, and the tentacle whip that had taken over Osten the day before during his test. Osten lay on the table positioned in front of the tentacle whip's cage, for he intended to try once more to bond with that particular aberration. Lirra had asked him about his choice not long before the experiment began. "I know the thing, and it knows me," Osten had told her, as if that was reason enough. And perhaps it was, but Lirra couldn't help feeling that Osten had chosen to bond with the whip again because he had something to prove to himself— and perhaps to the aberration as well. For their parts, the symbionts seemed to sense that something important was about to take place, for they writhed restlessly in their cages, occasionally testing the doors, as if eager to taste the flesh of a new host.

She glanced at Rhedyn then. His shadowy aspect was more prominent, making his features barely discernible. Perhaps he was merely gathering his shadow sibling's strength in case anything should go wrong.

Elidyr wore a leather satchel slung over his shoulder, containing tools of the artificer's trade, and for the last several minutes he'd been using one device or another to poke and prod at the Overmantle as he performed a last check to make certain everything was in working order.

"How much longer?" Vaddon said, an edge of irritation in his voice.

Elidyr stood hunched over the Overmantle, holding a device made of two thin glass rods with silvery webbing stretched between them. He waved the device in front of the Overmantle's opening, nodding to himself as he did so.

"That should just . . . about . . . do it."

Elidyr abruptly straightened, tucked the glass rods back into his satchel, and then turned and grinned at Vaddon.

"We're ready to begin whenever you are, General."

"Let's get it over with," Vaddon said evenly.

Elidyr nodded once then turned back to the Overmantle. He slid a tray of crystals halfway out of the containment framework and began touching them in a precise order. He didn't bother explaining what he was doing, but there was no need since Elidyr had covered the basics the day before in Vaddon's office.

"The Overmantle will do two things," he'd said. "First, the psi-crystals will strengthen a host's mental defenses, allowing him or her to resist all attempts at mental dominance by a symbiont. Second, the dragonshards will open a tiny portal to Xoriat, one no larger than a pinprick. The crystals will draw forth a small controlled stream of chaos energy through that portal and transfer it to a host. Once that energy is inside a host, it will insulate him or her from a symbiont's corrupting influence, much the same way our bodies are more resistant to a particular disease after we've contracted it and recovered. Once a host is cloaked by these powerful twin protections—hence the name Overmantle for my device—he or she should be able to control a symbiont with ease."

Elidyr turned to Sinnoch. "Open the cage doors."

A clawed hand emerged from a sleeve of the dolgaunt's robe. Clutched in his spider-leg fingers was a glass sphere the size of an apple. Sinnoch circled his thumb over the top of the sphere's surface, and in response the locks on the four symbiont cages disengaged with audible clicks and the doors began to rise. The symbionts were intelligent enough to sense that something strange was going on, and they were reluctant to expose themselves to danger willingly. And yet, there was a host for each one of them, laid out on a table like food at a feast, just waiting for them to come forth from their cage and take it. Eventually, instinct won out over caution, and one by one the symbionts began to move out of the cages and toward the steel tables.

The tentacle whip was the first to emerge. It slithered quickly toward Osten, as if somehow sensing he was the same man it had dominated before and it was eager to claim him once again.

Elidyr turned his head back and forth, watching closely as the quartet of symbionts climbed onto the tables and drew near their soon-to-be hosts. Elidyr had explained to them that it was important the bonding process between human and aberration already be underway before he activated the Overmantle—if for no other reason than to keep from scaring the symbionts off—but it couldn't be too far along, else it might be too late for the device to prove effective. He had to activate the Overmantle at just the right moment, and not before.

The tentacle whip fastened its beaklike mouth on Osten's inner forearm, and the thin crimson tendrils that surrounded the mouth wrapped around the man's elbow before burrowing into the flesh. Osten's teeth were gritted tight and his jaw muscles clenched. Sweat poured off him, and his every muscle was wire-taut as the symbiont began altering the internal structure of his body. His brow furrowed in concentration, and Lirra knew he was fighting to resist the pain of the foul creature merging with his physical body as the psychic corruption as the whip joined with his mind.

Lirra turned toward Ksana and saw that the cleric's eyes were closed, her lips moving silently. No doubt the cleric was seeking her patron goddess's blessing for the volunteers as well. Lirra hoped the gods were in a beneficent mood today. She knew Osten and the others could use all the help they could get.

The tongueworm slithered over the length of a woman's body, reversing its position as it neared her mouth. It inserted the tip of its tail between her lips, and the woman closed her eyes and opened her mouth wide to receive it. The worm hesitated for a moment, as if not quite able to believe it was being welcomed, and then it plunged its tail down the woman's throat. Tears streamed from her eyes, and her body convulsed as the tail wriggled its way down into her stomach, intending to anchor there. When the bonding process was complete, the tongueworm—whose hood resembled a human tongue— would lie flat over the woman's true tongue. She would still be able to speak, but the tongueworm could lash out whenever she willed it to deliver a paralyzing poison strike using its concealed barb. Lirra turned to see how the host on the third table was faring.

The crawling gauntlet had scuttled across the man's body like a large crustacean and settled over his right hand and forearm. The bonding process for this aberration was far less disturbing than for a tongueworm. The host wore it like a natural gauntlet, and the symbiont extended tiny tendrils into the flesh to bind itself to the host body. The man winced as the gauntlet joined with him, but the procedure looked much less painful than it was for Osten and the woman, and Lirra was glad for the soldier, though she had no doubt he'd have an equally difficult time resisting the psychic influence of the evil creature.

The last symbiont was a stormstalk. It resembled something like a fat, fleshy serpent with a single large white eye in the center of its otherwise featureless head. A static discharge of energy like a miniature lightning storm danced over the surface of the eye as the aberration slithered across the chest of the woman who would serve as its host. Once coiled over her breastbone, its tail wriggled toward her neck and slid around the base of her skull. The creature plunged tendrils into the host's skull, burrowed through the bone, and dug into the brain to take root. As the process began, the woman screamed—the only one of the four volunteers to make a sound as their symbionts joined with them—and Lirra didn't blame the woman one bit.

Lirra looked to Elidyr. The artificer was in motion, rapidly touching the Overmantle's crystals in a complex pattern, his hands moving with the speed and grace of a master musician playing a familiar, beloved instrument. Several seconds passed without result, and Lirra began to fear that the device wasn't going to work, that Elidyr simply hadn't had enough time to complete it. But then the crystals began to pulsate with an eerie blue-white light, and four streams of energy emerged from the Overmantle's framework and lanced through the air to strike the four crystalline rods affixed to the tables where the hosts lay. The rods shimmered with the same light as the Overmantle's crystals, and the tables began to gleam blue white as the rods transferred energy to the steel. In turn, the magical energy was fed directly into the host's bodies, and by extension, into the symbionts as well—just as Elidyr had said it would.

Now all four of the volunteers cried out in pain, but their shouts were drowned out by a chorus of shrill shrieks, like the high-pitched screams of animals in intense agony. The shrieking was so loud that Lirra clapped her hands over her ears to drown it out, but the action did no good. The sound remained just as loud, and Lirra realized that it wasn't an actual sound at all, but rather something she was hearing in her mind. She was experiencing the combined psychic cries of distress from the symbionts as the Overmantle's energy coursed through them.

She glanced at the others and saw that Vaddon and Ksana both held their hands over their ears, as did the guards and Elidyr. Not Sinnoch, though, and not Rhedyn, either. Of course they would be immune to the cries, Lirra thought.

The expression on Rhedyn's face was neutral, while Vaddon's was one of intense concentration as he observed every detail of the experiment going on before him, weighing and judging, just as he always did. Ksana looked worried, no doubt concerned for the volunteers' safety, but along with the worry was a taut alertness. The cleric intended to hang back and let the experiment run its course, but Lirra knew that at the first sign any of the volunteers needed her, Ksana would spring into action. Elidyr's face was wild with joy, like a Karrnathi child receiving his first weapon on Blades' Day Eve. Sometime during the proceedings, Sinnoch had lowered the hood of his robe, and the dolgaunt observed the scene around him with a sly, inhuman smile that disturbed Lirra more than anything she'd witnessed since the experiment began.

Suddenly both the symbionts and their hosts grew still and lay motionless on the tables. The psychic screams of the aberrations died away, and their absence felt as if a great pressure had been removed from Lirra's mind. As the hosts continued lying there, the Overmantle still feeding streams of mystic energy into the tables, Lirra feared that something had gone dreadfully wrong with the experiment, and that the men and women were dead. But then, almost in perfect unison, the four volunteers sat up, their expressions beatifically calm, and Lirra allowed herself to hope that the Overmantle had worked, and the hosts were in full control of their symbionts. If it were true, if Elidyr had finally succeeded, then perhaps Bergerron would continue to support the Outguard's work, and they could—

Before Lirra could finish her thought, the hosts leaped off their tables and rushed toward the guard standing closest to them. The guards were still off balance from having experienced the symbionts' psychic screams. They had dropped their handling rods to cover their ears, and while the psychic screams were over, none of the guards made a move to draw their swords as the hosts approached.

"Arm yourselves!" Lirra called out in warning, but it was too late.

All four of the guards wore Elidyr's enchanted armor, and the spells worked into the metal should've repelled the symbionts or at least slowed their attack, but for some reason the armor's magic had no effect and the hosts didn't so much as pause as they closed in. None of the guards wore any protection for their heads or faces, for the Outguard had needed none before, and it was a lapse the hosts exploited with swift, ruthless efficiency. The woman with the tongueworm opened her mouth, and her symbiont shot forth like a striking snake, its barbed tip striking one of the guards just below the left eye. The flesh there instantly became swollen and discolored, and the guard stiffened as the tongueworm's paralytic poison took hold. As the tongueworm flew back into the woman's mouth, the host walked forward, drew the paralyzed guard's sword, and laid open his throat with a single savage swing of the blade.

The man with the crawling gauntlet slashed open a guard's throat with the symbiont's razor-sharp claws, while the woman with the stormstalk sent a crackling burst of lightning from her symbiont's eye directly into the third guard's face. The man screamed as his flesh blackened and his hair caught fire. He fell to the ground, crying in agony, and the woman moved in to finish him off with a second burst of lightning. Osten stepped toward the last guard, the tentacle whip lashing out and wrapping around the woman's neck. Osten yanked back hard on the whip, and there was a loud crack as the guard's neck broke. The whip uncoiled and the woman slumped to the floor of the chamber, dead.

Not only had the Overmantle failed to give the hosts control of the symbionts, the reverse had somehow taken place—the symbionts had complete control over their host bodies. More, the energy fed into the aberrations by Elidyr's device seemed to have made the symbionts stronger than normal. It had taken them only a few seconds to slay the guards, and the hosts—or rather, the host bodies under the symbionts' control—turned toward Lirra and the others.

Elidyr gazed with stunned disbelief at the carnage the hosts had wrought.

"This can't be happening!" the artificer cried out.

Standing next to him, Sinnoch pointed toward the air several feet above the Overmantle.

"I believe you have something slightly more important to worry about, Elidyr," the dolgaunt said with a sickening grin.

Everyone's eyes—including those of the symbiont-hosts—turned toward the point in space Sinnoch had indicated. The air rippled, distorted, and then a seam opened . . . at first it was a small tear only a few inches long, but it soon began to widen until it measured more than a foot in length.

"What is it?" Lirra demanded.

"It's a portal," Elidyr answered in a frightened whisper. "To Xoriat."

A chill raced down Lirra's spine at her uncle's words. She was looking at a hole in space . . . a doorway between this world and the Realm of Madness. What awful things lay on the other side of that door—and what if those things chose to come through?

"I thought you said the Overmantle would only create a small portal to Xoriat!" Lirra said.

"That's right!" Elidyr stared up at the slowly widening portal in complete bewilderment. "I . . . I don't understand!"

"You don't need to understand!" Lirra snapped. "You just need to close it!"

"Right." Elidyr didn't sound very sure of himself, but he began frantically manipulating the Overmantle's crystals. Sinnoch continued to stand next to the artificer, but the dolgaunt made no move to assist him, Lirra noted.

Lirra turned to Vaddon, Ksana, and Rhedyn. "We need to deal with the symbionts before they start moving again. We'll each take one and do whatever is necessary to stop them." Her expression was grim. "Understand?"

They nodded and drew their weapons as they chose a target and began their approach. Vaddon headed for the man with the crawling gauntlet, while Ksana made for the woman with the stormstalk and Rhedyn for the woman with the tongueworm. That left Osten for Lirra. Despite what she'd told the others, she was determined to stop the tentacle whip without harming Osten if she could. Twice Lirra's actions had resulted in Osten being taken over by the symbiont, and she felt it was her responsibility to make up for those errors in judgment—and if it should come down to her having no choice but to kill Osten, then she'd make sure to do the deed as swiftly and painlessly as possible. She owed him that much at least.

The host bodies remained standing motionless and gazing upon the portal to Xoriat. As the symbionts were creatures born of madness and corruption, they doubtless could sense what lay on the other side of the rent in space, and they stood watching almost reverently, as if they were waiting for something to emerge. The thought chilled Lirra, but she pushed it aside. They were lucky that the symbionts were mesmerized by the portal, but there was no telling how long they'd remain like that, and Lirra and the others had to take advantage of the situation while they had the chance.

As she moved toward Osten, she couldn't resist sneaking a quick glance at the portal hovering in the air above the Overmantle. It was two feet long and nearly a foot wide, and Lirra could see through to what lay on the other side. But what she saw didn't make any sense. Swirling images, some blurry and indistinct, some so clear and sharp that it almost hurt to look at them. Things that appeared to be geometric shapes one instant, only to shift into amorphous blobs the next, and then into something so nightmarish it defied description after that. Sounds came through as well—mad laughter, grating low-pitched words spoken in a language she'd never heard, cries like those of exotic animals from deep within the darkest jungles of Xen'drik. Smells filtered into the chamber through the portal too—the foul stink of swamp gas, the cloying odor of thick perfume, the rank stench of decay, the oversweet smell of fruit on the verge of spoiling, and the coppery tang of blood.

The Realm of Madness, indeed, and Lirra found herself almost giggling at the thought. She immediately clamped down hard on the urge.

Careful, soldier, she told herself. The influx of disorienting sensations coming through the portal was starting to affect her mind, and she needed to maintain control of her thoughts. Otherwise, she risked succumbing to madness.

She started to tear her gaze away from the portal, but just as she did she caught a glimpse of a pair of hands reaching through—inhumanly long fingers covered in hard gray armor that reminded her of an insect's shell with pulsing red muscle visible between the segments. The sight of those alien hands filled her with fear and loathing so strong that for an instant she wanted nothing more than to drop her sword to the floor and flee the lodge in terror. But she kept a tight rein on her emotions and forced herself to look away from the portal. The fear subsided then, though it didn't entirely leave her. She didn't know what the creature reaching through the portal was, and she didn't *want* to know. Hopefully, Elidyr would find a way to close the portal before the damned thing could make it all the way through into Eberron. In the meantime, she had a job to do.

She started toward Osten.

CHAPTER SEVEN

Osten's head turned toward her as she approached, and eyes that no longer contained even a shred of humanity focused on her. Osten's lips stretched into a cruel smile, and Lirra felt a cold pit open in her stomach as she realized the tentacle whip recognized her.

She didn't waste time on words. The fastest way to stop the symbiont was to weaken it, and to do that, she needed to deprive it of its blood supply—Osten. She rushed forward, sword in her right hand, dagger in her left. The symbiont was intelligent in its own way, and if nothing else it possessed a certain amount of animal cunning. But one thing it didn't have was battle experience, and Lirra intended to use that failing against it. As she drew near, she raised her sword, feinting with the weapon to draw the symbiont's attention while she struck with her dagger.

Sorry, Osten, she thought.

The tentacle whip did nothing, and for an instant she felt a surge of hope. Perhaps the aberration was still too mesmerized by the portal to react in time to stop her.

But as her sword arm came around in its feint, Osten grinned, stepped aside, and the tentacle whip lashed out and wrapped its coils around the wrist of her dagger hand. The whip yanked her off balance, and Osten reached out with his free hand, grabbed hold of her other wrist and twisted. His grip was inhumanly strong, and she felt bones grind and a sharp pain shot through her arm. Her fingers sprang open, releasing their grip on her sword, and her weapon tumbled to the chamber floor. Next the tentacle whip squeezed the wrist of her dagger hand, forcing her to drop that blade as well.

Her right wrist blazed like fire, but she grabbed hold of the tentacle whip, grimacing at the warm, greasy feel of the thing's flesh, planted her feet solidly on the floor, and hauled backward with all her might. The whip was taken by surprise, and Osten's body stumbled toward her. Lirra lashed out with her foot and swept the man's left leg out from under him. Osten fell onto his side, hitting the stone floor hard. With the tentacle whip joined to him, the impact wouldn't do much to slow him down. What she'd wanted was to get Osten's head—or more specifically, his throat—within striking distance of her boot. She kicked out hard and crushed the man's windpipe.

Osten's body stiffened, and she felt the tentacle whip vibrate, as if it were reacting to the blow as well. Osten's mouth gawped open like a fish's as his body struggled to draw in air, but the soft wet clicks that emerged from his throat indicated that Lirra's blow had had the desired effect. He could no longer breathe and would rapidly lose strength and die, rendering the tentacle whip, if not helpless, than greatly reduced in strength. Hopefully weak enough that Lirra would be able to deal with it then. As if its host's plight were already having an effect on it, the whip released its hold on her wrist and fell to the floor. Lirra decided to take the opportunity to retrieve her weapons. Keeping an eye on the tentacle whip in case it decided to strike again, she reached down and grabbed both her sword and dagger. Osten's face had turned red and was beginning to shade toward purple. His eyes bulged as he fought a losing battle to breathe, and though Lirra knew that she'd had no other way to stop the symbiont possessing his body, she found herself unable to watch the man's face as he died. The whip itself still lay limply on the chamber floor, and she decided to risk a quick glance to see how the others were faring.

Vaddon had dealt with the crawling gauntlet in the most expedient way possible—by cutting off the arm of its host at the elbow. The man sat on the floor, white-faced and grimacing in pain, bleeding stump jammed against his midsection to staunch the flow of blood, while the crawling gauntlet—still attached to his severed arm—scuttled across the stone floor searching for somewhere to hide, leaving a trail of crimson in its wake.

Ksana stood before the woman possessed by the storm-stalk. The serpentlike creature unleashed a bolt of lightning at the cleric from its overlarge eye, but the cleric raised her hand and the energy discharged harmlessly inches before striking her. Ksana then stepped forward and swung her halberd like a staff, striking the woman on the side of the head with the end. The woman took a stagger-step to the side, and before she could react, Ksana—moving with a savage speed and grace that seemed at odds with her rational, accord-seeking personality—reversed her strike and struck the woman in the side of the neck with her halberd's axe blade. Blood fountained from the wound and the woman fell onto her hands and knees. Ksana then flipped her halberd around for a new strike and brought the axe head down upon the juncture where the stormstalk had buried its tail into the base of its host's skull. The stormstalk had no mouth with which to scream, but the way its body quivered told of the pain it suffered from the blow, and the aberration immediately yanked itself free of its host and began frantically slithering away before Ksana could strike at it again. Once the symbiont had left, Ksana dropped her halberd to the floor and rushed forward to place her hands upon the wounded woman and begin healing her.

Rhedyn stood before the woman possessed by the tongue-worm, his body cloaked in shadow, sword in his right hand. The worm had attempted to strike at him, but he'd managed to grab hold of the aberration with his left hand before its barb could sink into his flesh and paralyze him. The tongueworm writhed in obvious pain, and Lirra knew that Rhedyn was using the corrupting touch of his shadow sibling to hurt the creature, and through it, to hurt the host body as well. Maintaining his grip on the tongueworm, Rhedyn yanked hard and pulled the host body toward him. When she was close enough, he rammed the sword into her stomach, seeking the spot where the tongueworm was anchored. The woman's eyes flew open wide and a gout of dark blood spilled past her lips. It was followed by the length of the tongueworm as it abandoned the wounded body of its host. Its mouth end whipped toward Rhedyn's face, as if it intended to seek him as a replacement host. But Rhedyn cast aside the worm and it fell to the floor in a blood-slick coil and began rapidly slithering away. Rhedyn withdrew his sword from the woman's body and she slumped forward onto the floor, a pool of blood spreading out from beneath her. Rhedyn didn't once look at her. His gaze swept the room, searching for more symbionts to deal with.

Rhedyn was a soldier doing a soldier's work—Lirra knew this. Hadn't she dealt just as ruthlessly with Osten and the tentacle whip? But there'd been a brutal efficiency to Rhedyn's motions, along with a casual cruelty she'd never seen in him before, and she found herself wondering how much of that had come from him and how much from the symbiont he was bound to. She thrust the thought aside for later contemplation and looked to the center of the chamber, where Elidyr continued to struggle with the Overmantle.

The artificer had pulled out all three of the device's trays, and his hands were blurs as they moved back and forth across the crystals. Whatever he was doing was having some effect—no longer did streams of energy stretch from the Overmantle to the crystalline rods attached to the steel beds, and while the obscene insect-shelled hands still gripped the inner edges of the portal to Xoriat, the opening in space itself had shrunk significantly since Lirra had looked upon it last. She had the impression the portal might've been closed by now if the creature on the other side, whatever it was, hadn't been struggling so hard to keep the doorway open.

Sinnoch continued to stand next to Elidyr, but the dolgaunt still did nothing to help her uncle. Instead, the creature was laughing wildly, taking mad delight in the chaos surrounding him.

She gripped her sword tighter and started walking toward the center of the chamber. She doubted there was anything she could do to help Elidyr, but she could stop Sinnoch from making the situation any worse and, if nothing else, see to it that he paid for his betrayal . . . assuming, that is, her uncle managed to close the portal. If whatever those insect-armored hands belonged to made it through to their world, Lirra had the distinct feeling that none of them would survive very long after its arrival.

But before she could do more than take two steps, she felt something grab hold of her ankle. She looked down and saw a hand clasping her boot—a hand that belonged to Osten. The man lay prone on the ground, arm outstretched, holding onto her ankle with an iron grip. He grinned up at her, and she saw the ragged, bloody hole at the base of his throat, and she realized what had happened. She'd seen the technique performed on the battlefield before when a soldier's airway was obstructed and no cleric was available. Cutting a hole in the throat, like a tiny second mouth, allowed air to bypass the obstruction and make it into the lungs. The soldier would then be able to breathe until such time as he could be seen to by a cleric and healed. But the last time she'd looked at Osten, he'd seemed on the verge of losing consciousness. How had he managed to perform the procedure on himself? And then she realized that he hadn't. The tentacle whip had used its barbed tip to dig into the tender flesh at the base of Osten's neck and create a crude opening. It seemed the aberration was more intelligent than she'd given it credit for.

She glanced toward Osten's left arm where the symbiont was attached, but as she did so, its length unfurled toward her, and its coils wrapped around her throat. She instantly tightened her neck muscles before it could squeeze too hard, yanked her boot free from Osten's hand, and spun around, intending to bring her sword up and strike at the aberration. But before she could do so, she watched in horror as the tentacle whip's mouth detached from Osten's arm, anchor tendrils tearing free from his flesh with tiny sprays of blood. Then, using its grip in her neck for leverage, the whip flexed, bringing its mouth end swinging toward Lirra's left arm. It happened so swiftly that she had no time to react, and then the beaked mouth bit into the inner flesh of her forearm and its anchor tendrils burrowed into her skin, seeking purchase in the muscle beneath.

Lirra screamed.

―――――

Elidyr's terror was eclipsed only by his confusion. This couldn't be happening, it just couldn't!

He was dimly aware of the separate battles taking place around him—the volunteers going mad, the guards dying, Vaddon and the others engaging the symbiont-controlled hosts—but his attention remained fixed on the portal that had opened in the air above the Overmantle. The portal was supposed to be there, of course, its chaos energy fueling the dragonshards in the Overmantle, but it was supposed to be so small as to be invisible to the naked eye. This portal was hundreds, no, *thousands* of times larger, and Elidyr simply could not account for that. Nor, unfortunately, could he do anything to reverse the portal's growth. He frantically tried to recalibrate the crystals' energy matrices, but it seemed that his efforts only made matters worse.

Inhuman hands gripped the insides of the portal and began to widen it. Which was yet another impossibility. One couldn't physically touch a hole in space, let alone make it larger through sheer physical effort. But that's exactly what appeared to be happening.

Xoriat is on the other side, he reminded himself. *The rules of existence are different there. If such a word as rules could even apply.*

But the artificer forgot all about whether or not a dimensional portal could be grasped by hands when he realized exactly who—and what—those hands belonged to: a daelkyr lord.

Nausea ripped through his gut and pain like a white-hot dagger seared his brain, as the presence of the daelkyr lord assaulted his sanity. He had to retain hold of his faculties at least long enough to shut down the portal and prevent the daelkyr from coming through, even if doing so cost him his sanity in the end.

He turned to Sinnoch. The dolgaunt was looking up at the daelkyr's carapaced hands with wild joy. Elidyr opened his mouth, intending to call for the dolgaunt's help, but the sounds that emerged from his lips in no way resembled human speech, and all they did was make Sinnoch laugh. Realizing he was on his own, Elidyr focused his attention back on the Overmantle and did his best to hold off the burgeoning insanity roiling within his mind.

In the end, he didn't know whether he managed to figure out the right combination or if he stumbled upon it by accident, but when he finished touching the last dragonshard, the portal to Xoriat stopped growing and slowly began to close. The daelkyr fought to hold it open, but as powerful as the lord was, he couldn't keep the rift open without the Overmantle's help. As if the daelkyr realized this, he withdrew his hands, and Elidyr felt a moment of elation that he'd succeeded in preventing the foul creature from emerging into their world.

But even as the portal rapidly closed, the daelkyr shoved his arm through, hand stretching toward Elidyr until the claw tip of the index finger gently touched the artificer's forehead. And then, just as swiftly, the hand withdrew and the portal snapped shut and vanished.

Elidyr stood frozen for a long moment, staring up at the spot where only an instant before a doorway had been open upon the Realm of Madness.

"Of course," he whispered. "It's all so clear now."

And he began to laugh.

Vaddon was furious with himself for giving into his brother yet again. Though he hadn't admitted it to the others, he'd been just as upset that Bergerron had ordered the Outguard to cease operations and vacate the lodge. Not that he cared about proving the worth of using symbionts in warfare, but he hated leaving a job undone. So when Elidyr had told him they might have one last chance to salvage a victory, Vaddon had decided to gamble on his brother a final time. Unfortunately, it was rapidly becoming clear that this was one gamble Vaddon had lost.

The guards were dead, and the four others who'd volunteered to be subjects of the experiment were either wounded or, in one case, dead, and the symbionts that had possessed them were running loose in the chamber. Worse yet, there was some kind of distortion in the air above the Overmantle, and while Vaddon was no expert in magic, he'd witnessed enough to recognize that whatever was happening, it wasn't good.

Vaddon turned toward Lirra and was about to inform her of his orders, when he saw the tentacle whip wrap around his daughter's throat, then detach itself from Osten and latch on to her. Lirra screamed as the symbiont fused with her flesh, and Vaddon thought he hadn't heard a sound so awful since the dying scream of his wife when she fell at Jaythen's Pass.

Osten slumped to the floor, unconscious. Lirra still held her sword in her right hand, and she raised the blade, clearly intending to bring it slashing down upon the tentacle whip, but the instant she began to swing the sword, the muscles in her arm locked, freezing the blade in place. The aberration was exerting control over Lirra's body in order to protect itself, and though his daughter fought valiantly, Vaddon knew with every passing second the tentacle whip was solidifying its hold on her. If there was any chance to get the damned thing off her, it was now.

Vaddon moved forward, sword gripped tight, his soldier's mind—honed from years of training and decades of battle experience—rapidly calculating the best way to attack. There were really only two choices: cut the symbiont off Lirra or kill it while it remained attached to her. Neither was without risk for Lirra. Given that she was now physically and mentally joined with the tentacle whip, she would feel the aberration's pain as if it was her own, and she'd suffer the same shock to her system as it did. But Vaddon knew his daughter's strength. She could withstand whatever he did to her—assuming he could find the strength to do what needed to be done.

The contest of wills between Lirra and the tentacle whip continued, sweat running down the sides of Lirra's face as she fought to regain control of her sword arm, the tentacle whip lazily, almost mockingly, undulating in the air as it continued to prevent her. Vaddon knew he had no chance of making a stealthy approach—the enchanted armor prevented him from moving silently—but he hoped that the contest of wills Lirra and the symbiont were locked into would occupy them both long enough to give him the opportunity of getting in close.

Vaddon continued toward Lirra, armored feet clanking on the chamber's stone floor. But when he was within three yards of her, the tentacle whip's barbed tip suddenly swung in Vaddon's direction, almost as if the aberration could sense the soldier, and it lashed out at him. Vaddon instinctively dodged to the right, and if he hadn't been wearing armor, he might've been able to move swiftly enough to avoid the tentacle whip's strike. As it was, the symbiont's barbed tip grazed his left cheek, and Vaddon hissed in pain. The wound itself was minor, but that wasn't what concerned Vaddon. The big question was how much venom did the barb manage to inject into his body during its glancing blow? The general received his answer a split second later when a fiery sensation began spreading through his cheek, along his jawline, and down into his neck. A wave of weakness passed through him, and his sword slipped from his gauntleted hand as he fell to one knee. He felt the venom's fiery touch move swiftly down into his left arm, and vertigo struck him, nearly causing him to collapse. But Vaddon hadn't survived hundreds of battles by giving up easily, and he fought to keep his head clear. His daughter still needed him, and he'd be damned to every hell that had ever existed before he failed her.

Though it took every ounce of willpower he possessed and then some, Vaddon picked up his sword, hauled his body to a standing position, and started toward Lirra once more, doing his best to ignore the poison fire spreading throughout his body.

~~~~~~~

Lirra felt pressure in her head as if there was something inside—something *big*—trying to claw its way deeper into her brain. Accompanying the pressure came the whispering of a sly, sinister voice that sounded too much like her own, though she knew it wasn't. With each word the thought-voice spoke, the pressure inside her head mounted.

Submit . . . give yourself over to me . . . let us be One . . .

She tried to ignore the voice as she concentrated on moving her sword arm so she could cut herself free of the damned tentacle whip. But no matter how hard she fought against the symbiont's influence, she could not make her arm budge even a fraction of an inch more toward the creature. Its will to survive was simply too strong. As soon as the thought passed through her mind, she felt an answering surge of elation that she knew didn't originate in her own heart. It was the whip, excited that it had managed to dominate her to such an extent, and eager to assert its control over her further.

You might be able to prevent me from harming you, Lirra thought, *but that doesn't mean you own me.*

The thought-voice whispered in her mind. *We'll see about that.*

Lirra was about to redouble her efforts to cut the symbiont off of her when she caught a flash of movement out of the corner of her eye. She turned to see her father coming toward her, expression grim, sword held tight. She understood instantly that he thought he was coming to her rescue, and while she loved him for it, she inwardly cursed him too. The whip was too wild, too dangerous, and she couldn't—

She watched helplessly as the tentacle whip lashed out, its barbed tip grazing Vaddon's cheek. The wound swelled red as the symbiont's poison went to work, and her father staggered and fell to one knee. She sensed the whip's elation at having brought down an enemy, and she knew it intended to strike again, this time to deliver a full dose of poison, killing Vaddon.

NO! she shouted in her mind, and the tentacle whip froze, poised for a second strike but unable to complete it. The terrible pressure assaulting her mind eased slightly, and Lirra managed a smile. *Now who owns whom?* she thought. She felt the whip's answering rage as if the emotion were her own, so intense that it almost knocked her off her feet, but she rode it out and the feeling subsided to the point where it became manageable. She wanted to go to her father's aid, but she knew she couldn't risk bringing the tentacle whip any closer to him. She might've been able to stop it from attacking once, but that didn't mean she'd be able to do so a second time. Better to keep the symbiont away from everyone while she fought to get rid of it.

She glanced at Vaddon then and saw he'd managed to stand and was coming toward her once more. The entire left side of his face was swollen, as was a good portion of his neck, and his gaze was bright and feverish. But still he continued forward. If she could just keep him away . . .

As if in response to her thought, the tentacle whip lashed out, grabbed hold of Vaddon's right ankle, and yanked the man's leg out from under him. The general flew backward and cracked his unprotected head on the chamber's stone floor. He moaned once and then lay still. Before Lirra could react, the whip released its grip on Vaddon's ankle and coiled about her arm. She sensed a certain amount of dark amusement coming from the symbiont, but there was something else, too, a more subdued, almost compliant thought that seemed to say, *See? I can be useful when I want to.*

Lirra feared the worst for her father. Tentacle whip venom was raging through his system, and he'd just received a severe blow to the head. Either condition alone might prove fatal, but together . . .

Evidently Ksana was thinking along the same lines, for the cleric dropped her halberd and ran to Vaddon's side. The half-elf laid a hand upon the general's swollen cheek, closed her eyes, and began softly murmuring prayers to her goddess. Confident her father was in good hands, Lirra looked away and turned her attention toward Elidyr and Sinnoch. She was just in time to witness the closing of the spatial portal above the Overmantle. When the rift between realms was sealed, the malignant presence that had filled the chamber vanished, and the atmosphere immediately felt less oppressive, almost like the aftermath of a terrible thunderstorm.

Lirra was thrilled. Her uncle had succeeded in closing the portal and preventing whatever had been on the other side from coming through. It was over.

She sensed an amused thought from the tentacle whip: *Not quite. Watch.*

Elidyr began laughing, but it wasn't the relieved laughter of a man who'd just survived a close call with death—or worse. This was the cackling mad laughter of an unhinged mind. As she watched, Elidyr raised his arms above his head and spoke two simple words.

"To me!"

A trio of distorted shapes moved swiftly forth from the shadows, and Lirra recognized the other symbionts that had been used in the failed experiment. All three of them—the crawling gauntlet, the tongueworm, and the stormstalk—rushed toward the artificer with frightening speed and launched themselves at him. If Elidyr felt any pain as the symbionts grafted themselves to his flesh, he didn't show it. He merely stood, arms raised, a beatific look in his eyes as if he were a religious supplicant receiving his god's blessing. Within seconds the aberrations had fused with Elidyr's body, and the artificer lowered his hands and looked at Sinnoch.

"What do you think?" Elidyr asked.

Sinnoch grinned. "It suits you, my friend."

Elidyr's answering smile was lopsided and his eyes blazed fiercely. "My thoughts precisely."

It shouldn't have been possible for her uncle to have three symbionts attached to his body. There shouldn't have been enough blood in him to sustain more than one aberration, and the strain on his system of hosting three should've killed him. But he looked perfectly healthy. Almost *too* much so, as if bonding with the symbionts had increased the strength of his life-force. Perhaps it had something to do with the power generated by the Overmantle—or with the chaos energy that had filtered through the portal to Xoriat. Whichever the case, not only did Elidyr appear to be suffering no ill effects from fusing with the symbionts, he appeared stronger than ever. And from the wild, mad expression on his face, he had become completely insane.

If bonding with the symbionts had driven him to lunacy, then he was a greater threat than all of the aberrations combined. For he still stood before the Overmantle, and though it was now shut down, he might well choose to reactivate it again—and reopen the portal to Xoriat. And this time, whatever was on the other side might well make it all the way through.

Lirra glanced at Ksana and saw the cleric was still tending to her injured father. With the other soldiers dead, that left only Rhedyn to help Lirra deal with her uncle. She'd lost track of Rhedyn in all the confusion, but she found him standing next to the body of the woman he'd slain. He stood watching Elidyr, sword held at his side, the dark aspect of his shadow sibling full upon him, so that he appeared to be standing in deep shadow. Lirra had a difficult time making out his facial features, but his expression seemed to be one of wonder and . . . she wasn't certain, but she thought it might be satisfaction. What was wrong with him? He shouldn't just be standing there! He was a soldier; he should be fighting!

A thought whispered through her mind. *He's one of us . . .*

I'm not US! Lirra thought, but in response the tentacle whip only coiled more tightly around her forearm.

"Rhedyn!" she shouted. "Help me!"

He didn't react at first, and Lirra feared that something had happened to his mind during the time the Xoriat portal had been open. But then he turned to her and slowly smiled behind the shadow that cloaked him. The sight of that smile hit Lirra like a blow to the gut. Rhedyn—*her* Rhedyn—had gone mad just like Elidyr. Following on the heels of that thought was a worse one: What if he'd been mad for some time now, perhaps from the moment he'd fused with his shadow sibling? She remembered the words he'd spoken during his visit to her room last night.

I cannot—will not—give up my shadow sibling. As an impure prince, I can serve Karrnath in ways others could never hope to. And as long as I remain bound to a symbiont, I will repulse you physically. But if you were to accept a symbiont . . .

Of course Rhedyn was smiling, for he'd gotten his wish. She was bound to a symbiont. At least for the moment. But as long as that was the case, she might as well make some use of the damned thing.

She turned away from Rhedyn and started toward Elidyr.

CHAPTER EIGHT

It looks like I'm not the only one who's made a new friend today," Elidyr said, eyeing the tentacle whip coiled about her arm. He nodded approvingly. "It suits you, Lirra."

She felt an intense surge of rage at her uncle's words. He'd become a loathsome monstrosity, as much an aberration as the dolgaunt standing next to him, an unclean, unnatural thing that needed to be removed from the world, and she wanted nothing more than to strike him down. Her fingers tightened on her sword, and she felt the coils of the tentacle whip go slack around her forearm as it prepared to attack.

It was the whip's reaction that helped her understand why she felt such rage. The whip was using the repugnance she felt upon seeing her uncle's transformation to goad her into attacking him. She hadn't realized the creature could be that subtle. There was no way she was going to allow the tentacle whip to control her, and so she stopped three feet from her uncle and lowered her sword to her side.

She gritted her teeth against the rage still roiling inside her and forced herself to speak calmly. "I don't know what went wrong with the experiment, Uncle, but you have to let us help you. You can't survive long with three symbionts attached to your body."

Elidyr grinned at Lirra as if what she'd said was the funniest thing he'd ever heard. But it wasn't her uncle who responded to her words: It was Sinnoch.

"If your uncle was an ordinary human, you'd be correct," the dolgaunt said. "But he's become something more, something *better*. He's far more than a mere human now." The dolgaunt paused, and though it didn't have eyebrows exactly, Lirra had the impression the creature frowned. "Though to be honest, I'm not certain precisely *what* he is, but I imagine we'll have a great deal of fun trying to find out. Don't you?"

You should kill him too, whispered a voice in her mind, and she'd have been hard-pressed to say whether the thought originated with her or the symbiont. Again she felt the rage, so strong this time that it nearly overwhelmed her, but she fought it down and managed to stay in control, if only just.

"Be silent, dolgaunt," she said. "I'm not talking to you; I'm talking to my uncle."

Sinnoch's inhuman mouth twisted into an amused smile, but from the way the tendrils on top of his head writhed, Lirra knew the dolgaunt was irritated with her. She'd never been able to read the aberration's body language before, and she realized that becoming bonded with the tentacle whip had somehow granted her a deeper understanding of the denizens of Xoriat. But sympathy did not accompany that understanding. She still wanted to ram her sword blade into the dolgaunt's cadaverous chest and thrust the needle-sharp tip through his heart—assuming the foul thing even *had* a heart. But she resisted. Just because she was bound to a symbiont didn't make her a creature like Sinnoch. Not even close. As satisfying as it would be to destroy the dolgaunt—and the way she felt right now, it would be most satisfying indeed—Lirra was a highly trained soldier, and she only killed when there was no other course of action available to her.

A sullen thought drifted through her mind: *Spoilsport.*

"Nothing went wrong today, child," Elidyr said. "Everything went very, very right." He flexed the fingers of his crawling gauntlet, and the stormstalk draped around his shoulders swayed back and forth, keeping Lirra fixed with its single overlarge eye. "I've been cooped up in this damned lodge too long. I'd like to take a stroll, get out and stretch my legs a bit. I see things so very differently than I did before. I wonder what the world will look like through these new eyes of mine." He grinned. "I can't wait to find out." He turned toward Sinnoch. "Look after the Overmantle for me, will you? I'll be back for it."

The dolgaunt inclined his head. "As you wish."

Elidyr then looked over to where Ksana was ministering to his fallen brother. "I'd say farewell to Vaddon, but it appears as if he's somewhat preoccupied at the moment." He turned back to Lirra, still grinning. "Be a good girl and tell your father that while I've enjoyed working together, I think it's time I went into business for myself. And as for you, my dear, have fun with your new pet. I think the two of you are going to get along magnificently."

And with that, Elidyr began walking toward the chamber's exit.

Lirra started after him. "I can't let you go, Uncle. You're not in your right mind, and in your condition, you're a danger to yourself and others."

Elidyr stopped and turned around to face her. His grin was even wider than before, and his gaze shone bright with madness.

"My sweet child, you have *no* idea what a danger I truly am."

Elidyr made no movement, but the stormstalk perched on his shoulders suddenly stiffened and a bolt of lightning blasted forth from its eye. Crackling energy struck Lirra full on the chest. She staggered backward as pain coursed through her body and her muscles went rigid. Her vision grayed at the edges and she thought she would lose consciousness, but as quickly as it came, the pain receded, her muscles unlocked, and her vision cleared.

You're stronger now, a voice whispered inside her. *We're stronger . . .*

Without thinking, she flicked her left arm forward, and the tentacle whip uncoiled, sending its barbed tip flying toward Elidyr's face. Moving with inhuman speed, the artificer raised his crawling gauntlet in time to intercept the whip. Crustacean-like claws closed around the whip's barb, and Elidyr gave a vicious yank. The artificer was now far stronger than he had been before becoming fused with his symbionts and receiving the touch of a daelkyr lord, and Lirra—unable to resist his strength—was pulled stumbling toward Elidyr. Overwhelming fury surged through her. She was a Karrnathi warrior, and she refused to be defeated!

She still retained a grip on her sword, and she brought it swinging around in a wide arc toward the stormstalk, determined to slice through the grotesque thing and, if possible, through her uncle's neck as well. Part of her was horrified at the realization that she was ready to kill Elidyr when only a moment before she'd wanted to help him. But that part was as nothing compared to the white-hot battle-fury raging inside her, and she gave herself over to it completely, unable to resist.

Elidyr opened his mouth wide and the tongueworm shot forth. It wrapped around Lirra's wrist and pushed her sword arm upward, deflecting her strike. The blade whistled through the air above Elidyr's head, doing no damage to either the stormstalk or its master. She fought to bring her sword back in a reverse strike, but the tongueworm held her arm fast, preventing her.

Two can play at this game, she thought.

She gave a mental command to the tentacle whip, and though its barbed tip was still held tightly in Elidyr's gauntlet, it had plenty of length left to fight with. Its coils extended upward toward the artificer's head, looped around his neck, and began to squeeze. However strong Elidyr had become and whatever fell powers he now possessed, he still needed to breathe.

Elidyr had been grinning the entire time they fought, and though his face began to turn a dark red as the tentacle whip strangled him, his grin didn't waver. The stormstalk swiveled its head toward the whip and unleashed another bolt of lightning, but though Lirra felt the same agony course through her body as before as the energy passed through the whip and into her, she was ready for the pain now, and it came and went quickly. Let the damned stalk loose bolt after bolt of energy at her. She'd endure the pain and stand strong while Elidyr's lungs cried out for air. It would only take a few moments before he lost consciousness, and a few more after that for him to die. And then she, with but a single symbiont, would've defeated an opponent who wielded three! A glorious victory indeed!

No! We can't kill him! she thought.

Watch us! came the reply, and she couldn't tell if the thought was the whip's, hers, or if it belonged to them both.

The coils tightened further around Elidyr's neck, and the artificer's face edged toward deep purple. Still grinning, he raised his left hand, the one without the gauntlet, and extended it palm forward toward Lirra. The air around the artificer's hand wavered, like heat distortion rising off the ground in the summertime. A sudden wave of vertigo gripped Lirra and her stomach twisted with nausea. Her vision blurred, sharpened, blurred again, and all the strength drained out of her body. Her muscles were weak as water, and she slumped to the floor, dropping her sword in the process. Whatever Elidyr was doing, it affected the tentacle whip as well. The symbiont's coils loosened around Elidyr's throat, and he released its barbed end from the grip of his crawling gauntlet. The whip hung slack from the artificer's neck, and Elidyr reached up with both hands and easily removed the coils from around his neck and dropped them to the floor. The tongueworm then released its grip on Lirra's wrist and retracted into Elidyr's body. When the worm was once again concealed, the artificer gazed down at his niece.

"Did you enjoy that? It's a little taste of Xoriat chaos energy. Don't worry. You'll recover in due course, though I'll be long gone by then." He paused and tilted his head, as if considering. "You know, I really *should* kill you right now while you're helpless. I have a sneaking suspicion that it would make my life much easier if I did. But then again, what would be the fun in that? Farewell, Lirra."

"Hold, artificer!"

Lirra couldn't move her head to turn toward Rhedyn, but he quickly stepped into her line of sight, cloaked in shadow and gripping his sword. Seeing him filled Lirra with hope. It seemed he had finally shaken off the effect of whatever had held him motionless, and he was ready to rejoin the fight.

Elidyr looked at the warrior for a long moment, his eyes dancing with amusement, and Lirra couldn't help feeling her uncle was laughing inside at some private joke. Then he raised his left hand once more.

"You really need to pay more attention, Rhedyn. Didn't you hear what I just told Lirra?"

Elidyr unleashed a fresh blast of chaos energy at Rhedyn, and the warrior's dark aspect vanished, as if his shadow sibling had retreated deep within his body, and he collapsed to the floor.

Without another word, Elidyr turned and walked out of the chamber, moving with an unhurried gait and humming brightly to himself. Lirra, still suffering the aftereffects of the chaos energy Elidyr had attacked her with, was too weak to do anything more but glare at her uncle as he departed. She made a vow to herself at that moment—the instant she could stand again, she was going after him.

A weak thought drifted into her mind from the tentacle whip. *That's my girl . . .*

———✦———

Vaddon opened his eyes and tried to sit up, but he felt a gentle hand on his forehead urge him back down.

"After what you've been through, you need to rest," Ksana said.

An old joke from his days commanding a regiment of undead came back to him, and he uttered it without thinking. "I'll rest when I'm dead—and maybe not even then." He pushed the cleric's hand away and sat up, though he was unable to keep himself from groaning as he did so. You're getting old, soldier, he thought, and not for the first time. "What happened? I don't—"

A quick glance around the chamber brought his memory back in a sudden rush.

Lirra!

All weakness fled at the thought of his daughter, and the general rose to his feet, sword in hand, ready to fight. But another glance around the chamber revealed that the battle was already finished. Seven of his men and women lay dead—the volunteers for the experiment and those who'd been selected to guard them. Only Osten still lived. The young soldier was sitting up, fingers gently probing a ragged wound at the base of his throat. Sinnoch stood next to the Overmantle—which seemed to have been deactivated, thank the Host—but there was no sign of Elidyr. Rhedyn crouched on his hands and knees, struggling to stand but having a hard time of it. Vaddon had no idea what had happened to the lad, but it seemed something had knocked the starch out of him. And then he saw Lirra, and the sight of her nearly broke his heart. She stood not far from Rhedyn, and while she looked none too steady on her legs, she appeared to be uninjured. Vaddon was grateful for that, but the sight of the tentacle whip fused to her flesh filled him with almost unbearable sorrow. The general was in charge of the Outguard's project, and Lirra was his second in command. They were supposed to oversee the experiments at the lodge, not actually take part in them, not like *this*. The thought of his daughter's body being joined with an aberration—being one with it—made him feel physically ill, and he would go to the grave before he'd allow Lirra to be afflicted with an inhuman parasite a moment longer.

Vaddon picked up his sword from the floor, rose to his feet through a sheer effort of will and started toward his daughter. Ksana stood and without a word headed over to tend to Osten. Undoubtedly the cleric would've preferred Vaddon continue resting, but she understood why he had to do this, and so she said nothing.

Vaddon cautiously approached his daughter, mindful of the way the symbionts had taken over the bodies of their hosts during the experiment. Was Lirra in control of her body or was the tentacle whip?

"Lirra . . . can you hear me?" he asked.

She faced the chamber entrance, as if she were looking at something—or perhaps *for* something—but the doorway was empty. She didn't respond right away, and Vaddon tightened his hand on his sword, fearing the worst. But then she slowly turned to look at him. Vaddon expected her features to be twisted by the evil of the symbiont attached to her, but he was surprised to see how normal she looked. Her skin was paler than usual, but Vaddon was well familiar with the expression of grim determination on his daughter's face, and for the first time since seeing the tentacle whip attack Lirra, he allowed himself to hope that her iron will had allowed her to resist the aberration's attempts to usurp control of her body.

"He got away, Father."

There was an undercurrent of anger to Lirra's words that Vaddon found disturbing.

"Who did?" But even as he asked the question, he knew the answer. There was only one person missing from the chamber.

"Elidyr." Lirra practically spat her uncle's name. "I was just about to go after him. He can't have gotten far. If we hurry, we'll be able to catch him."

Without waiting for Vaddon to reply, she turned and started toward the chamber door. The tentacle whip was coiled around her left forearm, its barbed tip quivering in the air, as if the symbiont was excited by the prospect of the hunt to come.

"Wait!"

Vaddon hurried toward Lirra as fast as his armor would allow. Lirra stopped and turned back around to face him, but the instant Vaddon was within striking distance, the tentacle whip uncoiled from around Lirra's forearm and lashed toward him. Vaddon quickly raised an armored forearm to block the aberration's attack, but he needn't have bothered. Lirra yanked her left arm backward violently, throwing off the tentacle whip's aim, and the barbed tip missed Vaddon's face by several feet.

"He's not a threat!" Lirra snapped.

At first Vaddon had no idea who she was talking to, but then he realized that she was addressing the tentacle whip. From what Elidyr had told him back when they first began the symbiont project, the aberrations possessed a certain amount of intelligence, could understand spoken language, and even communicate telepathically with their hosts, if only in a rudimentary way. But hearing his own daughter speak to one of the damned things as if she were scolding a misbehaving hound deeply disturbed him.

But her words had the desired effect. The whip—somewhat reluctantly, Vaddon thought—drew its length back toward Lirra, wrapped around her forearm once again, and settled down. He slowly sheathed his sword. Lirra appeared to be in control of her body, at least for the time being. And while it might not have been the most strategic of moves, holding a sword against his own flesh and blood didn't sit well with Vaddon, so battle strategy be damned.

He remained standing where he was, several yards away from Lirra, and he made sure to keep his hand well away from his sword, sheathed or not.

"What happened to Elidyr?" he asked. "I was unconscious for a time and didn't see."

"A daelkyr lord reached through the portal to Xoriat and touched him," Lirra said. "The creature's touch drove Elidyr mad. He called to the other three symbionts and they bonded with him. It shouldn't have been possible—a person can't serve as host to more than one—but Elidyr managed it. That creature's touch did more than destroy your brother's sanity, Father. It changed him somehow." She paused and then slowly turned and trained a suspicious, narrow-eyed gaze on Sinnoch.

Almost faster than Vaddon could track, Lirra dashed across the chamber toward the dolgaunt, unfurling the tentacle whip as she ran. With a flick of her arm, the whip's coils wrapped around Sinnoch's chest, pinning his arms and back tentacles in place. The barbed tip of the symbiont hovered in front of the dolgaunt's face, swaying back and forth as if it was a serpent that might strike at any moment. Sinnoch didn't struggle against the tentacle whip's grip, and he appeared undisturbed by Lirra attacking him. He merely grinned that oversized grin of his.

Seeing Lirra move that swiftly made Vaddon realize that Elidyr hadn't been the only one changed during the course of the experiment. Becoming bonded with a symbiont normally enhanced a host's strength, speed, and ability to heal to a certain degree, but nothing like what Vaddon had just witnessed. What had happened to his poor daughter?

Lirra leaned close to Sinnoch's face, and the tentacle whip's barb tapped the dolgaunt lightly on the nose several times, as if to make sure he was paying attention.

"You were Uncle's assistant, and you know more about Xoriat and its creatures than any of us here. You must know what happened to him."

"I might have an idea or two," the dolgaunt said, still grinning.

Lirra scowled and her lips drew back from her teeth in an expression that was almost a snarl. Though she made no outward move, the tentacle whip's coils tightened around Sinnoch's chest, and the dolgaunt let out a pained gasp, followed by an amused chuckle that sent a shiver down Vaddon's spine.

"Keep making jokes and I'll keep squeezing," Lirra said.

Not *the whip will keep squeezing,* Vaddon noticed. But rather *I will.* A mere slip of the tongue, or was it a sign that Lirra was beginning to lose her individuality? Vaddon was mindful that Osten had hosted the tentacle whip for several days before the aberration had taken control of his body. Just because Lirra appeared to be in control at the moment didn't mean she was going to stay that way.

"You humans have no sense of fun," Sinnoch said, almost sounding as if he was pouting. "Very well. Elidyr designed the Overmantle so that a host might join with a symbiont and remain in complete control, but—if you were paying attention—you also know that the device clearly failed. And very spectacularly so, I might add. Instead of bolstering the host's psychic defenses to resist a symbiont's dominating influence, the chaos energy drawn from Xoriat made both host and symbiont stronger." Sinnoch smiled. "That's the problem with trying to control chaos, of course. The harder you try, the more you're bound to fail. I tried to explain that to Elidyr on numerous occasions, but he's human, and your kind can be so very stubborn."

"That only explains part of it," Lirra said. "Something else happened to Elidyr." She leaned her face close to Sinnoch's and bared her teeth, almost as if she were prepared to bite him if he didn't answer to her satisfaction. Vaddon found the naked ferocity on his daughter's face more disturbing than the eyeless visage of the dolgaunt. "Did you have anything to do with it?"

"I did not. Your uncle was blessed by the touch of a daelkyr lord. With that single touch, he reshaped Elidyr, made him into something more than human. Precisely what, I couldn't tell you, but I'm sure he's going to have fun finding out."

Lirra glanced to the side and muttered, as if speaking to herself. Or maybe, Vaddon thought, a sinking feeling in the pit of his stomach, speaking to her symbiont.

"That's why he can host three aberrations and unleash blasts of chaos energy. I wonder what else he can do." She looked down at where the tentacle whip joined to her forearm. "I wonder what *we* can do."

We, Vaddon thought. She said *we.*

She turned back to Sinnoch and flexed her forearm. In response, the tentacle whip tightened its coils around the dolgaunt further, and the creature hissed in pain. One corner of Lirra's mouth edged up in a half smile, and a dark look came into her eyes. Vaddon realized she was enjoying the dolgaunt's discomfort, and the sight sickened him to the core.

"Stop it, Lirra!" Without thinking, he started to reach for her left arm, intending to pull her off Sinnoch, but he restrained himself. All he'd earn for his effort was another attack by the symbiont.

Lirra relaxed her forearm, and the tentacle whip loosened its coils, though it did not release Sinnoch. She then slowly turned to Vaddon and gave him a calculating look, as if she was reappraising him in some way. "This is a supreme irony, Father. You, defending an aberration. You hate the things more than anyone else in the Outguard."

"I don't care about the damned dolgaunt," Vaddon snapped. "I care about you! Can't you see what's happening? That symbiont is poisoning your mind . . . filling your heart with fury, making you act irrationally . . . Let us help you, Lirra."

"Your father's right."

Vaddon turned to see Ksana standing by his side, halberd held in a tight grip. He glanced over his shoulder to see Osten was sitting up. The lad looked dazed, but the wound on his throat had vanished, and his color looked good. Rhedyn had managed to get to his feet, but the soldier made no move toward Lirra. He just stood watching the drama play out before him, as if he was unsure how he could best help.

Ksana continued. "We can help you separate from the symbiont. It won't be an easy process, you know that, for you've witnessed it before, and in your case I fear it will be even more difficult if what Sinnoch says is true about the symbiont having been strengthened by the Overmantle's energies. The creature will not let go of you easily, I'll warrant. But you're a fighter, my child, born and bred, and with Dol Arrah to lend me strength, I will do everything in my power to make certain you are free of that abomination."

"Neither of you understand," Lirra said. "The Overmantle may not have functioned as Elidyr had hoped, but it did achieve its ultimate aim. It produced a weapon—*me*. You said yourself that you were unconscious when Elidyr changed, Father. You didn't see what he's become. He's incredibly powerful and absolutely insane. If there's any hope of stopping him, it lies with me—and my symbiont. After I've dealt with Elidyr—"

Vaddon interrupted. "Listen to yourself. *Dealt* with him? What do you plan to do? Kill your own uncle? Don't delude yourself into thinking you can control your symbiont, Lirra. If there's anything this whole misbegotten project has taught us, it's that creatures of chaos cannot be controlled."

"I don't plan to control it, Father. I plan to *use* it." She smiled grimly. "There's a difference."

Vaddon knew then that reason wasn't going to work on Lirra. How could it, when she obviously wasn't in her right mind?

"Lirra, I am your father, but I'm also your commanding officer. I order you to release the dolgaunt and surrender yourself into my custody. Immediately."

Lirra looked at Vaddon for a long moment, her expression unreadable. When she finally spoke, her tone was calm, almost casual.

"I have never disobeyed an order from a superior, Father. Unfortunately, after today, I'll never be able to say that again."

She spun around and hurled Sinnoch toward Vaddon and Ksana. The tentacle whip uncoiled, releasing the dolgaunt so swiftly that neither the general nor the cleric had time to move out the way. The creature slammed into them hard, and all three of them fell to the chamber floor.

Ksana was back on her feet before Vaddon, whose armor slowed him down, and the half-elf helped him to his feet. But it was too late. Lirra was gone.

CHAPTER NINE

Ranja had been watching Bergerron's hunting lodge for three stultifying days when something interesting finally happened. The shifter had taken up a perch in an oak tree that provided an excellent view of the lodge, but which also had thick enough foliage to keep any of the soldiers stationed there from spotting her when they patrolled the area. Her mottled green clothing helped camouflage her, though given how obviously thick-headed the soldiers were, she doubted they'd have seen her if the tree was completely bereft of leaves and she was lounging naked among the bare branches. But that was Karrns for you. Steel in their spines, icewater in their veins, and fire in their hearts, but not a whole lot going on upstairs.

It was late morning on the fourth day of Ranja's vigil when a man came strolling out of the lodge's entrance, whistling gaily as if he were looking forward to a pleasant stroll. Except this man had three symbionts fused to his body. Ranja had worked as a mercenary since she was young—mostly doing scouting and spywork, though she'd fought if the money was right—and during her career she'd seen any number of strange if not downright bizarre sights that if nothing else made for good storytelling over a pint of ale or three. But she'd never seen anything quite like this before. She'd seen symbionts bonded to hosts before, sure, but not three! Within moments the man had disappeared into the surrounding forest. Ranja was tempted to follow him simply to satisfy her curiosity, but her employer's instructions had been quite clear.

"I want to know what's going on in Bergerron's lodge, and I want to know now. Don't even *think* about coming back until you find out."

Arnora Raskogr was a haughty bitch, but she paid well, and that was what mattered most to Ranja. So while she might find out the true nature of the secret work going on in the lodge by following the amazing three-symbiont man, she might also miss out on some important development here if she left her observation post. Besides, as a shifter, her senses were keener than a human's, and symbionts offended her on a primal level. Simply put, the damned things were just *wrong,* and she couldn't stand being around them—and that man had *three* of them fused to his body. How could he even survive with that many symbionts attached to him? No, maybe she'd be better off erring on the side of caution for a change, at least in this particular instance. So Ranja had decided to stay in her tree, sore though her muscles were, and watch a little longer—not that she had all that long to wait until someone else left the lodge.

The first thing Ranja noticed was that the woman also had a symbiont, just one, and hers was different from any the man possessed. The second thing she noticed was that the woman was definitely not in as good a mood as the whistling man had been. She rushed out of the lodge, sword in hand, and swept a fury-filled gaze around the area, obviously searching for something . . . or someone. The woman—whom Ranja thought of as Curly because of her hair—then shouted, "I know you're out there! Show yourself!"

Ranja's stomach muscles clenched, and she thought Curly had somehow detected her presence, maybe because of some power the symbiont had granted her. But then the woman shouted again.

"Elidyr! Where are you? Can you hear me, Uncle?"

Ranja relaxed a bit then. Obviously Curly was addressing the man who'd left the lodge earlier. And, unless *Uncle* was some kind of nickname, it seemed the two of them were related. This was getting more interesting all the time.

Curly waited for a moment, as if she actually expected Elidyr to answer her. Then she picked a direction, seemingly at random, and ran off in pursuit of the man. Unfortunately for her, the direction she chose wasn't even close to the one her uncle had selected. She plunged into the forest surrounding the lodge and was quickly lost to sight.

Ranja was puzzled by the woman's behavior. From the way the woman held her sword and carried herself, she was obviously a trained soldier. But she'd taken no time to determine in which direction Elidyr had gone; instead, she'd just started running. Ranja had heard that bonding with a symbiont adversely affected one's mind. Perhaps Curly wasn't thinking straight. Then again, how could anyone think clearly with some unnatural parasite attached to your flesh and feeding on your blood?

A group of soldiers burst out of the lodge's entrance. An old man wearing armor shouted for the soldiers to find Elidyr and Lirra—no doubt Curly's real name—and the men and women under his command raced off into the woods, some on foot, some on horseback. The old man didn't join them, however. He was pale and looked weak, and he went back inside the lodge, leaning on a half-elf woman for support.

Once the area around the lodge was empty again, Ranja grinned. She was glad she'd resisted the urge to go after either Elidyr or Lirra. Now that she'd watched the little drama unfold outside the lodge, she thought she had a basic idea of what had been going on here—and what had gone wrong. It looked like Raskogr's suspicions about this place and what Bergerron's people were up to here were correct.

She'd learned enough to return to Raskogr's keep and make her report to the warlord, but Ranja didn't depart right away. She'd seen enough to earn her admittedly high fee, but if she could learn even more about what had happened here today, she might be able to squeeze even more silver pieces out of Raskogr. Besides, Ranja's curiosity was piqued now, and if there was one thing the shifter loved more than silver, it was adventure, and she sensed that a goodly amount might be found in sticking with this job a little longer. So she flipped a mental coin to see which one she would follow—Elidyr or Lirra—and in the end the curly-headed woman won.

Grinning, Ranja slipped down from her tree perch with a silent grace and started running noiselessly through the forest.

Vaddon walked down a long hallway, flanked by a pair of warforged guards wearing long swords belted at their waists. One guard was short and squat, with huge, blocky hands, while the other was tall and lean with long, sturdy legs and metal toes that tapered to needle-sharp spikes. Vaddon tried not to resent the guards' presence. All Bergerron's visitors were accompanied by guards within the warlord's keep, friends and allies included, regardless of rank and standing. The fact that Vaddon had only two guards shepherding him was a testament to how much Bergerron liked and trusted him. Vaddon wondered if the warlord would feel the same after today's visit.

It was the evening after the failed experiment. Vaddon had left the lodge on horseback and ridden to the town of Geirrid where he'd caught the lightning rail. Though there wasn't an official stop near Bergerron's keep, Vaddon's rank—along with a sizeable gratuity—had convinced the railmaster to drop him off not far from the keep, and the general hiked the rest of the way. He'd made good time, but he was tired physically as well as emotionally, and his nerves were on edge.

The guards led him to a chamber at the end of the hallway and halted before a large black oak door. The lean guard knocked and Bergerron immediately called out for them to enter. The lean warforged opened the door and stepped inside, and then the squat guard executed a half bow and gestured for Vaddon to go in, as if he were a butler ushering a guest into his master's den. Vaddon entered the room without bothering to acknowledge the guard's gesture, which may or may not have been a clumsy attempt at humor. It was sometimes hard to tell with warforged, especially given their complete lack of facial expression. Veit Bergerron preferred to employ warforged as his personal guards, for to him they seemed the ultimate soldiers, created for the sole purpose of engaging in battle and possessing no human weaknesses: no need for food, drink, rest, or sleep. Vaddon had fought both alongside and against warforged during the Last War, and on the whole, if he had to work with nonliving beings, he preferred zombies. At least they had been human once. To him, warforged were nothing more than animated weapons, like swords that had magically sprouted arms and legs and which could fight on their own, and they should be treated as such.

Still, Bergerron's fondness for warforged had made him more amenable to backing the Outguard and the symbiont project, something Vaddon had been grateful for at the time. Now he wished the warlord had withheld his support. If he had, the events of yesterday wouldn't have occurred. His brother would still be sane, and his daughter would still be uncorrupted.

You can't blame Bergerron, Vaddon told himself. It was your project. You were in command. Whatever went wrong was your responsibility, no one else's.

This was Bergerron's library, and the warlord sat in a luxuriously soft leather chair before a fireplace, an open book resting on his lap, a glass of red wine in one hand. The chair and a small mahogany table next to it were the only furnishings in the room. Shelves filled with books lined every inch of the walls, leaving the doorway as the only open space. This truly was the warlord's library, not meant for anyone else to use but him.

Bergerron didn't look up as the lean warforged guard approached with Vaddon in tow. This wasn't necessarily a bad sign, Vaddon knew. Bergerron had the ability to focus single-mindedly on a task, concentrating so deeply that he wasn't aware of his surroundings. Vaddon hadn't seen Bergerron for months, not since the symbiont project began, but the warlord hadn't changed all that much. He'd put on a few pounds, but given his love of good food and drink, that was hardly a surprise. Despite the extra weight, and the fact that the man was in his mid-sixties, Bergerron still resembled the strong soldier he once was. He was broad-shouldered, strong-jawed, and though his shoulder-length hair was silver, his full beard still held a goodly amount of black. Though Bergerron was a powerful, wealthy man, he dressed simply, as was the fashion for Karrnath's warlords, who wished to prove that despite their exalted rank, they were still in touch with the common soldiers they had once been.

The lean warforged stopped in front of the warlord's chair and waited to be recognized, while the squat guard took up a position near the door. Bergerron continued reading until he finished the page he was on, then closed the book and looked up.

"General Brochann to see you, Warlord," the warforged said in a hollow, unemotional voice.

"Thank you, Longstrider. You and Shatterfist may leave."

The warforged named Longstrider turned toward Vaddon and regarded him for a moment. Longstrider's stone features remained fixed and unchanging, as was normal for his kind, but Vaddon had the feeling the creature was sizing him up and trying to decide whether he could be trusted alone with his master. Evidently Vaddon passed muster in the end, for the warforged departed, followed by Shatterfist, who closed the library door behind them. Vaddon knew the guards would take up positions on either side of the door in the outer hall and wait for Bergerron's summons should he need them. Bergerron may have implicitly vouched for Vaddon's trustworthiness by telling the guards they could leave, but that didn't mean the two warforged would go far.

Bergerron smiled at Vaddon. "Sorry it took me a moment to realize you were here. I often get lost when reading poetry."

"I prefer military histories, myself."

Bergerron smiled. "Spoken like a true son of Karrnath. Still, it never hurts to broaden one's horizons, does it? Remember what they teach at Rekkenmark: 'One never knows what knowledge may turn the tide of battle.' "

"True." But even so, Vaddon didn't think he'd be borrowing any of Bergerron's poetry collections in the near future.

"To what do I owe the honor of your visit?" Bergerron asked. "I assume you received my message to shut down the Outguard's project and vacate the lodge." He frowned. "I hope you're not here to try to get me to change my mind."

"No, Warlord. I received your message. I'm here to report what I did upon reading your message"—he paused—"and what happened afterward."

Bergerron raised an eyebrow, but he said nothing, merely waited for Vaddon to continue.

Despite his rank and decades of experience, right then Vaddon felt like a green recruit called on the carpet in front of his commanding officer. He took a deep breath and without preamble launched into his report, though it was a struggle for him to maintain control of his emotions toward the end. Bergerron listened without expression or reaction.

"So, the project *was* a success of sorts," he said after a moment.

Vaddon started to object, but Bergerron held up a hand to forestall him. "Of course what happened to your brother and daughter is regrettable, but their transformations have proven Elidyr's basic theory: Symbionts can make significant weapons. Perhaps not controllable ones at this point, but even if the hosts remained wild and chaotic, they could still be of use. We would only need to aim them at an enemy and turn them loose . . ."

Vaddon didn't believe what he was hearing. When he was a young soldier, he'd served under Bergerron in numerous campaigns, and he'd always admired the man's bravery and sharp, strategic mind. That was why he'd continued to serve the warlord even though the Last War was over. Whenever the Next War inevitably came, Vaddon wanted to be leading troops under Bergerron's banner. But the words coming out of the warlord's mouth now were madness.

"My lord, did you not listen to my tale? The experiment was a disaster! Not only were Lirra and Elidyr turned into uncontrollable monsters, we almost allowed a daelkyr lord to come through into our world!"

Bergerron gave Vaddon an icy glare. "You are understandably distraught over what has happened to your family members, Vaddon, and for that I shall forgive your impertinence. This time. But try to remember your training—in battle, emotions are often the real enemy we must fight."

Another platitude they passed along at the Rekkenmark Academy, and up to this point, one Vaddon had believed in. But now it was just a hollow saying, bereft of meaning. How could he ignore the hideous transformation that had befallen his beloved daughter and brother? But Bergerron was his warlord, and Vaddon had pledged his allegiance to the man, and so he would do his best to keep a tighter rein on his emotions.

Vaddon inclined his head stiffly. "Please accept my apologies, Warlord, along with my gratitude."

Bergerron made a dismissive gesture, and a thoughtful expression came over his face.

"You did the right thing by coming here as soon as possible to inform me of what occurred," Bergerron said. "Tell me, what are the rest of the Outguard doing right now?"

"I gave them orders to complete our withdrawal from the lodge, and then to return to the garrison at Geirrid when the task was finished. Three of my people will make camp on the town's outskirts where they will guard the dolgaunt Sinnoch until my return. The creature swears he had nothing to do with the Overmantle's malfunction, but I don't trust him. I'd have killed him if I didn't think he might still be of some use in finding Lirra and Elidyr."

Bergerron nodded. "Very good. And what of the Overmantle?"

"Elidyr damaged it before departing the lodge, but it remains with those guarding the dolgaunt. There is no danger of the creature repairing it and using it for his own purposes, not without my brother's guidance."

"I see." Bergerron paused for a moment then, as if trying to decide whether or not to continue. "Do you have any idea why I ordered you to shut down the symbiont project so abruptly?"

"I'd assumed that the project's secrecy had been compromised somehow. I intended to look into the matter after we had vacated the lodge."

"You assumed correctly, Vaddon. One of my spies informed me that Arnora Raskogr had somehow gotten wind that something strange was going on at my hunting lodge and that she was planning on letting Kaius know." Bergerron gave Vaddon a thin smile. "We couldn't have that now, could we?"

"No, Warlord."

Vaddon had guessed it was something like that. The intrigues between Karrnath's warlords were constant and never-ending, and they'd only gotten worse with the cessation of hostilities. Warriors needed battles to fight, he supposed, even if they had to manufacture the reasons for those battles themselves.

"I thought you and Warlord Raskogr were on relatively good terms," Vaddon said.

"The key word is *relatively.*" Bergerron grimaced. "For a time she was allied with those of us who believe Kaius to be too weak to lead our nation, but recently she's begun cozying up to him in order to gain his favor. I doubt she's suddenly had a change of heart regarding Kaius's suitability as a ruler. But if nothing else, Arnora has always been a pragmatic woman, and she's likely come to believe that the winds of fortune are currently blowing in Kaius's direction. If she could cast suspicion on me, and Kaius learned of my true feelings about him and the steps I've taken to, if not overthrow him, at least undermine his power, Kaius would be grateful, and Arnora would rise significantly in status."

"How did she find out about the symbiont project?"

Bergerron shrugged. "No doubt from one of her spies serving in my keep. Oh, don't look so shocked, Vaddon. We all have spies planted in each other's homes." He grinned. "Keeps us on our toes."

It all sounded more than a little childish to Vaddon, and he was beginning to regret his pledge to serve Bergerron. "At least the lodge is vacant now, and all traces of the experiment have been removed. Warlord Raskogr will never learn of what happened there."

Bergerron scowled. "I wouldn't be too sure of that. In order to provide Kaius with more than idle speculation, she would've dispatched agents of her own to investigate what was happening at the lodge. It's entirely possible my message—though sent as swiftly as possible—arrived too late, and you were already under surveillance. If that was the case—"

"Then someone might've witnessed both Elidyr and Lirra leaving the lodge," Vaddon finished.

Bergerron nodded. "And the whereabouts of both remain unknown?"

Despair clutched at Vaddon's heart, but he did his best to keep his feelings from showing. "Yes, Warlord. We searched the environs around the lodge before I left, but we found no trace of them. None of the horses were missing, so we know both are on foot." Considering the way a horse would react to a rider bonded to a symbiont, it wasn't surprising both Lirra and Elidyr had chosen to walk. "This leads me to the main reason I've come before you. I request permission to keep the Outguard together for the time being and to remain in command of them, so that I might search for my daughter and brother. Not merely because I am personally concerned for their safety," he hastened to add, "but because I believe that in their current state they pose a very real threat to the people of Karrnath. And while the safety of our fellow countrymen is no doubt of most importance to you, it would be awkward for you if one of the other warlords—Raskogr, say—should learn about Lirra and Elidyr and capture them first."

Bergerron looked Vaddon up and down as if reappraising him. "I imagine you spent quite a lot of time working up that little speech."

Vaddon kept his expression carefully neutral. "As a matter of fact, I did."

"Well, it worked. I'm actually rather impressed. You always struck me as less of a thinker and more of a reliable, stolid man at arms. Looks like you have a bit of warlord in you, Vaddon."

Vaddon's gut curdled at what he took to be an insult, but he forced himself to say, "Thank you, Warlord."

"Very well, permission granted." Bergerron held up a pair of fingers. "With two conditions: One, when you capture your brother and daughter, I want them brought here to my keep. If there's any chance we can train them to be . . . cooperative soldiers, I want to make sure we give them every opportunity. Agreed?"

Vaddon's face remained impassive but inside he seethed with anger. He wanted to capture Lirra and Elidyr so that the aberrations that corrupted their bodies and minds could be removed and, the Host willing, their sanity restored. He knew that he'd never be able to turn them over to be used as tools in Bergerron's intrigues—Lirra especially. The symbiont project was misguided and misbegotten from the start. Vaddon regretted ever taking part in it, and once Lirra and Elidyr were returned to normal, he intended to do everything he could to make certain that symbionts were never used as weapons in Karrnath again. But he knew that if he told Begerron any of this, he'd never obtain the man's permission to continue commanding the Outguard. And that meant, for the first time in his career, Vaddon would have to lie to a superior.

He didn't hesitate. "Agreed."

"Excellent. Now for the second condition." He raised his voice. "Shatterfist, Longstrider, come in, please."

The library door opened and the two warforged guards entered and crossed the room to stand before their master.

Begerron looked at Vaddon. "These are two of my best warforged. As of this moment they are assigned to the Outguard under your command, Vaddon, but while they shall take orders from you, ultimately, they will answer to me." A slow smile spread across the warlord's face. "If Lirra and Elidyr have truly become as dangerous as you say, I figure you could use the extra muscle. Agreed?"

Vaddon knew he had been outmaneuvered. Bergerron had guessed that he'd had no intention of delivering Lirra and Elidyr to him, and so he'd decided to send along his pet warforged to make certain Vaddon did as he wanted. Though Vaddon raged inwardly at this development, on one level he couldn't help admiring the warlord's keen grasp of strategy.

"Agreed," he said through clenched teeth.

At least for the time being, he thought darkly, giving the two warforged a narrow-eyed glance.

The artificial constructs gazed back at him with their armorlike faces, and whatever thoughts they might've had about their new assignment they kept to themselves.

CHAPTER TEN

Lirra had no memory of the sun setting. It seemed that one moment it was day, the next it was night. She had no clear idea where she was either. She was walking across a grassy field that she took to be pastureland for cows, based on the occasional pile of dung she passed, though she'd seen no actual cattle so far. There were no farms of any sort in the vicinity of the lodge. The closest she knew about lay outside the town of Geirrid, but it wasn't possible that she had traveled that far since leaving the lodge . . . was it?

She remembered leaving the lodge in search of Elidyr, remembered making her way through forestland, hiding when necessary to avoid Outguard patrols her father had sent out to search for her. While her symbiont granted her no special abilities when it came to concealment, it did possess a certain animal cunning that she was able to draw on, and combined with her battle experience, it allowed her to evade detection and capture. She'd been surprised and, though she was reluctant to admit it to herself, pleased to discover that her symbiont was proving to be an even more useful tool than she'd originally thought.

Too bad it hadn't sharpened her sense of time. Hours had to have passed since she left the lodge, but though she searched her memory, she couldn't account for them all. Her hours traveling through the forest were a blur of trees and fields seen through a white-hot rage that only seemed to intensify as the time passed. She was furious at Elidyr for having bungled the experiment so badly—and for having the idiocy to conceive of the symbiont project in the first place. She was furious at her father for not understanding why she needed to find and stop Elidyr and sending forth the Outguard to get in her way. She was furious at Rhedyn for standing stupidly by and watching as the tentacle whip attached itself to her and for not finding the stones to act against Elidyr until it was too late to make a difference. And to make matters worse, she was hungry, thirsty, and her feet ached from all the walking she'd done this day.

The night sky was overcast, as it often was this time of year, and the cloud cover blocked the moons. Though Karrns preferred straightforward battle—which normally meant fighting by daylight—Lirra was no stranger to making her way across country in the dark, and it seemed that her night vision had grown a bit sharper, no doubt another benefit granted by her symbiont. But even so, she was having trouble navigating through the shadows that surrounded her. Her mind felt sluggish, almost feverish, and she was having trouble making sense of the things she saw and heard. It was almost like the confusion that came with being drunk, except without the accompanying pleasant numbness. Most likely she was still adjusting to having joined with a symbiont. Hopefully her mind would clear eventually. In the meantime, she had to find Elidyr, and when she did . . .

She heard a sound off to her right, a snuffling as if something large was breathing close by. Without thinking she spun and flung her left arm in its direction. Her tentacle whip unfurled, and as the barbed tip flew through the air, wild elation filled her, and she couldn't tell whether it originated from the symbiont or her. She saw the shape standing before her, a dark outline framed against the night, and for an instant she allowed herself to believe she had caught up with her uncle at last. But she quickly realized the shape was the wrong size—too long and low to the ground—and whatever it was, it possessed four legs instead of two. Elidyr might've fused with a trio of symbionts, but when he'd departed the lodge, he'd done so on a single pair of legs.

She felt more than saw the barbed tip sink into flesh, sensed poison being injected into whatever creature the whip had struck. Lirra yanked the whip away from its victim, but it was too late. The poison had been delivered, and the creature swayed and collapsed heavily on its side without making a sound. For all Lirra knew, the creature could've been some dangerous wild animal, and while the symbiont's poison had brought it down, that didn't mean the creature was dead yet. But she was too horrified at the ease with which she'd lost control of the whip, how she'd lashed out without thinking, and she walked over to the downed beast and kneeled beside it, the tentacle whip undulating in the air over the creature, almost quivering in its excitement to strike again. Lirra ignored it and placed her hand on the beast's side. She felt short-haired hide over solid muscle, and she knew what she had brought down before she heard the animal's soft, pained exhalation of breath. The whip had poisoned a cow.

The animal began to pant, sides bellowing in and out as she struggled to draw air into her rapidly failing body. It didn't take long for the symbiont's poison to do its work. Several moments later the cow's breathing slowed, she shuddered once, and then lay still. But though the animal was dead, Lirra slowly stroked the cow's side.

An accident, she thought. Nothing more. And it wasn't as if she'd killed a human. She had nothing to feel guilty about. So why were trails of hot tears streaming down her face?

You're overtired and dehydrated, she told herself. That's all.

Thoughts whispered in her mind, then—but though she heard them spoken in her own voice, she knew they weren't hers.

It was just a stupid animal. Scrawny too, from the feel of it. You did it a favor by killing it quickly. It was obviously sickly and would've succumbed to illness before long—or perhaps fallen to the jaws of a predator. Either way, it would've done its owner no good if it had lived. Too skinny to give good milk, too slight of frame to provide much beef. This way, at least it won't eat any more grass that could go to feed stronger animals.

The tentacle whip swayed lazily in the air before her eyes, almost as if mocking her.

Lirra had struggled to maintain control ever since leaving the lodge, but all at once her fragile hold on her emotions slipped. She released a cry of rage and leaped to her feet. She struck out with the tentacle whip, slashing the cow's body with the symbiont, the barbed tip scoring the animal's flesh and spraying the air with blood. How long she stood there ravaging the cow's dead body, she didn't know, but eventually her rage began to drain away, replaced by a bone-deep weariness. She stopped lashing the cow and with a tired thought commanded the tentacle whip to wrap around her left forearm. The whip obeyed, moving almost sleepily, as if sated. Lirra felt the slick warmth coating the symbiont as it coiled around her flesh, but she thought nothing of it. She was too tired to think. All she wanted to do was find someplace where she could lie down, close her eyes, and escape into the emptiness of sleep for a time.

"Here now, what do you think you're doing?"

At first Lirra didn't react to the voice, for she assumed it was merely another thought planted in her mind by the symbiont. But after a moment she realized that someone else was speaking, and that he'd done so aloud. Barely able to stay on her feet, she turned toward the man, and just then the cloud cover broke. Silver moonlight filtered down from the heavens, illuminating the pasture and giving Lirra a good look at who she was facing. The man was middle-aged, big and broad-shouldered, and though his belly was rather sizeable, he had the look of a man who'd been in good shape once. He was mostly bald, with thick, fleshy features, and a prominent scar that bisected his left cheek. He wore a leather vest over a simple homespun tunic, leggings, well-worn boots, and a large hooded black cloak. He carried a crossbow, bolt loaded and ready to release, and from the way the man held it, it was obvious that he knew how to use it. He wore a pair of crystal-lensed glasses over his eyes, and from their design, Lirra recognized them as a magical device that granted the wearer the ability to see in darkness almost as clearly as if it were full daylight.

Probably a veteran, Lirra thought. Which would explain the scar on his face, not to mention the crossbow and glasses. The man had likely been a scout who specialized in night reconnaissance or perhaps served as an assassin. Either way, she knew he wouldn't hesitate to loose the bolt if he thought she was a threat. Her sword was sheathed at her side, and she made certain to keep her hand well away from the pommel as she raised her arms.

She opened her mouth to explain, but no words came out. How could she possibily explain what she was doing in this man's field at night, standing over the bloodied corpse of one of his cattle? Lirra imagined what she must look like to the farmer: haggard, wild-eyed, and spattered with blood. She must seem like some manner of fiend, or at the very least a lunatic.

The farmer took one look at her and immediately raised his crossbow and prepared to loose the bolt, ready to shoot first and ask questions later. She flicked her left wrist and the tentacle whip uncoiled and shot toward the farmer just as he squeezed the crossbow's trigger. The bolt released, but the symbiont snatched it out of the air before it could travel more than a couple inches. It then swung the bolt around and stabbed it point-first toward the farmer's eye.

No! Lirra thought.

The tentacle whip moved slightly to the right, and the bolt missed the farmer's eye.

Render him unconscious, but do not harm him, she thought.

The whip hesitated, which gave the farmer enough time to grip his crossbow as if it were a club and swing it at the symbiont. The whip took the blow, and Lirra winced as the aberration's pain was transferred through their link to her. The symbiont swiftly recovered, dropping the bolt and coiling around the farmer's neck. His eyes bulged as the tentacle whip squeezed, cutting off his air. He dropped the crossbow and clawed at the symbiont's coils in a futile attempt to try and loosen them. But the whip was too strong, and it took only a few moments for the farmer's eyes to close and his body to go limp.

Drop him, Lirra ordered.

The whip continued to squeeze, and Lirra repeated the command in her mind, more forcefully this time. Reluctantly, the whip obeyed, releasing the unconscious farmer and allowing him to drop to the ground. Lirra ordered the tentacle whip to wrap around her forearm, and then she kneeled to check the farmer's pulse. His heartbeat was steady. The man would probably wake up with a severe headache, but at least he'd be alive.

Lirra stood and regarded the farmer's unconscious body for several moments. She could no longer pretend that her mind was adjusting to the tentacle whip's influence. The aberration was just as strong as it had ever been while she was weakened from lack of food and water, not to mention all the traveling she'd done that day. With her resistance lowered, the whip had been able to keep her confused, goad her into killing the cow and savaging its corpse, and it almost had managed to get her to kill the farmer as well. If she planned to use the symbiont as a weapon to help her against Elidyr, she was going to have to keep herself strong, physically as well as mentally, in order to resist its corrupting influence. So, as much as she wanted to continue her pursuit of Elidyr, she needed to attend to her basic needs first: food, drink, and rest.

The farmer likely had a home close by, and she was tempted to seek it out so that she could "borrow" some food and drink, but she resisted the urge. It was possible the farmer had a family, wife and children, and the last thing she wished to do was expose them to the tentacle whip. If she were to lose control of the symbiont around them . . . No, she'd just have to continue on her way and see what she could forage on her own. If this was cattle country, though, that meant she was probably near Geirrid. Given the location of the lodge, Geirrid was most likely north, northeast of her current position, and probably not too many miles away either. If nothing else, she would be able to find food and drink at an inn. But not, she reflected, covered with cattle blood and wearing a symbiont coiled around her forearm.

Her gaze fell upon the large black cloak the farmer was wearing.

She hated to steal it, especially considering that she had killed one of the man's cattle. If she could find a stream, she could do her best to wash the worst of the blood from her clothes, but even so, she still needed a way to conceal the symbiont from curious eyes if she were to go about unnoticed in Geirrid—and that meant she needed the cloak.

As she bent down to remove it from the unconscious farmer, she spoke. She knew she was babbling, but she couldn't help it. "My apologies. If I had any extra silver on me, I'd leave you some in payment. But I can't afford to part with any of my coin. I'll need all the resources I have to draw on to complete my mission."

She stood and put on the cloak and fastened the clasp. It was military issue—in fact, she had one like it back at the lodge—and while it was a bit large on her, that was good. The extra cloth would help conceal the symbiont. As an afterthought, she also took the man's night-seeing glasses. They'd likely come in handy as well. She donned the glasses, drew the cloak's hood up over her head, and with a last apologetic look at the unconscious farmer, she headed off in the direction of Geirrid.

As she walked, Lirra felt the tentacle whip's sullen anger over leaving the farmer alive. *Go ahead and pout,* she thought. *Just as long as you don't slow me down.*

Lirra continued on into the night.

Averone's throat felt sore and he swallowed painfully several times as he struggled to sit up. His head pounded and he thought something must've happened to his eyes because everything was so dark.

She took your glasses, fool, he thought, and that's when he remembered the blood-covered woman, the one with the trained serpent or whatever it had been. The memory cut through the fog enshrouding Averone's mind and he groped around on the ground, searching for his crossbow. He found it and quickly saw that it was unloaded. He remembered loosing the bolt at the woman, but then her serpent had somehow managed to pluck the bolt out of the air, and then it had tried to jam it into his eye. . . . Things got hazy after that, but

Averone decided not to worry about the details. Though he'd traded in the life of a soldier for that of a cattle farmer, his military training told him that he was alive and that was all that mattered. But if he wished to stay that way, he needed to make sure the area was secure. He hadn't brought an entire quarrel of bolts with him as he owned only a handful left over from his soldiering days. He carried the extras with him in one of his cloak pockets. He started to reach for a bolt, and that's when he realized that the woman had taken his cloak as well.

"At least she didn't take your head," he muttered resignedly. In retrospect, he decided coming out to investigate the noises he'd heard—noises he now knew had been made by the woman when she slaughtered his cow—hadn't been the wisest choice he'd ever made.

Without his night-seeing glasses or additional bolts for his crossbow, Averone decided that the smartest thing to do would be to head back to his cabin. He could put up a better fight there, if need be. He could barricade himself in and he had a sword he kept mounted on the wall above his fireplace. And come morning he could patrol his fields and see if any more of his cattle had been killed. His wife had left him before last winter for, of all things, a weaver who lived in Geirrid, and they'd had no children; therefore, he had no one to worry about protecting except himself. He felt a twinge of disappointment in himself for being so ready to retreat. After all, he *was* a Karrn, and his people were tougher than that. But his military career had lasted long enough for him to learn the value of pragmatism on the battlefield. It was night, he was unarmed, and he knew next to nothing about his enemy—or enemies. One of the first things he'd been taught during his training was that a dead soldier was a useless soldier. So it was back home for him, and he would resume playing soldier once the sun had risen.

Averone was just about to start walking in the direction of his cabin, when he heard the sound of someone approaching. He fought an urge to run, knowing that it would do him no good without his night-seeing glasses, especially if it was the woman returning and she was wearing them.

"Good evening, gentle farmer."

The voice was male and friendly enough. There was enough moonlight for Averone to make out the silhouette of a man approaching, though something struck him as odd about it. It appeared as if the man had something riding on his shoulder, such as an animal. A familiar, perhaps? Was the man a wizard of some sort? Averone didn't trust wizards. He'd never met one yet that was entirely right in the head.

Just in case the man's night vision wasn't any better than Averone's, the farmer raised the crossbow as if he was making ready to attack. A soldier used whatever weapons were ready to hand, even if all he had to fight with was a bluff.

"Get off my land." Averone tried to speak in a strong, confident tone, but he couldn't keep his voice from quavering.

The man continued approaching. He glanced at the dead cow as he passed it and shook his head.

"You really should take better care of your animals. This poor thing looks as if it was slaughtered by a blind butcher with a dull cleaver and a bad case of arthritis."

The man let out a high-pitched giggle at his joke, and the sound sent a chill racing down the length of Averone's spine. It was not the sort of sound a sane person would make.

The man stepped closer, and Averone was able to make out his basic features, enough to see that he was a thin, middle-aged man. At first, Averone relaxed a bit. The farmer was young and strong, and if it came down to a physical contest, he had no doubt he'd be able to take the older man. But there was that thing on his shoulder, and Averone noticed that one of the man's hands was significantly larger than the other. He remembered the serpent the woman had commanded, and for the first time he wondered if it had been a serpent at all. Whatever the woman had been, he had a feeling that this new arrival was something similar, and that scared him. He'd been lucky to survive his encounter with the woman, and now he was being confronted by a second lunatic. Even more, there was something about the man's manner that told Averone he was far more dangerous than the woman.

Despite his training, Averone found himself backing up several steps as the man approached.

"I don't want any trouble, so why don't you just be on your way?"

The man smiled, his teeth gleaming blue-white in the moonlight. "I'm not here to cause you any trouble. I'd just like to you stand still for a bit."

Before Averone could react, the man opened his mouth and a thin tendril not unlike the serpent thing possessed by the woman shot forth. A barbed tip struck Averone at the base of the throat, and a sensation of coolness swiftly spread throughout his body. His muscles spasmed and locked tight, and within seconds he could no longer move, though he could still breathe, if only shallowly.

The tendril withdrew into the man's mouth. "That's better," he said.

Averone calmly wondered how the man could speak with such a strange tongue, and a distant part of his mind realized that his body wasn't the only thing that had been paralyzed. His emotions had been too. He felt no fear, no concern over what might happen to him while he was unable to move. Only a mild curiosity.

The man walked around Averone, looking him up and down as if the farmer was a steer he was considering purchasing.

Averone was still able to blink, although he couldn't move his eyes or turn his neck to follow the man with his gaze. But the man was now close enough that when he moved in front of Averone's eyes, he could see that the shape he had taken for a familiar was some manner of snakelike creature with a single large eye. If Averone hadn't been in the grip of the strange paralysis, he would've recoiled at the sight of the thing. As it was, he still found it somewhat disturbing.

"I saw you talking with my niece," the man said. "Lovely girl, isn't she? A bit on the serious side, but she gets that from her father. We've been playing hide and seek all day, but of course I have an unfair advantage. I always carry a few toys around with me—including a device called a concealer that allows me to roam about undetected if I wish. For the last few hours I've been within shouting distance of Lirra and she didn't know it. It's been amusing watching her adjust to the presence of her new friend, and I was especially intrigued by her encounter with you. After she took the life of your cow, I thought for certain that she wouldn't be able to resist taking yours. The lust to spill blood runs strong in symbionts, you see, and once they start killing it becomes almost impossible to stop them. But Lirra was able to resist the symbiont's influence and spare your life. I always knew my niece was strong, but I'm beginning to see that she's far stronger than I ever imagined. I'm going to have so much fun plumbing the depths of her strength and learning what it takes to finally break her."

The man stopped in front of Averone and grinned.

"But in the meantime, there's something else I'd like to try. You might have noticed that I've recently acquired several new friends of my own." The man raised his misshapen clawed hand, and the sinuous creature draped across his shoulders trained its single milky white eye on Averone. "But my symbionts aren't the only gifts I've received. A powerful benefactor graced me with his touch, and not only did he open my eyes to the true nature of reality, but he granted me certain abilities as well—abilities that I've been dying to try out."

The man reached toward Averone's face with his left hand—this one perfectly normal—and brushed the tips of his fingers across the farmer's cheek. Averone felt his flesh grow warm beneath the artificer's touch, and when the man pulled his fingers away, the skin stuck to them, stretching like warm tree sap.

"I can now shape flesh and bone the way a potter shapes clay, and you, my dear farmer, are going to be my first work of art."

Averone could see the light of madness shining in the artificer's gaze as the man shook loose the strands of cheek flesh from his fingers and reached toward his forehead. He paused for an instant and then plunged his hand into Averone's skull, fingers passing through flesh and bone as easily as if they were made of water. Still paralyzed, Averone stood completely still as the artificer went to work molding, shaping, and rearranging his mind, but inside he screamed in agony.

⟶ ⟵

Ranja crouched on a hilltop a quarter of a mile from where the two men stood. She kept low to the ground, her mottled green clothing helping to conceal her from them. She'd been following Lirra at a distance and watched as the woman savagely killed a cow for no apparent reason. She'd seen the farmer confront Lirra, and she'd fully expected the woman to slay him as well, and she'd been surprised when Lirra had turned away and departed, leaving the man alive. Fusing with a symbiont had clearly taken a toll on Lirra's mind, but she'd been able to resist the urge to kill the farmer. It seemed the woman hadn't completely succumbed to madness yet, and that intrigued Ranja.

She respected strength and courage, and it appeared Lirra had an abundant supply of both.

When Lirra rendered the farmer unconscious and departed, Ranja had fully intended to follow her, though she'd planned to wait before doing so to allow the woman to put some distance between them. But as she waited, she was shocked by the sudden appearance of Elidyr. And "appear" was precisely what the man had done. One moment he wasn't there, the next he was. Ranja didn't know what sort of magic the man had used, but she was familiar with any number of spells or devices that could accomplish the task, and the specifics didn't really matter to her. As this was the first time she'd seen Elidyr since he'd walked away from the lodge, she decided to stick around and see what he'd do. She could always catch up to Lirra later.

But Ranja regretted her choice when she saw a symbiont burst forth from Elidyr's mouth to paralyze the farmer, and she *really* regretted it when he touched the farmer's face, stretching the man's flesh as if it were bread dough. And when he actually stuck his hand *inside* the farmer's head . . .

The hackles rose on the back of Ranja's neck, and a low growl sounded deep in her throat. Instinctively, she changed form, teeth and claws lengthening, hair thickening and becoming furlike, her face assuming a more bestial aspect.

Perhaps it was her growling, soft though it was, or perhaps it was due to some preternatural sense that Elidyr possessed, but the man looked away from the farmer and turned his gaze toward the shifter. He grinned, as if delighted to see her, raised his oversized claw of a hand and waved.

That was too much for Ranja. She bolted and fled as swiftly as her bestial form would allow.

CHAPTER ELEVEN

The town of Geirrid lay in the center of Warlord Bergerron's lands, surrounded by open fields and dense forests beyond. It was the kind of place you stopped briefly at on your way to somewhere else, and that was precisely why Lirra hoped she'd be able to move about without drawing too much attention to herself.

The guards stationed at the town's main entrance hadn't given her a first glance, let alone a second, as she entered. Though identification papers were still required and checked in the larger cities and bordertowns, those living in Karrnath's interior were able to travel freely and only had to show their papers if they caused a disturbance or were suspected of a crime. As a soldier, Lirra had been against such lax discipline, but she was grateful for it now, as it allowed her to enter Geirrid unchallenged and unnoticed.

After leaving the farmer lying unconscious in his field, Lirra had walked all night to reach Geirrid, and while her symbiont made her physically stronger, she was bone-tired, and it took an effort of will for her to keep putting one foot in front of the other. She'd managed to find water during her journey, but nothing to eat, and her stomach was so empty she thought it had probably forgotten what food was by now. Concealed by the folds of her "borrowed" cloak, the tentacle whip continually squeezed her forearm in a rhythmic pattern. She could sense the symbiont's hunger. After all, it drew nourishment from her blood, and if she didn't put food in her belly, the symbiont would have nothing to sustain itself. The way the aberration squeezed her arm reminded her of a hungry pet whining and pawing at its owner's leg in order to get fed.

Patience, she told the whip. *We need to find a place where we won't be noticed.*

But the tentacle whip refused to be mollified and continued squeezing Lirra's forearm.

She felt a wave of irritation, but she was too weary for the emotion to build into anger. She knew she couldn't afford to wait much longer to eat though. She needed her mind strong and clear if she was to continue resisting the aberration's corrupting influence—*and* so she could plan a strategy for tracking down Elidyr. She didn't know why she'd ever thought that she'd find her uncle by simply wandering around Karrnath's countryside hoping to stumble onto him. Elidyr might not have been a soldier, but he was an intelligent man and an artificer as well, and even before his transformation yesterday, Lirra would've had a difficult time locating him if he didn't want to be found. But now he had additional abilities to drawn on, and just because he was insane didn't mean he was any less intelligent. To find her uncle, she would need a better plan, a *real* plan. But first she needed a decent meal.

This wasn't Lirra's first time in Geirrid. When her father had formed the Outguard, he'd drawn a number of members from the town's garrison, Osten among them. Lirra had helped with the interview process, and thus had spent a number of days in town, though she'd spent most of the time in the garrison's barracks and had taken her meals there. Still, she remembered Osten telling her of one particular tavern the soldiers often ate at when off duty. The food was simple, but there was plenty of it, and best of all, it was cheap. Osten had also told her that the owner had originally come from Thrane and was friendly to foreigners, so outlanders often patronized the establishment as well. It sounded perfect for her needs. Now if she could just remember where it was located . . .

As she continued walking, she had the sudden feeling that someone was following her. When she turned a corner, she ducked into the nearest alley and waited to see if anyone suspicious passed by, but in her current weary state of mind, *everyone* seemed suspicious. Finally, she decided it had only been her imagination, and she left the alley and resumed her search for the tavern.

She wandered the streets for another fifteen minutes before finally giving up and asking a halfling wearing an eyepatch if he knew the way to the Wyvern's Claw. As he was giving her directions, the tentacle whip squeezed her arm more violently, causing her to let out a surprised yelp and earning her a curious look from the halfling.

"Hunger pangs," she explained. The halfling eyed her dubiously, and she thanked him for his help and headed for the tavern.

The Wyvern's Claw wasn't much to look at from the outside—a plain stone facade, with a simple wooden sign hanging above the door displaying a crudely painted lizard's claw.

When she stepped inside, she saw that the tavern's interior was even less impressive than its exterior: dirt floor covered with straw to soak up spills, lopsided wooden tables and chairs that looked as if they'd been built by a particularly clumsy-handed child, and a pervasive odor of boiled cabbage and unwashed bodies. But Lirra had endured far worse conditions in her time as a soldier, and she walked into the room and took a seat at an empty table. She made sure to lower herself onto the rickety-looking chair carefully, as it appeared incapable of supporting anything heavier than a mouse. But the chair held, and Lirra signaled for the serving woman to come over.

Lirra ordered a bowl of beef stew, along with some bread and cheese, and a mug of ale to wash it all down. After the woman left, Lirra started to reach up to pull back her hood, but she stopped herself. It had been several months since the last time she'd been in town, but there was a chance, however remote, that someone might recognize her. Her father would be looking for her, and knowing Vaddon, he wouldn't stop until he found her. Best not to give him any help, she decided. So the hood would stay up and with any luck, she'd remained unrecognized.

The patrons of the Wyvern's Claw were the usual mix of travelers and down-on-their-luck vagabonds that passed through Geirrid, most of whom kept to themselves and looked as if their fondest wish was to be left alone. Good, Lirra thought. She should blend in here without any trouble.

There were soldiers, of course, wearing the uniform of Geirrid's garrison, which wasn't much different from that worn by the Outguard—another reason she was grateful for the concealment of her robe. There were a half dozen of them, men and women, laughing, talking, and drinking as if they were having a night out on the town instead of a late breakfast. Lirra guessed they'd gotten off night duty not that long ago and had decided to have a little fun before taking to their bunks for the day. A trio of dwarves sat not far from from the soldiers, and from their dress, Lirra took them to be merchants or perhaps bankers.

She was startled out of her thoughts by the sound of the chair opposite her being pulled back from the table. She looked up to see a smiling shifter woman wearing the mottled green clothing of a scout or hunter sit down.

"Hello, Lirra. I have to warn you—the stew here isn't very good."

Lirra tensed and she felt the tentacle whip loosen around her forearm, preparing itself to be deployed if need be.

So much for blending in, she thought. She felt a spark of anger ignite inside her, and she struggled to keep it from fanning into a flame. The last thing she wanted to do was to reveal her symbiont in a crowd like this. If she intended to continue keeping a low profile, she was going to have to maintain control of her emotions, and maintain control of the tentacle whip. She forced herself to speak calmly as she replied to the woman.

"Who are you, and how do you know my name?"

"I'm Ranja, and it's my business to know things. I get paid—and quite well, I might add—to find them out and then report what I've learned to my employer. Right now, that's Arnora Raskogr."

Before Lirra could say anything more, the serving woman returned with her food. As the woman set the wooden bowl on the table, Ranja ordered some stew and ale for herself.

When the serving woman departed, Lirra said, "I thought you disliked their stew."

The shifter shrugged. "I do, but I'm hungry enough that I don't care what it tastes like. You're not the only one who was wandering the countryside all night, you know."

Lirra gritted her teeth against a rising tide of irritation. She felt the tentacle whip's barbed tip slither toward the edge of her sleeve, and she commanded it to remain hidden. The whip hesitated, and for a moment she thought it was going to reveal itself anyway, but then it reluctantly retreated.

She's a threat and must be dealt with, her voice—but not her voice—whispered in her mind.

Maybe so, Lirra thought back. *But not here and not now.*

"I'm not one for playing games, Ranja. Tell me straight out: What are you doing here?"

Despite Lirra's determination to keep a tight reign on her emotions, a sharp edge crept into her voice, and she saw the shifter's eyes narrow, her nostrils flare, and her lips tighten. She drew back, only by an inch or so, but it was noticeable. She's afraid of me, Lirra realized.

No, her inner voice said with smug satisfaction. *She's afraid of* us.

She leaned forward and allowed a cold look to come into her gaze. In response, Ranja's hair grew slightly coarser, and her nails lengthened a touch. But when the woman spoke, her voice sounded relaxed enough.

"Arnora got wind of your experiment at Bergerron's lodge, and she sent me to spy on you and find out what you were up to. I was watching yesterday when Elidyr left the lodge, and I saw you follow close on his heels. Well, not all that close, considering you set out in the opposite direction than he did, but you get my meaning."

So Bergerron hadn't been acting out of paranoia when he'd ordered the symbiont project to shut down, Lirra thought. Ranja continued.

"I was intrigued, so I decided to follow you to see what I could learn. I tracked you all day and night." She nodded at Lirra's left arm. "Not even your little friend was aware of me."

Lirra wanted to argue that she hadn't exactly been performing at the peak of her abilities yesterday, given how confused her mind was by the fusion with the symbiont, but she said nothing. Even with a clear head, Lirra might not have detected the shifter's presence—not if the woman hadn't wanted her to.

Nearby, one of the garrison soldiers, who couldn't have been long into his adulthood, laughed a bit too loudly and said to his companions, "Those are awfully fancy clothes for people who live in a hole in the ground, don't you think?"

The man's comment had obviously been about the dwarven merchants sitting close by, and it had just as obviously been said loudly enough for them to hear. The dwarves scowled but they didn't rise to the bait.

Lirra gritted her teeth upon hearing the young soldier's taunt. She was tempted to go over to the soldiers' table and give them a quick refresher on manners, and she actually started to rise from her seat, but she stopped herself. There was no way she could confront the rude soldier, not in her current . . . condition. She decided to do her best to ignore the idiot and refocused her attention on Ranja.

"Why did you follow me instead of Elidyr?" she asked.

Ranja shifted in her chair uncomfortably. "To be honest, he frightened me. Not only does he have three . . . pets compared to your one, the man struck me as completely mad. Not the best combination, in my book."

Ranja broke off as the serving woman brought her stew and ale. As soon as she departed, Ranja dug into her food, and Lirra realized she hadn't touched hers at all. Lirra had no intention of letting her guard down around Ranja, but she'd come to the Wyvern's Claw to fill her belly, and it would be foolish of her to ignore the food sitting right in front of her. So she too ate, and the women continued talking between mouthfuls.

"Why tell me these things?" Lirra asked. "I thought spies were supposed to be secretive."

Ranja grinned. "My curiosity still isn't satisfied. I know in general what you were doing at the lodge, but I want to know the whole story. And while skulking around in the shadows can be a great deal of fun, sometimes it's more effective to take the direct approach when you want to know something." She paused to take a long swig of her ale. "And to be blunt, there are certain business considerations at work."

It took Lirra a moment to understand what the shifter was getting at. "You're hoping that Bergerron will pay you more than Raskogr to keep your mouth shut about our project."

She grinned. "It wouldn't be the first time I've played one Karrnathi warlord against another to maximize my profit."

Lirra was about to respond when the table full of soldiers broke out in fresh laughter.

"I agree," one of the soldiers—a red-headed woman—said. "The feathers in their caps are quite colorful. It puts one in mind of a trio of exotic birds imported from Xen'drik, does it not?"

"A trio of *small* birds!" amended the young soldier who'd first taunted the dwarves.

The soldiers laughed once more, and this time one of the dwarves slammed his fist down on the table and glared at them. One of his companions laid a hand on his arm, shook his head, and spoke softly. Lirra couldn't hear the words, but she could well imagine them: We're here on business, just passing through. No need to antagonize the local military—even if they are fools.

Anger roiled within Lirra's heart, and she felt the tentacle whip stir in response. Karrnath had a long, proud military tradition, but even in the Karrnathi army there were those who abused the power and authority granted them by their rank, even if they were only low-ranking garrison soldiers in a small farming town like Geirrid.

Are you going to let those fools disgrace everything you've believed in your entire life? What would your father do if he were here? What would your mother do? Or your brother?

Lirra recognized the thoughts as not her own—or at least, not *entirely* her own—and she knew her symbiont was attempting to goad her into confronting the soldiers. She clamped down on her anger and concentrated on finishing the last of her stew. When she was done, she pushed the empty bowl away from her and looked at the shifter sitting across from her.

"You're wasting your time. Not only won't I tell you anything about the project, I can't put you in touch with Bergerron."

"Can't or won't?" Ranja challenged.

"Both, I suppose," Lirra admitted.

The shifter glared at her for a moment before shrugging again and draining the last of her ale.

"I figured as much. If you were in the good graces of your people, you'd have returned to the lodge and rejoined them to hunt down Elidyr. I'm not sure what you did, Lirra, but it must've been serious. They had patrols out looking for you last night, you know."

Despite her determination to keep silent, Lirra said, "It's not what I did. It's what I've become."

"Not your choice, eh? Don't bother denying it; I can hear it in your voice." Ranja leaned forward and spoke more softly. "You can get rid of it, or so I understand. I've heard it's a difficult, but not impossible."

The shifter's words caused the tentacle whip to rustle within Lirra's sleeve like a restless serpent. She ignored it.

"Right now I need it."

Ranja nodded. "To help you deal with Elidyr. I suppose what happened to him wasn't his choice either? No answer? Ah, well. Still, you're a brave woman, Lirra. Braver than I am. After what I saw Elidyr do last night, I wouldn't want to come within a hundred miles of him."

"What are you talking about?" Lirra's body tensed, and it took all the control she had not to reach across the table and grab Ranja by the front of her tunic and shake the answers out of her.

Ranja told her of how she'd witnessed Lirra slaying the cow last night and her subsequent encounter with the animal's owner. She also told her that Elidyr had appeared after she'd departed, and he'd done something to the farmer once the man had regained consciousness . . . something awful.

"I didn't stick around to watch," Ranja said. "My curiosity only carries me so far. But it looked as if Elidyr was somehow using his bare hands to . . . to *mold* the man's flesh." The shifter shuddered. "It was horrible."

Lirra knew that none of the symbionts that had fused to her uncle's body granted such a power, and she doubted the ability was due to some magical device he'd created. Then she remembered something Elidyr had once told her about the denizens of Xoriat. The aberrations were created by the daelkyr lords, and they often took ordinary creatures and reshaped their flesh to turn them into dolgaunts, dolgrims, and the like. Somehow yesterday—whether it was due to the malfunction of the Overmantle or the touch of the daelkyr who'd reached through the portal or a combination of both—Elidyr had gained the power to mold flesh. Lirra wondered to what mad purpose her uncle might turn his newfound ability, and the thought terrified her. She was now more determined than ever to find and stop him—but in order to accomplish that task, it was becoming clear to her that she was going to need help.

"I have a proposition for you, Ranja. You came to me in hope that I'd be able to introduce you to Lord Bergerron. I will do so—*if* you help me track down my uncle."

The shifter's eyes narrowed. "Earlier, you said you couldn't put me in touch with Bergerron."

"Not now," Lirra admitted. "But once my uncle has been dealt with, I'll be able to give up my . . . pet."

The symbiont tightened painfully around her arm, but she ignored it.

"After that, I won't have to avoid my people any longer. My father was in command of the symbiont project, and he has Bergerron's ear. If you assist me in stopping Elidyr, I will ask my father to introduce you to Bergerron, and I have every confidence he will do so. He may not trust me right now, given my condition, but he wants Elidyr stopped as much as I do. And once I'm free of my pet, as you put it, I have no doubt things between us will return to the way they were."

At least, that was her hope. What if, even with her symbiont removed, Vaddon saw her as irredeemably tainted by corruption? Would he still trust her judgment as a soldier? Would he still regard her as his daughter? Would he still love her? Or in his eyes would she always remain a monstrous thing?

Ranja regarded Lirra for several moments while she thought, and Lirra took the time to finish off the last of her ale.

"Tempting," Ranja said. "But it seems something of a gamble. First off, I'd rather not go anywhere near your uncle. Secondly, you can't put in a good word for me with your father if Elidyr kills you, and from what I've seen of the man so far, he wields more power than you do. We have a saying in my line of work: 'A promise of payment is always an empty one.'"

Lirra shrugged. "Then forget we talked and go take your information to Lady Raskogr. But if you help me, you'll learn even more about the symbiont project, and that will give you more bargaining power with Bergerron. And the more of his secrets you know, the more likely he'll be to pay you to keep quiet about them."

"If he doesn't kill me outright to keep me from talking," Ranja said. "Still, I didn't get into this line of work to play it safe." She grinned. "All right, Lirra. You've got yourself a deal."

The shifter stuck out her hand to shake, but before Lirra could reach for it, the woman quickly drew it back, an expression of near panic on her face.

"I'm sorry," Ranja said. "I just . . . I mean, I can't . . ."

"That's all right." Lirra understood. This must have been how Rhedyn had felt when she'd been reluctant to touch him, and she felt guilty for ever having made him feel this way.

"Let's settle up and we can get started." Lirra raised her hand to get the serving woman's attention, but just as the woman started toward their table, one of the garrison soldiers loudly said, "Bankers, eh? Well, they must deal in *small* change then!"

Fury blossomed inside Lirra like a red-hot flower. Gritting her teeth and doing her best to hold in her anger, she reached into her purse, removed a couple silver coins and tossed them onto the table. "That ought to take care of the bill," she said to Ranja, her voice tight. "Let me know if it doesn't." She then stood and forced herself to move slowly as she made her way to the soldiers' table.

All three of the dwarves were glaring at the soldiers, and two of the dwarves had their hands on the pommels of the long knives they wore at their sides. The dwarves were of a type—all male, black hair, black beards, squat noses, thin lips—and she assumed they were family based on their resemblance. Brothers, or perhaps cousins. Dwarven businesses were usually family ones.

The soldiers were laughing too hard to notice her at first, but before long the young soldier who'd been the first to start taunting the dwarves looked up at her. He was younger than she'd thought at first, younger even than Osten, and she doubted he'd been with the garrison more than a couple months.

The youth regarded her for a moment before giving her a sneer. "I'd say 'Look what the cat dragged in,' but not even the most flea-bitten feline would go anywhere near something as ratty looking as you."

The tentacle whip twitched beneath Lirra's robe, eager to strike out at the loudmouthed youth, and Lirra restrained it with an effort of will. She forced herself to speak calmly as she addressed the soldier. "You may be off duty, but you're still wearing your uniform. I don't think Rol Amark would appreciate the way someone under his command has been mocking visitors to his town. Do you?"

The youth was clearly taken aback by her mention of the garrison commander's name. He glanced at his friends, saw them looking at him with amusement that he was being called out by a stranger, and he turned back to Lirra, determined not to be made a fool of.

"What gives you the right to lecture us? We're Karrnathi soldiers. We don't answer to civilians." He looked her up and down. "And certainly not ones who look as if they spent the night sleeping on a dung heap."

Fresh anger surged through Lirra, and she imagined drawing her sword and lopping the fool's head off. *That* would silence him right enough. She felt the tentacle whip's excitement at the thought of the loudmouth losing his head, and she concentrated on keeping her sword hand relaxed at her side.

The other soldiers started to laugh at the insult their comrade had delivered, but their merriment quickly died away when they saw the grim expression on Lirra's face. Up to this point, she'd allowed her cloak to cover her uniform, and she was tempted to reveal it to the soldiers now, but she resisted. She didn't want anyone in town to know who she was.

"I'm a veteran," she said, "and I doubt I'm the only one in here."

Everyone in the Wyvern's Claw had gone silent as they watched the confrontation taking place in their midst. More than a few of the patrons cheered at Lirra's words. She noticed the dwarves were watching her carefully, and while they hadn't made any comments of their own so far, all three of them now gripped the handles of their long knives and had drawn them halfway out of their sheaths. Lirra continued, her tone becoming increasingly strained as she went.

"The way you're acting is a disgrace to your homeland and your family. I suggest that you apologize to the three gentlemen sitting over there"—she nodded toward the dwarves—"and then go back to the barracks to sleep off all the ale you've swallowed before you embarrass yourselves or Karrnath any further."

Though Lirra currently looked like any other down-on-her-luck ex-soldier, her military bearing and confident tone of command caused the soldiers no small amount of confusion. A couple looked as if they thought it best to do as she said and depart, but of course the loudmouth wasn't having any of it. The last thing he wanted to do was lose face in front of his friends.

He stood and turned to face Lirra. He was taller than she was, and he stepped toward her, clearly intending to use his height to intimidate her, but she didn't move so much as a fraction of an inch away from him. He scowled, displeased that his petty tactic hadn't worked. He then held out his hand.

"Travel papers."

Lirra groaned inwardly. She had her papers with her, of course. Karrnathi citizens were required to keep them on their person whenever they weren't in their homes, and soldiers carried their papers all the time, regardless of where they were. But her papers would reveal her to be Lirra Brochann, Captain in the Karrnathi army, and a member of the Order of Rekkenmark. She outranked every soldier here. Indeed, she outranked every member of the garrison, with the exception of Rol Amark, who was also a captain. But she couldn't afford to expose her true identity just to put a wet-behind-the-ears soldier in his place.

She held up her right hand in what she hoped was a gesture of conciliation. "Look, why don't you just apologize to the dwarves, and then we can—"

The youth drew a dagger from the sheath on his hip, stepped forward, and pressed the tip to the underside of Lirra's jaw.

He leaned in close to her face, and she could smell the stew and ale on his breath. "Perhaps you didn't hear me, bitch. I said present your papers—*now.*"

The anger she'd fought so hard to contain now roared through Lirra like an uncontrollable wildfire, and an instant later the tentacle whip uncoiled from around her forearm and grabbed hold of the young soldier's wrist. It squeezed and the bones inside snapped like kindling. The soldier cried out in pain as his fingers sprang open and the dagger tumbled to the floor.

Lirra leaned forward until her mouth was close to his ear. Her voice was cold and dagger-edge sharp. "A couple words of advice: First, never draw a weapon on an opponent until you've taken the time to gauge his or her strength. And second, never call me bitch."

With a thought, she commanded the tentacle whip to hurl the youth away. He soared through the air and slammed into the wall next to the tavern's fireplace, bounced off, and hit a table occupied by a half-elf who only barely managed to jump out of the way in time. The table collapsed into kindling and the youth hit the ground, groaned once, and lay still. Lirra had no idea how badly injured the fool was, and at that moment, she really didn't care. As angry as she was, he was lucky to be alive.

The youth's fellow soldiers sat for a moment, stunned, but they quickly gathered their wits. They leaped to their feet, drew their swords, and glared at Lirra with undisguised loathing. She realized what she'd done then. Despite her best intentions, she'd revealed her true nature. She was a host to a symbiont, an impure thing to be reviled. Seeing the mingled fear and disgust in their eyes caused Lirra's anger to drain away. She didn't want to hurt anyone else.

A voice came from someone standing at her side, startling her. She hadn't heard anyone approach.

"You've seen what my companion can do," Ranja said, her words coming out as a near growl. Her full bestial aspect was upon her, and she looked more animal than human. "Your friend undoubtedly needs a healer. Why don't you collect him and leave before there's any more trouble?"

The soldiers looked at each other, clearly unable to decide what the best course of action was. Lirra could almost read their thoughts. As Karrnathi soldiers stationed in Geirrid, they were pledged to protect the town, and one of their own had just been put down by a woman bearing a symbiont. On the other hand, they *had* been acting like children, and their friend *had* drawn a dagger on Lirra when she'd made no aggressive move toward him. In the end—and in the absence of orders from a superior officer—they gathered up their unconscious comrade and carried him out of the tavern, casting dark looks back at Lirra as they departed. With the soldiers gone, the show was over and the noise level in the Wyvern's Claw returned to normal as the patrons went back to their various conversations.

Lirra commanded the tentacle whip to withdraw into her sleeve and coil around her forearm once more. The symbiont wasn't pleased about having its fun cut short, but it did as it was told. Lirra then turned to Ranja, weary from fighting so hard to control her anger and disappointed that she'd failed. She'd have to do better if she were to have any hope of using the symbiont instead of being used by it.

"Thank you," she said.

The shifter's bestial aspect was already fading, and by the time she finished speaking, she appeared fully human again. "You're welcome." She grinned. "Besides, I can't have you getting killed before you can get me my introduction to Bergerron, can I?"

"Then let's get going. The sooner we track down Elidyr—" But before Lirra could finish the thought, one of the dwarves rose and walked over to her. He carried himself with great dignity, and if he was afraid of her at all, he didn't show it. The conversation in the room died down once more as the patrons sensed more entertainment might be in the offing.

"I am Quarran Delletar, Secundar of Clan Delletar." The way he spoke his family's name told Lirra that he expected her to recognize it, but when it was clear she didn't, he went on. "You have our thanks for standing up for the honor of our clan, though it was unnecessary. We are perfectly capable of defending our name."

His tone was gruff, and his gratitude obviously grudging. There was also an edge of challenge in his voice, as if he was angry with Lirra for what she'd done. She glanced over at Quarran's two companions and saw their expressions were neutral.

They're waiting to see what I'll do, she thought.

She inclined her head in acceptance of his thanks. "It was my honor, Secundar Delletar. Those soldiers needed a lesson in manners, and as a veteran of the Karrnathi military, it was my duty to see that they received it."

Quarran's gaze strayed to her left arm and then returned to her face. "You have an unusual . . . skill. There are those who would look askance at such talent, but my people are practical first and foremost. We have a saying: 'A tool is only as effective as the one who wields it.' You wielded yours most effectively, and with restraint. I appreciate restraint. I believe in control, and I loathe waste."

He seemed to consider for a moment before reaching into a vest pocket and removing an iron token shaped like a coin. He flipped it to Lirra and she caught it easily. She examined it and saw that on one side was a design of a pick and shovel with their handles crossed, and on the other side was a series of runes she couldn't decipher, but which she recognized as Dwarven letters.

"That's a token of Clan Delletar. If you ever have need of assistance, show this to any trader in Karrnath, and you shall receive aid. Any cost incurred by their assistance will be covered by my family."

Lira wasn't sure when or if she'd ever have need to redeem the dwarf's token, but she had no desire to offend him, so she tucked it into one of her uniform pockets.

"Thank you, Secundar. You are most gracious."

"Not at all, Lady . . ."

The question hung in the air, and Lirra didn't know how to respond to it. She didn't want to give her real name, but she also didn't want to lie to Quarran. Still, she had little choice. But as she struggled to come up with a false a name to give the man, Ranja stepped in.

"She is known as Lady Ruin," the shifter said.

Quarran raised an eyebrow at this, but then he slowly smiled at Lirra. "It suits you, my lady. Good travels to you." He nodded to Ranja. "And you as well."

The dwarf started to turn, but before he did, Lirra said, "One more thing, Secundar."

He paused and gave her a questioning look.

"Why did you and your friends stop in here? It's a humble tavern, to say the least, and the stew leaves more than a little to be desired."

Quarran laughed. "You humans lack the discerning palates of dwarves. This tavern serves the best stew in the entire country—and they charge almost nothing for it!"

Chuckling, Quarran turned and walked off. The other two dwarves rose from their table and joined him, and the three departed the tavern without a backward glance. The patrons of the Wyvern's Claw once more went back to their conversations, but they were hushed, more than a few men and woman tossed furtive glances Lirra's way, and once or twice she heard the words *Lady Ruin* pass their lips.

She turned to Ranja, but the shifter just grinned.

"My people have a saying, too: 'A name is what your friends call you.' " She glanced in the direction of the table that had been broken when Lirra flung the loudmouthed soldier through the air. One of the servers was busy clearing away the splintered remnants of the table and trying not to look at Lirra as she worked. "Lady Ruin has a certain ring to it, don't you think?" the shifter said. "And you have to admit, it's appropriate."

"It's not exactly the name of someone who wishes to travel unnoticed," Lirra said, irritated, "but I suppose it will do as well as any other."

"Fortune smiled upon you this day, my friend. Clan Delletar is one of the most powerful banking families among the dwarves, and they don't hand out their tokens lightly. You must've really impressed them. And it's not a one-time thing, you know. The token is yours to keep for life, and you can use it as many times as you wish. It's a very handy thing to have indeed."

The greed in Ranja's voice was unmistakeable, and Lirra reached into her vest to pull out the token. "Do you want it? Perhaps we can count it as partial payment for your helping me find Elidyr."

"I'd love to take it from you, but I can't. It's only good for you. Quarran and his friends will soon begin spreading the word among the dwarven community that they gave a token to a woman with a symbiont who goes by the name Lady Ruin. And if anyone else ever tries to use your token, Clan Delletar will make them regret it."

Lirra didn't know how she felt about that. It was possible that the token would come in handy somewhere down the line, but she wasn't thrilled with the idea of the name Ranja had saddled her with being spread throughout Karrnath, and perhaps beyond. Still, there was nothing she could do about it, and she placed the dwarven token back into her vest pocket and decided to forget about it for now.

"All right," Lirra said. "*Now* if we can get started?"

The two women crossed the room to the door, Lirra uncomfortably aware of the patron's gazes following them as they left. So much for keeping a low profile, she thought.

Once on the street, Ranja starting ticking off a list of things they would need.

"We could probably use a pair of horses. And we'll need packs and other supplies. I don't know how much silver you have on you, but I suppose I can cover the cost of whatever we buy for now." She grinned. "Unless we get lucky and can find a dwarven merchant in town. In which case we can start putting that token of yours to good use."

Before Lirra could reply, she heard shouts and cries of alarm coming from the far end of the street. She looked and saw a mass of people running toward them, and her first thought was that word had gotten out that a woman with a symbiont had been brawling in the Wyvern's Claw, and the outraged citizens of Geirrid had banded together to come after her. She drew her sword and the tentacle whip uncoiled and slipped free of her sleeve. Beside her, Ranja shifted and raised her claws, a low growl rumbling in her throat.

But the wave of townsfolk broke around the two women as if they were a pair of large rocks in a rushing river, and it was quickly clear to Lirra that the people weren't interested in her. Indeed, from the way they kept casting glances behind them, it appeared they were running from something.

She felt suddenly strange, almost dizzy. There was a tingling sensation at the base of her skull, and cold nausea filled her stomach. She knew instinctively that something was wrong here—very wrong.

Without waiting for Lirra's command, the tentacle whip lashed out and grabbed a fleeing man by the arm and yanked him to her. The man was middle-aged, lean, with sun-weathered skin that spoke of a lifetime working outdoors. His simple home-spun tunic further marked him as a farmer, probably come into town to buy supplies or sell some of his farm's products. The man was obviously terrified, so much so that he didn't seem to be aware that he'd been snagged and reeled in by a symbiont. As a battlefield commander, Lirra had dealt with frightened men and women on more than one occasion, and she used a strong, harsh tone to cut through the man's fear.

"What's wrong?" she snapped.

The wild look in the farmer's eyes persisted, and she commanded the symbiont to give him a shake as she barked her question again. This time the man's gaze cleared and his eyes focused on Lirra.

"Something awful has entered the town . . . they look human, but they're not, they're . . ." He shook his head. "I don't know what they are, but they're killing everyone they see, and nothing seems to stop them! Not swords, not magic . . . You have to let me go before they get here!"

The man struggled to pull free, and Lirra ordered the whip to release him.

During the few moments Lirra had questioned the farmer, the fleeing crowd had diminished, and there were only a handful of people running down the street. Lirra turned to Ranja to ask what she made of the sudden panic when a line of men, women, and children, more than a dozen in all, came into view. Before them stood a smattering of garrison soldiers—several of whom Lirra recognized as those that had been taunting the dwarves in the Wyvern's Claw. The soldiers fought a retreating battle as they attempted to halt their enemies' advance, but their efforts were to no avail. They hacked and slashed with their swords, but every wound they inflicted on their enemies refused to bleed and healed within seconds. A number of different races were represented in the advancing line—human, dwarven, halfing, half-elf—but they all shared a similar appearance. Their eyes were completely white, almost glowing, in fact, and the flesh of their faces was scarred and distorted, as if they'd all been through a fire some time before.

Lirra felt a strange recognition upon seeing their mis-shapen visages. They were aberrations of some sort, tainted by the corrupting influence of Xoriat. The tingling at the base of her skull and the nausea in her gut intensified, and she knew that the sensations were caused by the presence of these bizarre new aberrations.

As Lirra and Ranja watched, the white-eyed men and women made fast work of the soldiers, ripping off limbs and snapping necks without taking so much as a lasting cut from any of their blades. When the soldiers were dead, the white-eyes tossed them aside as if they were nothing more than broken toys that were no longer fit to play with, and the distorted creatures continued marching down the street toward Lirra and Ranja.

Lirra felt a clawed hand grasp her elbow.

"I don't know about you," Ranja said in a bestial voice, "but I'd rather not be standing in the middle of the street when those things get here. Let's go!"

But Lirra resisted the shifter's urging. She felt a compulsion to stand her ground and fight the oncoming creatures, even though she and Ranja were seriously outnumbered. At a guess there were a dozen of them, and given the way they rapidly healed their wounds, Lirra knew there was nothing either she or her shifter companion could do to stop them. Nevertheless, the feeling that she *had* to stay here and fight was so strong it was as if her feet were magically affixed to the ground. An instant later, she understood why.

Following close behind the advancing white-eyes, Elidyr saw her and waved cheerfully.

"There you are, my dear! My new friends and I have been looking all over town for you!"

Ranja leaned her mouth close to Lirra's ear. "Remember the deal we made that I'd help you find your uncle? Well, there he is."

"Yes," Lirra said, tightening her grip on her sword. "Yes, he is."

CHAPTER TWELVE

Still no word?" Ksana asked.

Vaddon sat upon one of the logs arranged around their campfire, a mug of hot nestleberry tea in his hand. He looked up as the cleric approached and sat down next to him. A metal teapot sat at the edge of the fire, resting in a bed of coals, and Vaddon offered his old friend some, but she declined.

"I've already had two cups this morning," she said. "More than that, and I get jittery."

Vaddon smiled. "Given your usually placid nature, you being jittery is like another person being half asleep."

Ksana smiled back. "How many campaigns have we been on together, Vaddon? How many times have we sat around campfires like this, waiting for news—for orders or intelligence—that would tell us it was finally time to act?"

"Too many times to count," he said. There was a hint of warmth beneath his gruff tone. Ksana might not have been related to the Brochanns by blood, but she was as much a member of the family as if she had been. The bonds forged in battle among Karrnathi soldiers were as strong as any formed by familial relationship, and often stronger. Ksana had stood by Vaddon's side, as a fellow soldier, advisor, and friend, for more years than he liked to think about. But there was no one he'd rather have by his side during trying times, with the exception of Lirra, and given that his daughter had become possessed by an aberration and had taken leave of her senses, the cleric's presence was, as always, a great comfort to him.

The Outguard had set up camp on the outskirts of Geirrid, less than a mile from the city. Vaddon wanted to be near the town garrison in case he needed to call upon reinforcements, but he didn't want to stay at the town's barracks in order to avoid any of the other soldiers learning about the symbiont project and what had happened to Lirra and Elidyr. A dozen tents were pitched in a circle around the campfire, and about the same number of horses was tethered to stakes not far from camp. Sinnoch remained in his tent—indeed, the dolgaunt hadn't left it since they'd made camp yesterday, and Vaddon had set Bergerron's two warforged to stand guard. A half-dozen other soldiers, including Rhedyn and Osten, busied themselves with maintaining their weapons, caring for the horses, or running practice drills to keep in shape.

The rest of Vaddon's people were out riding across the countryside in search of Elidyr and Lirra, all of them in possession of communication amulets containing psionic crystals. The amulets allowed the wearers to send and receive brief telepathic messages to each other, though the crystals only contained enough power for two or three exchanges before they burned out. Vaddon wore one of the amulets around his neck, and his crystal was larger than the others, allowing it to retain a charge longer. Elidyr had originally created the devices for the Outguard's use, and the irony that his brother's handiwork would now be used to track him down wasn't lost on Vaddon. His own amulet had already seen a significant amount of use that morning.

"I've received some reports," Vaddon said. Each time someone had contacted him, he'd felt a surge of hope that there would be news about Lirra, but he'd been disappointed every time. "None of our people have sighted either Lirra or Elidyr, but they have run across a number of abandoned farms—all of them in a more or less direct line between the lodge and Geirrid."

"Do you think either Lirra or Elidyr had anything to do with it?"

"There's no evidence to suggest that, but you know as well as I that coincidences are never to be trusted in a campaign. I've ordered a couple of our soldiers to ride to Geirrid and see what, if anything, they can learn there."

"Do you think Lirra or Elidyr would head for the town?"

Vaddon shrugged. "Who's to say what either of them will do now? My brother is clearly insane, and Lirra . . ." He paused and sighed deeply. "She may retain more of her sanity than Elidyr, but her fusion with the symbiont affected her mind as well, and every moment she remains bonded to the foul thing corrupts her further. It's only a matter of time before she loses her mind as well."

"I wouldn't be so certain of that," Ksana said softly. "Lirra is strong in body, mind, and spirit. If anyone is able to resist the corrupting influence of a symbiont, it will be her."

Vaddon dearly wanted to believe that Ksana was right, that his daughter would be able to maintain her sense of self and not be overwhelmed by her symbiont. But it was precisely because he so badly wanted to believe it that he couldn't allow himself to do so. Lirra was his daughter, and it was tearing him up inside that she had become corrupted in body and mind because the symbiont project had failed—a project *he* was in command of. But if he was to have a chance of freeing his daughter from the parasite that afflicted her, he had to control his emotions and do what had to be done, just as he'd had to on a hundred previous campaigns, on a hundred different battlefields. But this time he would do it for Lirra.

As if sensing his mood, Ksana turned the conversation in a different direction. She nodded toward the two warforged guarding Sinnoch's tent. "So what do you think of our new recruits?"

Vaddon snorted. "You know how I feel about warforged. I will say this: They were useful for flagging down the lightning rail. I ordered them both to stand in the middle of the tracks and wave their arms until the engine stopped."

Ksana grinned. "And I bet you wouldn't have been disappointed if they'd been run down."

Vaddon smiled back. "I'll admit the thought had occurred to me. Unfortunately, the driver stopped in time." He glanced over at the warforged. Longstrider stood still as a statue—which, Vaddon supposed, came naturally to his kind—but Shatterfist kept talking to his companion, moving about as he did so, almost fidgeting, in fact.

"Bergerron sent them both to keep an eye on us, but they've been ordered to assist us as necessary, and I don't doubt they will." Vaddon paused. "I can tolerate the tall one," he said grudgingly. "He's quiet, does his job, and doesn't get in the way. As for the short one . . ." He shook his head. "He talks too much. I've begun to wonder if Bergerron didn't send that one with me as a form of punishment for bungling the symbiont project."

Ksana chuckled. "I've talked with Shatterfist a couple of times. He's different then most warforged, but that's his charm."

Vaddon turned to face the cleric. "You talked to him? Whatever for?"

"To get to know him, of course. I've spoken with Longstrider as well."

"Why would you want to do that?" Vaddon asked, honestly puzzled. "They're just constructs. They aren't alive. There's no more sense in getting to know them than there is getting to know a horseshoe. They're tools designed to fulfill a purpose, nothing more."

"We've had this discussion before, Vaddon. You know how I feel. Just because the warforged were created through magical engineering doesn't make them any less alive than you or I. The gods have many ways of working their miracles." She smiled. "Or to put it in a way you might better appreciate, there's more than one way to skin a wolf."

Vaddon couldn't help but return the cleric's smile. "Perhaps so." But he didn't truly believe it, and he knew his words didn't fool his friend. He took another sip of tea before going on. "I'm beginning to question the wisdom of keeping Sinnoch with us."

"The dolgaunt hasn't caused any trouble, has he?"

"No," Vaddon admitted. "He hasn't left his tent since we made camp. Rhedyn checks on him from time to time, but the dolgaunt never seems to need anything. I'm not sure if the damned thing even eats or drinks."

"Sits in his tent, make no demands . . . Sounds like a troublemaker to me."

"I simply don't trust him. He's like a coiled snake, lying motionless, waiting for the perfect moment to strike. I can't help thinking he had something to do with the Overmantle's malfunction."

"He denied any involvement when Lirra questioned him," Ksana pointed out.

An image flashed through Vaddon's mind: Lirra standing over the dolgaunt, fury twisting her features while her tentacle wrip wrapped around the aberration's throat and squeezed. He felt a pang of sorrow at the memory.

"She forced him to answer," he said. "The dolgaunt might well have said what he thought Lirra wanted to hear in order to save his life." He thought for a moment. "Then again, who knows why his kind do what they do? They don't think like you and me, Ksana. You know that. It's impossible to guess their motives." He glanced again at Sinnoch's tent. "I'm not even sure they *have* motives, not as we would recognize them."

"Elidyr trusted him," Ksana said, though she sounded less certain than she had before.

Vaddon nodded. "And look where it got him."

"If you don't trust him, why do you allow him to keep the Overmantle?"

"He claims that he'll be able to repair and adapt it so that it can be used to separate the symbionts from Lirra and Elidyr."

Ksana looked doubtful. "And you believe him?"

Vaddon shrugged. "Not really. He might have assisted Elidyr, but the dolgaunt's no artificer. And like I said before, there's no way to guess what his true motivations are. But if there's even a chance that Lirra and Elidyr can be freed from the aberrations that have claimed them . . ."

"And what if Sinnoch is repairing the Overmantle for his own reasons?" Ksana asked. "What if he wants to reopen the portal to Xoriat and free the daelkyr that touched Elidyr?"

"The thought had occurred to me," Vaddon admitted. "But I'm willing to take that risk if it means saving my daughter and my brother. I intend to keep close watch on the dolgaunt to make sure he doesn't betray us." He smiled. "That's the real reason Rhedyn keeps checking on him for me."

As if on cue, they saw Rhedyn approach Sinnoch's tent. The warrior paused and turned to look at Vaddon questioningly, and the general waved him on, giving him permission to talk to the dolgaunt again. Rhedyn nodded and then—after exchanging a few words with Shatterfist and Longstrider—he walked past the warforged guards and slipped into the dolgaunt's tent.

After a bit, Ksana said, "You may well be playing a dangerous game, Vaddon Brochann."

He smiled sadly at her. "What else is new? When you get a

spare moment, say a prayer to Dol Arrah for us, will you? We may need all the help we can get."

"I haven't stopped praying to the goddess since this whole mess began," the cleric said. She reached out and took Vaddon's mug from his hand. "I changed my mind about the tea," she said, and finished off what was left and refilled it.

The two of them sat in companionable silence for a time after that, alone with their thoughts, until Vaddon felt the amulet he wore grow warm against his chest.

He must've reacted visibly, for Ksana said, "What is it?"

"Someone is trying to contact me." He felt a surge of excitement. Perhaps this was it—news of Lirra at last. Vaddon touched his fingers to the amulet, closed his eyes, and opened his mind.

"Come to visit the dolgaunt again, I see," Shatterfist said. "That's . . . what? The dozenth time this morning?"

"Only the second," Longstrider said. "Don't exaggerate."

"Twelve *does* have a two in it," Shatterfist pointed out. "So from a certain point of view, I was correct."

"Only from your skewed prespective," Longstrider said. "I'm certain you took one too many blows to the head during the Battle of Atraex."

"Lord Bergerron had those dents repaired months ago," Shatterfist said. "I'm confident there was no lasting damage . . . certainly none that would impair my ability to think." The warforged turned to Rhedyn. "What do you think? About *my* thinking, I mean. I seem rational enough, don't I?"

Rhedyn wasn't sure how to answer. "I'm not really an expert on such matters. I'm a soldier, not a philosopher." Without waiting for a response, he ducked into the tent.

Inside Sinnoch's tent, Rhedyn found the dolgaunt in the same position he had the last time he'd paid a visit— sitting cross-legged on the ground, the remains of the Overmantle spread out before him, along with a number of Elidyr's artificing tools. A bedroll lay untouched to one side, and a small everbright lantern provided the dolgaunt illumination to work by. Alone in his tent, Sinnoch had removed his robe—it lay next to the bedroll—and sat naked, the numerous small tendrils that covered his body swaying like blades of grass in a soundless breeze. Anyone else might've found the sight of the unclothed dolgaunt disturbing, if not outright sickening, but Rhedyn could see the strength and strange beauty in the creature's form.

A small blue crystal rod encased in wire mesh lay on the ground next to Sinnoch. One of the dolgaunt's back tentacles stretched down and the tip brushed across the crystal. In response, it glowed briefly, and the air within the tent suddenly felt flat and dead.

Sinnoch spoke without looking up from his work. "Ah, it's my watchdog, come sniffing around again. I'm sorry I don't have a treat for you, doggie."

Rhedyn bristled at the dolgaunt's words, but the dolgaunt went on before he could respond.

"You may speak freely," Sinnoch said. "The device I just activated was another of Elidyr's little toys. It will prevent the sound of our voices from traveling outside the tent, so no one can overhear us."

"How goes the work?" Rhedyn asked.

"I've managed to make some headway in the repairs," Sinnoch said, "but only some. After assisting Elidyr all these months, I could probably construct a new Overmantle if we had the right materials—which we don't—but without his knowledge or experience, I highly doubt I'll be able to repair this one."

"So we need to get him back," Rhedyn said.

"Of course we do." The tentacles sprouting from Sinnoch's back reached over his shoulders, picked up a pair of artificer's tools, and began tinkering with the Overmantle. "But not to worry. We'll be reunited with our friend one way or another. Either Vaddon will capture him—which is extremely doubtful, given how powerful Elidyr has become—or he'll grow tired of playing with his newfound abilities and seek us out." Sinnoch turned to look at Rhedyn with his empty eye sockets and grinned, his shoulder tentacles continuing to work on the Overmantle. "He was touched by Ysgithyrwyn, you see. Not only did that touch change him, Ysgithyrwyn implanted the desire in him to complete my lord's release from Xoriat. Elidyr will have no choice but to reclaim the Overmantle, repair it, and once again attempt to open the portal between this world and the Realm of Madness. We have but to wait."

Sinnoch turned back around to face his work, though since he had no eyes with which to see, Rhedyn didn't know why the dolgaunt bothered. Rhedyn watched him work in silence for a time, and eventually Sinnoch said, "Something on your mind?"

The question startled Rhedyn out his thoughts. There'd been a mocking edge to Sinnoch's words, and Rhedyn doubted the dolgaunt was sincere in wanting to know, but the warrior found himself answering truthfully anyway.

"I'm worried about Lirra. You saw her yesterday . . . I'm afraid she may be having trouble adjusting to her symbiont."

"Afraid she's not going to return to you and be your little playmate, you mean," Sinnoch said.

Anger welled sudden and strong within Rhedyn, and he felt his shadow sibling whispering to him, urging him to strike out at the dolgaunt for taunting him. He felt a shadowy sheen cover him, and his hand dropped to his sword.

"Control yourself, boy," Sinnoch said calmly, without turning to look at Rhedyn. "Slaughtering me won't make her come back to you any faster."

Rhedyn fought the urge to attack the dolgaunt, and he felt his anger begin to subside. It helped that Sinnoch was right. His death wouldn't speed Lirra's return. Rhedyn's shadowy aspect retreated and he removed his hand from his sword.

"There now, isn't that better?" Sinnoch said in his mocking tone. "Don't fret about your paramour. She's strong-willed, and hosts like her take some time before they fully settle in to having a symbiont. Actually, as strong as her will is, she might well have resisted fusing with the tentacle whip if it hadn't been for the influence of the Overmantle. And because of the Overmantle, she won't be any ordinary combination of host and symbiont. She might not have been graced with my master's touch as was her uncle, but the Overmantle channeled the power of Xoriat into her during the joining process. It made both Lirra and the whip stronger than they would've been otherwise, and granted them abilities beyond what they would normally have. I don't fully understand the scope of their power, mind you, but I have no doubt it's there. Lirra's adjustment period will take longer because of this, but as I said, she's strong-willed, and I'm confident her sanity will remain more or less intact once the process has finished."

Rhedyn hoped the dolgaunt's words would prove true. Now that Lirra had a symbiont, there was nothing standing in the way of their being together. She'd come to understand that eventually. She had to.

"And once she's adjusted, will she be sympathetic to what we're trying to do?" Rhedyn asked.

The dolgaunt shrugged, the motion making the cilia on his shoulders ripple. "Perhaps. But she may well take some convincing and that task shall fall to you. You know her far better than I. How do you think she will react when she learns that you intend to help me free Ysgithyrwyn, that in fact you've been helping me all along?"

After Rhedyn had joined with his shadow sibling, he saw the world differently. It was as if he'd lived his entire life with his eyes closed, and by accepting a symbiont, he'd finally had them opened. He'd come to understand how limited the material world was. So many rules of nature that were inalterable, so many events that happened only one way, and once those events occurred, they were fixed in time, unable to be changed. Rhedyn understood all about wanting to change things but not being able to. When he was a child, he'd lost both his parents to the war, and he'd wanted them back so very, very much. Wanted it so badly, in fact, that his grandmother eventually took him to a garrison that had a significant contigent of zombie soldiers, and there she pointed out two particular undead to him—ones that had once been his mother and father.

"See? They're still alive," his grandmother had said. "Still serving Karrnath, still fighting to protect our borders and keep us safe."

But Rhedyn hadn't been reassured by the sight of his undead parents. Instead he'd been horrified. And on that day he'd come to understand a profound truth about the world. It was a place where awful things happened sometimes, unspeakable things, and once they happened, there wasn't a damned thing anyone could do about them.

But then he'd been granted the gift of his symbiont, and he heard the song of Xoriat singing through his mind. Xoriat . . . a realm where the laws of nature held no meaning, where time meant nothing, where reality itself could be molded and shaped, provided one's will was strong enough. *That* was what

Ysgithyrwyn and the other daelkyr promised for Eberron. Freedom from suffering and sorrow, freedom from the oppression of the *real*. The daelkyr wished to transform Eberron into a paradise, and Rhedyn intended to do everything he could to help them. To this end, he'd sought out Sinnoch and offered his services to the dolgaunt. He'd already sensed Sinnoch had ulterior motives for assisting with the symbiont project, and he'd been delighted when the dolgaunt had confirmed his suspicions. Things hadn't quite gone according to plan so far, Rhedyn had to admit, but all was far from lost. If the Overmantle could be repaired, the portal could be reopened and Ysgithyrwyn could be set free—the first of many daelkyr who would stride across the face of the material world and remake it in their own wondrous image.

"I don't know how she'll react," Rhedyn admitted.

"Then perhaps you'd best hope she's not quite as strong-willed as she seems," the dolgaunt offered.

That, Rhedyn thought wryly, is one hope that would definitely be in vain.

***

Osten sat perched on a large rock not far from the main camp, honing the edge of his sword with a sharpening stone, one slow stroke after another. As he worked, he kept an eye on the camp. He saw Ksana approach General Vaddon and sit with him, saw Rhedyn go to Sinnoch's tent and chat with the warforged guards a moment before entering. Osten was glad that the general had someone like Ksana to talk to. Even a strong, experienced leader like Vaddon Brochann needed someone to simply listen to him from time to time, and the cleric knew many ways to heal—and not all of them required drawing on divine power.

Though he'd certainly benefited from the latter. Twice now, in fact. If it hadn't been for Ksana, he would've been a dead man by now, and both times it would've been due to that damned symbiont. Yes, technically the second time he would've died because of the blow Lirra had given him to the throat, but he didn't blame her for that. She'd just been doing her duty. Once again, he'd lost control of his mind to the tentacle whip, and the creature had taken command of his body. Lirra had known that, and she'd struck quickly and efficiently in order to cause Osten the least amount of pain possible. Even though the symbiont had been holding the reins of his body, Osten had still been aware at the time, and he'd recognized what Lirra had done and why. No, it had been the symbiont's doing—that, and his own weakness that had twice allowed the aberration to take control of him.

And now Lirra had become cursed with the burden of the tentacle whip, and she was out there somewhere, doing what—and to whom—only the gods knew. Osten prayed that she was safe, and that whomever she came in contact with survived the encounter. Lirra Brochann was stronger than him, that he was certain of, and he doubted the tentacle whip would have an easy time controlling her. Even so, he knew better than anyone, save Lirra, how strong the whip's influence could be, how insidious, and he hoped her strength would prove sufficient to allow her to resist the symbiont's corruption.

Yesterday, when Osten had fully recovered from his latest wounds—the physical ones, that is; the emotional ones would take a bit more time to heal—he'd vowed that he'd do whatever it took to help Lirra. Since then, he'd followed the general's orders and traveled with the rest of the Outguard to the outskirts of Geirrid to make camp and await news of Lirra or Elidyr. He'd helped pitch the tents, take care of the horses, and gather firewood and water. Outwardly, he was still the good little soldier that had first joined the symbiont project. But inwardly, he no longer considered himself a member of the Outguard. He was Lirra's servant now, even if she didn't know it yet, and he was only biding his time until he could be reunited with his mistress once more. And once that occurred, he intended to stand by her side and aid her in any way he could, regardless of the cost to himself. And if he was called upon to kill Lirra in order to free her from the tentacle whip's influence, then he would do so, though with a heavy heart.

His thoughts were interrupted as Vaddon jumped to his feet.

"We've found Elidyr!" the general bellowed. "He's in Geirrid right now! Mount up!"

Osten smiled grimly as he put his sharpening stone away and quickly tested the edge of his blade with his thumb. A tiny sliver of flesh peeled away bloodless, and he nodded, satisfied. Perhaps they hadn't found Lirra yet, but Elidyr was the next best thing. He was looking forward to trying out his newly sharpened sword on the artificer.

He stood, sheathed his weapon, and started running toward the horses.

Inside the tent, Sinnoch and Rhedyn heard Vaddon's command, and the dolgaunt smiled.

"See?" Sinnoch said as he began gathering up the pieces of the Overmantle. "I told you we had only to wait."

CHAPTER THIRTEEN

Nothing personal, Lirra," Ranja said, "but I'm not sure Lord Bergerron has enough silver to get me to go up against those things! I'm not sure even Kaius has enough!"

Elidyr's white-eyed servants walked stiffly toward them, like puppets manipulated by unseen strings, and their vacant, slack-jawed expressions never changed, whether they were simply walking down the street or slaughtering someone who'd gotten in their way.

"Go then," Lirra said. "I won't think any the less of you for it."

Ranja grinned as she reached into one of her tunic pockets. "What, and miss all the fun?"

From her pocket, she withdrew a handful of what looked like iridescent pearls. The shifter pulled back her arm and hurled the tiny spheres toward the oncoming white-eyes with all her considerable strength. The pearl-like objects soared through the air and struck a number of white-eyes, exploding with bright, soundless flashes of light. Lirra had witnessed any number of magical weapons used during the Last War, but she'd never seen anything quite like these. Instead of tearing apart the white-eyes' bodies with concussive force as she expected, the energies released from the spheres caused the white-eyes to begin collapsing inward on themselves. Their bodies began to compress, as if they were being pushed upon by an invisible force from all directions. Their forms began to crumple and shrink, bones snapping, muscles tearing, skin splitting as their bodies were reduced to a fifth their original size. The process wasn't a smooth one, however. The white-eyes' healing ability struggled to fight off the effects of Ranja's spheres, and sometimes the compression would halt, even begin to reverse, but then the magic would intensify and the process would continue. When all was finally said and done, five white-eyes had been reduced to lopsided fleshy masses lying still upon the stone street.

"A working girl has to spend her money on something. I like to make sure I have the best toys." Ranja gave Lirra a wink.

Elidyr raised his hand and the surviving white-eyes halted.

"Most impressive, shifter!" Elidyr said, his tone holding all the enthusiasm of a young child who'd just witnessed a particularly entertaining feat. "Whoever made those for you did fine work. Now shall I show you one of my tricks?"

The stormstalk curled around Elidyr's shoulder straightened, trained its overlarge eye on Ranja, and an instant later a bolt of lightning leaped forth from the creature's orb and streaked toward the shifter. Lirra had anticipated Elidyr's move, and even before he'd finished speaking, she'd commanded the tentacle whip to grab hold of Ranja's arm and yank the shifter out of harm's way. The stormstalk's bolt sizzled through empty air and dissipated without doing any damage.

A soft whine escaped Ranja's throat as she frantically shook herself free of the tentacle whip's coils.

"Thanks but, *eew!*" The shifter shuddered. "It felt like being grabbed by a length of animated intestine."

"Stop complaining," Lirra muttered. "The whip kept you from getting your fur scorched, didn't it?" She turned to face her uncle. He hadn't commanded the white-eyes to continue their advance, and she had the feeling that he hadn't seriously been trying to injure Ranja, that he'd loosed the bolt of lightning at her more for amusement's sake than anything.

The sight of her uncle filled Lirra with conflicting emotions. It was because of him that she'd become a monstrosity, and while she wasn't sure how he'd done it, she was certain that he was responsible for whatever foul magic had created the hideous white-eyes. Elidyr had become a fiend, and he needed to be stopped before he could hurt anyone else. But she also felt overwhelming sorrow for the transformation that had befallen her uncle. He'd been a brilliant man, and while he could be arrogant and short-tempered at times, he'd been kind and loving as well, a good uncle to her, and despite the differences between him and Vaddon, a good brother to her father. She wondered if anything of the man Elidyr had been still remained buried somewhere inside, or if the dark influence of his symbionts—along with the daelkyr's foul touch—had irrevocably corrupted both his mind and soul. She hoped some way might be found to restore Elidyr to sanity, but she feared it was already too late to save him.

Elidyr came forward, stepping through pools of blood from the slaughtered garrison soldiers that lay scattered on the street. He paused to gaze down at the compressed masses that had been white-eyes and then kicked one as if it were a ball and sent it rolling down the street. He then continued walking forward until he stood within five feet of Lirra and Ranja. Lirra felt her symbiont's eagerness to attack before Elidyr could strike at them, and as dangerous as he'd become, she was tempted, but she restrained herself. She had to at least make an attempt to reach him.

"I wasn't joking when I said I was looking all over town for you, Lirra," he said. "The moment I set foot in Geirrid I sensed your presence. It took me a while to track you down, but then I'm still learning to use my new abilities. As are you, I imagine. Speaking of new abilities, what do you think of my creations?" He gestured toward the surviving white-eyes. "They take a little while to make, but the basic process is relatively simple. Akin to molding clay, when you get right down to it. I gathered them from several farms on my way to Geirrid, and once we arrived, I decided it would be fun to put them through their paces and see what they could do. They're wonderfully effective, don't you think? Strong, obedient, resistant to injury." He scowled at Ranja. "Most injuries, that is."

Lirra looked at the white-eyes in a different light. They might be monsters now, transformed by her mad uncle, but they'd been families—fathers, mothers, children . . . simple farmers whose only crime had been to be in the wrong place at the wrong time. Anger blossomed anew inside her, and the tentacle whip screamed out for her to attack, but she fought to keep her emotions under control. She needed to stay calm while she talked with Elidyr. If she lost her temper, she'd attack him without thought, without strategy, and she knew he was too powerful for her to beat in a straight fight—especially when he had the white-eyes to call upon. And besides, she didn't want to attack him, she reminded herself. Not unless she had no other choice.

"You need help, Uncle," Lirra said. "Bonding with so many symbionts has damaged your mind. Those things . . ." She gestured toward the white-eyes. "No sane mind could've created them. Surely you must see that!"

Ranja elbowed her in the ribs. "A word of advice," she whispered. "Try not to antagonize the scary man and his army of monsters. I have a few more toys at my disposal, but I don't have *that* many."

Elidyr looked at Lirra, and she saw nothing of the man he'd been in his gaze. Only the bright light of madness shone in his eyes. "Concepts like *sane* or *insane* no longer have any meaning for me, Niece. Nor should they for you. Instead, you should start thinking in terms of *limited* and *unlimited*. This world"—he gestured at the austere stone buildings surrounding them—"is limited. So much so that it can scarcely be said to exist at all. It's only one step up from an illusion, little more than a child's paint smears on a tissue-thin piece of paper. Crudely rendered and"—he gazed down upon the dead body of a solider—"so easily shredded." He returned his gaze to Lirra and reached up with the outsized claw of his living gauntlet to gently scratch the head of his stormstalk. "Xoriat is a higher realm than this one, Lirra. A boundless place of endless possibilities. It represents freedom in its most pure and absolute form. That's what we can bring to this world, and I'm giving you the chance to help me do it."

Lirra felt the last shred of hope that she might be able to help her uncle fade. He was clearly insane. "Do what, precisely?"

"What do you think?" Ranja hissed. "Help him to achieve whatever megalomaniacal scheme he's cooked up. I ought to know. I work for Karrnathi warlords, and they practically invented megalomaniacal schemes!"

Elidyr laughed. "The shifter is right enough as it goes, though I'd quibble with her terminology. You and I both needed a period of adjustment, a chance to acclimate ourselves to our new condition, explore our gifts, and better understand our new perspective on the world. But that time is over. Now I intend to do everything in my not inconsiderable new power to bring the glory and wonder of Xoriat to this world. To Karrnath first, then Khorvaire, and finally to all of Eberron! Until the barriers between the planes completely break down and there is no longer any difference between one world and the other. Then, and only then, will everyone know the same joy we've discovered."

Lirra was sickened by her uncle's words, but she did her best not to show it. "Why me? If you truly are so powerful now, why do you need anyone's help?"

"I may be powerful, child, but I'm not a god. And as I told you, I'm *not* insane. I know that the task which lies before me will not be an easy one, and I will have need of strong allies if I'm to succeed. I can't think of anyone more suited to stand by my side than you. You're an intelligent woman, a soldier trained at Rekkenmark and seasoned by battle. You bear a symbiont and—through the Overmantle—you have also experienced the power of Xoriat. And in the end, you are family." He held out his hand, the one covered by the crawling gauntlet. "Come with me, Lirra, and together we shall reshape the world."

"You're not really thinking of doing it, are you?" Ranja whispered in her ear. "Because if you are, let me know, so I can turn tail and run like blazes in the other direction."

Lirra ignored the shifter. "I won't join you, Uncle. What you see as glorious, I see as horrible. What you view as gifts, I view as abominations."

"Young people. Always so rebellious." Elidyr sighed and then shrugged. "Oh well. You can't say I didn't try." He looked over his shoulder at the white-eyes. "Kill them both."

Elidyr's monstrous servants shambled forward. Lirra gripped her sword tighter and the tentacle whip swayed in the air, the symbiont gleefully anticipating the mayhem to come. Ranja assumed her bestial aspect as she pulled another object out of her tunic pocket, this one a crystalline shard wrapped in coils of fine silver wire.

"I'd tell you it's been nice working with you," the shifter said, as the shard began to glow with a crimson light, "but my mother taught me not to lie."

Just then a pair of warforged—one squat with large hands, the other tall and lean—came running down the street behind the white-eyes. The constructs were quickly followed by a half-dozen men and women on horseback, soldiers wearing the uniform of the Outguard, and leading them, sword in hand and raised high, was Lirra's father.

Lirra turned to Ranja and grinned.

"It's about time they showed up, don't you think?"

Then she turned back to face her uncle, shouted a war cry, and ran forward to battle. She sensed Ranja hesitate for a moment, and Lirra wouldn't have been surprised if the spy chose that moment to flee and save her own hide. But instead she charged forward as well, and the two of them ran side by side toward the advancing white-eyes.

Lirra told herself that whatever they'd been before, the white-eyes were no longer people. They were monsters under Elidyr's control, and the most merciful thing to do would be to kill them and release them from the horrible state of non-life her uncle had forced upon them. But that didn't make it easier for her to swing her sword at them—especially the children. But she'd been well trained and battle hardened, and she would do what had to be done. She raised her sword and swung at the first white-eye she came in contact with, one who had once been a young girl of no more than fourteen, and she kept on swinging until the creature went down.

As she fought, part of her mind stayed focused on what she was doing, but another part kept watch on what was happening around her. When Elidyr became aware of the Outguard, he ordered his white-eyes to attack the oncoming soldiers. Up to this point, the white-eyes had moved slowly, and Lirra was surprised when several of them leaped into the air and knocked soldiers off their mounts. Two of the Outguard were dead before they hit the ground, but the rest managed to roll with the impact and scramble away from the white-eyes' grasping hands before the monsters could catch hold. Once the soldiers were on their feet, they began hacking at the white-eyes, but Lirra knew their efforts would only succeed in delaying the monsters. The abominations would heal swiftly, and they did not tire, unlike the mortals who opposed them.

The two warforged fared far better against Elidyr's creations. Lirra didn't know where her father had come by them, but her best guess was that he'd reported to Bergerron after the failure of the Overmantle, and the warlord had given the constructs to Vaddon to help track down Elidyr—and likely her as well. Formed of far more durable materials than mere flesh and blood, the warforged fought like living suits of armor, and took little damage from the white-eyes, though the creatures fought with strength far greater than their natural bodies had possessed. Some warforged were highly skilled at the use of weapons, but others had been designed to *be* weapons in and of themselves, and these two were definitely among the latter. The shorter warforged swung his oversized fists like giant hammers, slamming white-eyes against buildings and onto the ground. Bones splintered and flesh pulped beneath the warforged's fists, but the moment he withdrew the injured white-eyes—none of whom made so much as a whimper as they'd been wounded—began to heal. As soon as their legs were functional again, they got back on their feet and resumed attacking, even if the rest of them was still in the process of being put right. White-eyes fought with shards of bone sticking out of their arms, with dented heads, with jaws hanging half off. But no matter how serious the injury they'd sustained, still no blood flowed from their wounds.

The tall warforged fought with his hands as well, but his primary mode of attack was to use his long legs and spiked feet. He leaped into the air and delivered one devastating spinning kick after another, and white-eyes were tossed about as if caught in the throes of a cyclone, their flesh torn by the force of the warforged's foot spikes. But even though the construct did just as much damage as his brother, the white-eyes refused to stay down, and within seconds they were up and fighting again.

Vaddon remained in the saddle, shouting orders as he swung his sword at any white-eye that came near. Next to him was Ksana, sitting astride a horse and carrying her halberd. The half-elf's eyes were closed and her lips moved silently as she mouthed a prayer. Lirra felt a wave of warmth pass over her, as if clouds had parted to permit a beam of sunlight to filter down from the heavens. She felt stronger, more alert, and the despair that had been begun nibbling at the edge of her awareness was pushed back. She'd experienced this effect on the battlefield before when Ksana called upon Dol Arrah for aid, but the experience remained as amazing and humbling as the first time she'd felt it.

Lirra knew the others, Ranja included, also felt the effects of Dol Arrah's blessing, for they fought with renewed vigor, and while the white-eyes continued to heal their wounds, they did so more slowly, and their movements became more sluggish. Her symbiont, however, not only didn't seem to receive a boost from the goddess's power, it actually seemed to lose strength. The tentacle whip continued to fight at her command, but it moved more slowly than usual, and its grip was no longer as strong.

What's wrong? she thought. *Surely a bit of divine power can't harm a big, strong symbiont like you.*

The whip didn't respond, but Lirra had the distinct impression that it would've liked to tell her to shut her damn mouth. She dismissed the whip from her mind and continued fighting against the white-eyes.

Rhedyn and Osten were there as well. Both had been among those soldiers who'd been knocked from their mounts during the white-eyes' initial attack, but they had survived and were standing back to back, swords flashing as they fought to keep Elidyr's creatures from tearing them apart. Rhedyn had called upon the strength of his shadow sibling, and he was cloaked by the symbiont's dark aura. Osten had no such special abilities to rely on, but he nevertheless fought like a man possessed, his features set in a grim mask of determination as he swung his sword in one vicious arc after another. Osten had always been a competent fighter, but Lirra had never seen him like this, and she feared that what had happened at the lodge yesterday had caused permanent damage to his mind and spirit. The way he fought, without caution or restraint, made him appear as if he didn't care whether he lived or died, just as long as he could get one more strike in at his opponent. Such an attitude could be a strong asset for a warrior, freeing him from fear and frightening enemies with his fierceness. But it could also be dangerous, not only for the warrior himself, but for any companions unfortunate enough to get too close to him during a fight.

One member of the Outguard hung back and merely observed as the battle went on. Sinnoch, his features completely hidden by his overlarge robe, sat upon the back of a small brown mare who'd been specially enchanted by an animal trainer bearing a dragonmark of handling so that the horse would carry the dolgaunt without complaint. Even so, the mare pawed the ground restlessly and shook her head, clearly unhappy with having an unnatural creature like Sinnoch sitting astride her. Lirra wasn't surprised that the dolgaunt only watched. Though he was not trained in the fighting arts, he was much stronger than a human and could've aided them if he wished, but that was not his way. She had no doubt he was sitting back and watching the battle unfold before him with great amusement. She wondered why her father had brought the dolgaunt along. Probably so that he might provide some insight into dealing with Elidyr, she decided. Otherwise, Sinnoch was useless. If she'd been in her father's place, she'd have run the dolgaunt through and tossed his body onto the side of the road for those few scavengers that could stomach the unclean carcass.

She felt a wave of satisfaction come from the tentacle whip.

See? came the thought-voice that sounded so much like her own. *We're becoming more alike all the time . . .*

Lirra ignored the symbiont's taunt and refocused her concentration on dealing with the latest white-eye before her. It was the fourteen-year-old girl again, wounds healed and come back for a second helping of punishment. Very well. Lirra would dish out some more for her.

Though Ranja had assumed her full shifter aspect, she fought with her glowing crystal just as much as she did with her claws. She pointed the magical device at white-eyes and a crimson beam of energy lanced forth to strike the creatures. The energy entered into their bodies, suffusing them, until they radiated a gentle crimson light. The energy didn't stop them altogether, but it slowed them down considerably, making it much easier for Ranja to gouge large chunks of flesh out of them with her claws.

Lirra kept an eye on Elidyr while she fought. Her ultimate goal was to get past these damned white-eyes and reach her uncle. She didn't know if there was a direct link between Elidyr and his creations, but during the Last War she'd seen wizards whose spells faltered the moment they went down, and so she knew it was possible that if she could render her uncle unconscious—or, if she was forced to, kill him—then the white-eyes might collapse like puppets who'd lost their puppeteer. But try as she might, she was unable to get past the white-eyes. Every time she put one down, another rose to take its place, and by the time *that* one fell, the first was back on its feet again.

Up to this point, Elidyr had taken no direct part in the fighting. He'd simply stood by and watched as Lirra and the others engaged his creatures and fought desperately to stop them. Four of the Outguard had been killed, and two others had sustained wounds, though they continued to battle on. It was clear to Lirra that if things kept going as they were, it was only a matter of time before she, Ranja, and the Outguard were dead, and Elidyr was victorious.

"This has all been great fun, but I have work to do," Elidyr said. "Time to finish this. But how? It has to be something good. After all, I don't want to do second-rate work, not where my brother and niece are concerned."

Elidyr reached up to stroke his beard, looking thoughtful. A moment later a gleam came into his eyes, and his mouth slowly stretched into a broad smile.

"I know just the thing!"

He raised his hands over his head and released a blast of chaos energy. Lirra felt it slam into her, and she staggered backward, suddenly disoriented. Her allies were similarly affected, and several of the surviving Outguard actually went down on their knees, unable to remain standing upright. Lirra expected that the white-eyes would take advantage of the situation to press their attack, but instead they broke off fighting, turned, and started walking unhurriedly toward Elidyr. They gathered in a group before him and huddled together, pressing their bodies tight one against the other. As they pressed, their flesh began to run like melting butter, and the white-eyes merged into a single large shapeless mass. No longer needed, their clothing slid away and piled on the street, and the skin of the combined creatures took on a whitish hue that resembled the eyes that were no longer visible.

Dozens of tentacles extruded from the mass and shot toward Lirra and her allies, encircling waists, arms, and necks like bands of iron.

One white-fleshed tentacle caught Lirra's sword arm by the wrist, and though she struggled, she was unable to free herself. Her symbiont struck at the tentacle, stinging it with its barbed tip several times in rapid succession, but though the whitish flesh took on a black tinge and the tentacle's grip slackened, it didn't weaken enough for Lirra to pull loose.

Everyone else was similarly bound by the white mass—everyone, that was, but Sinnoch, Lirra noted—and though they too tried their best to win free, they were held fast. Even the warforged were unable to get loose. Each of the constructs had multiple tentacles holding him by the arms and legs, and around the chest and waist, their sheer number negating the constructs' strength. And then, slowly, inexorably, the tentacles began to retract into the central mass, pulling its victims toward it.

Elidyr laughed and clapped his hands like a delighted child.

"I wasn't certain that was going to work. I'm so glad it did!"

Those Outguard members who'd remained on their horses—Vaddon and Ksana included—had been pulled off by the tentacles, and a number of riderless mounts stood in the street. Several of the steeds fled, terrified by the inhuman monstrosity in their midst, but these were warhorses, trained to stand steady in the face of battle, and many of them remained where they were. Elidyr walked up to the mount Vaddon had been using and swung into the saddle with an easy grace that Lirra had never known him to possess before. It seemed the touch of the daelkyr lord had done more to transform his body than she'd thought. The horse—a black gelding—was less than thrilled to have this human and his three symbionts sitting upon his back, but his training held and he did not rear or buck.

"Farewell, everyone," Elidyr said. "I'd love to stay and see what happens to you when you're pulled into the main mass, but I've dawdled here long enough, and it really is time for me to take my leave." He pulled on his mount's reins and the horse turned toward Sinnoch. "Are you ready, my friend? And do you have what we need?"

"I am, and I do." The dolgaunt reached behind him to pat a pack tied to the back of his saddle, and with a sinking feeling, Lirra realized what it contained—the Overmantle.

"Excellent! Then we can be off." Elidyr turned away from Sinnoch. "Choose a horse and hop on, Rhedyn. It's time to leave."

At first Lirra didn't understand what her uncle was talking about, but then she saw that the white tentacles had left Rhedyn alone just as they had Sinnoch. Rhedyn stood in the street, looking like a living shadow, and as Lirra watched, the dark aspect faded until Rhedyn resembled a man standing in light shade, despite the fact the sun was shining down upon him. The implications struck her as hard as any blow from the hammer-fisted warforged ever could have. Rhedyn was in league with Elidyr and Sinnoch. Despite the evidence of her own eyes, she couldn't bring herself to believe it. She told herself it was just more of Elidyr's insane ramblings and couldn't possibly be real.

"Rhedyn!" Lirra called out. "You can't go with them! You're a member of the Outguard and a soldier of Karrnath! Stay with us, fight with us!" She wanted to say: Stay with me! but she couldn't make herself speak the words.

Rhedyn gave her a look that was impossible to read before turning away and walking to the nearest horse. He swung himself up into the saddle, took hold of the reins, and then, with a last look at Lirra, he turned the horse about, touched his heels to the horse's sides, flicked the reins, and the animal began galloping down the street. Elidyr and Sinnoch followed close behind.

Lirra watched them ride off, despair welling up inside her. But the feeling was quickly choked off by a rising tide of anger. She remembered his visit to her bedchamber on the night before the test of the Overmantle, remembered the things he'd said, the feelings he'd attempted to express . . . Nothing but lies.

Fury roared through her like a firestorm, and she vowed that whatever else happened, she would not die this day, absorbed into a disgusting mass of flesh. If nothing else, she'd survive to make certain that Rhedyn paid for his betrayal of the Outguard—and for betraying her.

The thing the white-eyes had merged into had continued pulling Lirra and the others toward it while Elidyr, Sinnoch, and Rhedyn rode off, and they were within three yards of the main mass. At this rate, Lirra judged they had a minute at most before they were pulled into the pile of flesh, and what would happen then? Would their own flesh and bones liquefy as they became part of the creature? Or would they merely suffocate as their air was cut off? The warforged would likely survive in either event, but the rest of them would not. Lirra thought furiously, determined not to die before she could have her vengeance. She found herself remembering a lesson her father had taught her long ago, when she was a child learning to spar with a wooden practice sword.

"Every opponent has a weakness," he'd told her. "The trick is figuring out what it is in time to do you any good."

Assuming this creature had a weakness, what could it possibly be? And how could they exploit it in the few seconds remaining to them? Lirra rapidly went over what she knew about the monstrous conglomerate. It was comprised of the bodies of people whom Elidyr had reshaped into mindless, supernaturally strong servants. He'd transformed them using powers granted to him by a daelkyr lord, powers that originated in Xoriat, the Realm of Madness. She didn't know if those powers were, strickly speaking, evil, at least in a metaphysical sense, but they seemed close enough to her. And if they were based in evil, that meant . . .

"Ksana!" she called out.

Though Lirra couldn't see every member of the Outguard, for the fleshy mass of the creature stood before her and some of the others, she could still see the cleric. The woman was off to her left, and Lirra was glad to see she'd managed to retain hold of her halberd.

The half-elf's face was scrunched in concentration as she hacked at the tentacle encircling her waist with her halberd, but whatever damage she inflicted healed before she could strike again.

"What?" Ksana called back, not pausing in her attack on the tentacle that gripped her.

"Do you remember what you did at the Battle of Corran Ridge?"

At first Ksana looked at Lirra without comprehension, but then awareness slowly filtered into her gaze. "But that was an entirely different situation! The creature they sent at us was a battalion of Karrnathi zombies that had been abducted and merged into a single massive creature! This thing isn't undead! I don't know if I can—"

"It's evil, isn't it? Besides, whatever the damned thing is, it's going to be the death of us in less than a minute if someone doesn't do something!"

Lirra thought the cleric was going to protest further, but instead she nodded and then turned to face the conglomerate creature. Her expression grew placid, almost serene, and Lirra knew she was preparing her spirit for what was to come. And then Ksana gripped her halberd tight and stopped resisting the pull of the fleshy mass that had been the white-eyes. Instead she ran toward it, her halberd blazing with bright light as the cleric channeled the power of her goddess— the power of the sun—into her weapon. When the half-elf reached the main mass of the creature, she raised her halberd high and cried out, "In the name of Dol Arrah, I command you to begone, foul thing!"

And Ksana brought the halberd down upon the creature with all of her might, burying the axe head into its pulpy flesh.

Dazzling light burst forth from the wound Ksana made, and though the creature possessed no mouth, Lirra heard its death cry in her mind, accompanied by a pain like someone had jammed a white-hot dagger blade into one ear and out the other. But there was another voice within her mind. Voices, actually. Men, women, and children, all of them saying the same thing: *Thank you.*

And then the conglomerate creature exploded like an overripe melon, and a putrid, viscous slime gushed onto the street. The tentacles gripping Lirra and the others fell limp and collapsed to the ground, releasing them. The Outguard soldiers didn't stand around once they were free though. They rushed forward and began hacking away at the creature's remains with their swords, just to make sure the damned thing was dead. Lirra wasn't concerned about the creature anymore. She was worried about Ksana. The cleric, now that her work was done, staggered back from the remains of the creature, dragging her halberd because she was too weak to lift it. Her face was pale, her eyes unfocused, and Lirra knew Ksana was on the verge of collapse. The same thing had happened at Corran's Ridge, and Lirra remembered how Ksana had explained it to her afterward.

"I don't perform miracles, child. Dol Arrah does. I'm just the tool she uses to work her will in the world. But while my goddess has no limitations, the same can't be said about her servants. We are a vessel for Dol Arrah's holy might, but a mortal body can only channel so much divine power without sustaining damage. Stopping that undead monstrosity was nearly the death of me. I hope the goddess never calls on me to do anything like that again—at least, not anytime soon!"

Lirra saw her father heading for Ksana as well. No doubt he remembered what had happened at Corran's Ridge as well as Lirra did. After all, the general had been in command that day.

Ksana's legs began to buckle. Lirra flicked her left arm, and the tentacle whip sailed toward Ksana and wrapped around the cleric's midsection just in time to prevent her falling. Ksana's body went limp as she lost consciousness, but the symbiont held her upright. Shock showed on Vaddon's face, only to be quickly replaced by outrage.

Lirra and her father made it to Ksana at the same time. The general started to reach toward the cleric, but then he fixed his gaze upon the tentacle whip and withdrew his hands. He then looked at his daughter, fury blazing in his eyes.

"How dare you touch a holy woman with that unclean thing!" Vaddon said. "Remove it at once!"

Lirra was hurt by her father's tone and the expression of loathing on his face.

"I'll withdraw the symbiont," she said. "Just make sure you're ready to catch Ksana when I do."

Vaddon nodded. Lirra commanded the tentacle whip to release the cleric, and the symbiont slowly unwrapped itself from around the half-elf's waist. Vaddon was ready, and he easily caught the cleric's slight frame with his armored hands. He cradled her in his arms as if she were a child as the tentacle whip coiled around Lirra's left arm once more and lay still.

Evidently the symbiont's lust for violence had been sated, at least for the time being.

Vaddon looked at her, his expression difficult to read. He opened his mouth to speak, but then closed it again, as if thinking better of it, and turned his attention away from Lirra to check on Ksana.

Lirra looked away from her father to examine the aftermath of the battle. The people of Geirrid, who'd wisely remained hidden during the struggle with the conglomerate beast, poked their heads out of doorways and windows to see if it was safe to go back outside. The Outguard soldiers had finished carving up the creature's remains, and they were using its tentacles to haul the larger chunks into the gutter so they'd be out of the way. Garrison soldiers would be dispatched later to clear away the mess, although Lirra didn't know if there would be anything for them to clean up. The creature's flesh was beginning to liquefy at a fairly rapid rate, and Lirra wouldn't be surprised if there wasn't anything left before long. Ranja had assumed her fully human form once more, and she grumbled to herself as she scraped her boots against the street curb to get the viscous muck off them.

Lirra turned to see Osten approaching.

"Are you all right, Lirra?" The young warrior had sheathed his sword, and though he was sweaty from his exertions, he appeared little the worse for wear.

"I'm unwounded," Lirra said. She was glad to see that Osten looked at her directly, without suspicion or loathing in his gaze. The other Outguard soldiers kept sneaking glances at her, and while she had once been second in command over them, they now looked at her as if she were a stranger, and a dangerous one at that. But Osten had been host to the same symbiont she now carried, and if there was anyone in the Outguard who could understand what it was like for her, it was him.

Osten gave her a sad smile. "I wasn't referring to your physical health," he said softly.

She remembered then that Osten had fought back to back with Rhedyn against the white-eyes, and he'd no doubt witnessed Rhedyn betray them as he'd departed with Elidyr and Sinnoch.

"I'm fine." It was a lie, and from the look on Osten's face, he knew it, but the young warrior had the good grace to nod and say nothing more about the matter.

While Lirra had been talking with Osten, Ksana had recovered enough to stand on her own feet. Vaddon stepped away from her and approached Lirra. As he came, he drew his sword and leveled it at her. There was sadness in his gaze, but his voice was steady as he spoke.

"Lirra Brochann, in the name of King Kaius and his code, I place you under arrest."

Vaddon stopped when his sword point was a foot away from Lirra's heart, and though she could see the conflict in her father's eyes over holding a weapon on his own daughter, his hand remained steady and the sword point never wavered.

"You can't be serious, General!" Osten said. "Lirra is one of us!"

Vaddon's gaze flicked toward Lirra's left arm. "Not anymore," he said, his voice now thick with the emotions he struggled to contain. "Please, Lirra . . . don't resist. Let me help you."

Vaddon was pleading with her in the same way she had with Elidyr, and the irony didn't escape her. Out of the corner of her eye, Lirra noted the remaining Outguard soldiers moving in to surround her. She was also aware of Osten taking up a defensive stance next to her, and she knew he intended to fight with her, should it come to that. Ranja just stood off to the side, watching, as did Ksana, the cleric still too weak to participate in the drama unfolding before her.

Lirra had no doubt that she could escape if she wished to. She could use her whip to poison the soldiers if she wished, direct its barb to put out their eyes or command it to coil around their necks and snap them with a twist, and she would be free to go after her uncle. Elidyr was still at large, and now he had the Overmantle in his possession once more. He would be able to repair it in short order, and once the device was functional again, there would be nothing to stop him from opening a doorway to Xoriat, releasing the daelkyr lord and who knew what other abominations into their world. And she wanted to catch up to Rhedyn and demand to know how he could betray them like that, how he could betray *her*. All it would take was a single thought, a slight loosening of her mental reins, and her symbiont would do the rest. The tentacle whip would strike, Vaddon would go down, and she could flee to do what had to be done.

The thought-voice whispered in her mind then.

Do it! Rhedyn isn't the only one who's betrayed you this day. Your own father has drawn his sword against you. How many times have the two of you fought on the same battlefield? You supported each other after the deaths of your mother and brother, found a way to keep going when the grief seemed like it would swallow you both whole. And now here you stand, in the middle of a slime-covered street in Geirrid, and your father is demanding your arrest. Strike him down! He deserves nothing less!

Lirra's left hand twitched, and she felt the tentacle whip begin to uncoil from around her forearm, but then she regained control and commanded the symbiont to remain where it was. The whip was less than pleased but did as it was told.

Lirra still held onto her own sword, and she sheathed it. Then she bowed her head.

"I'll go with you, Father."

A number of emotions passed rapidly across Vaddon's face: relief, guilt, and sorrow. He then ordered his soldiers to take his daughter into custody. Osten stepped back, evidently unwilling to comply with Vaddon's order, but he made no move to stop the other soldiers as they advanced. Lirra was glad. She didn't want Osten getting hurt trying to defend her—especially when she didn't want to be defended.

As a pair of soldiers grabbed her arms, the thought-voice whispered in her mind once more.

You're going to regret not running when you had the chance.

And as the soldiers began to march her down the street, while the rest of the Outguard fell into line, Lirra wondered if the symbiont would be proven right.

CHAPTER FOURTEEN

You know, my mother always said that curiosity would be the death of me."

Lirra sat on the wooden bunk, the only furniture in the small cell, eyes closed, arms folded over her chest, listening to Ranja complain as she paced around the room like a restless caged animal.

"And she said if that didn't do it, greed would probably finish me off. I should've quit while I was ahead. If I had, I'd have a pocket full of new silver, which I'd no doubt be spending on good food, good wine, and questionable men. Instead, what am I doing? I'm stuck inside a garrison cell with you! I never did get all the muck the creature released when it died off my boots, and it's starting to stink something fierce. Even you must be able to smell it! The first thing I'm going to do when I get out of here is buy myself a new pair of boots and burn the old ones."

Lirra could smell the stench, and it was rank indeed. But she'd endured worse smells on the battlefield in her time. She spoke without opening her eyes.

"You could've fled when Ksana killed the creature. None of my father's soldiers would've been able to catch you. They probably wouldn't have even noticed, given how focused they were on capturing me. But you didn't flee. You stuck around and allowed yourself to be brought to the garrison. Why?"

Ranja stopped pacing and sat on the bunk next to Lirra.

"I plead temporary insanity."

Lirra smiled, though she still didn't open her eyes. "I see two other possibilities: One, you still think there's a way to turn this situation to your advantage—and increase your profit in the process. After all, given the skills you've acquired in your profession, you can probably escape whenever you want to." Lirra didn't want to refer directly to Ranja being a freelance spy, for the two warforged were standing guard just outside the cell door.

Ranja didn't deny Lirra's words. Instead, she asked, "What's the second possibility?"

"That you're not quite as much of a cold-hearted silver-hungry mercenary as you pretend to be, and you didn't want to abandon a new friend."

Ranja laughed, though it sounded a trifle forced to Lirra. "Shows what you know! Now I have no doubt that bonding with a symbiont has affected your mind."

The tentacle whip had been mostly still since they reached the garrison, but it moved slightly against her forearm, as if irritated by Ranja's words. Lirra ignored it.

"You must be getting used to my carrying a symbiont," Lirra said. "You no longer keep your distance like you did when we met."

"I suppose I am getting used to it . . . a little. Besides, the scent of the thing is mild compared to the stench of the white-eye muck." Ranja paused before going on. "I've seen you in action a couple times now, Lirra. I know you can control your symbiont, at least as much as anyone can. I may not trust the damned thing that's attached itself to your body, but I trust you."

More fool, you, the thought-voice said.

Lirra opened her eyes and turned to face the shifter. "Thank you."

Ranja looked uncomfortable, but she nodded. Then she turned to stare at the backs of the two warforged.

"So what happens next?" she asked.

"Father will send for you soon. He'll interview you to find out who you are and what you were doing with me. Just tell him the truth—that I hired you to help me track down Elidyr. And *only* tell him the truth."

Lirra gave Ranja a meaningful look that she hoped said, For the Host's sake, don't tell him you're a spy for Raskogr. The situation was complex enough without introducing another element to destabilize it. She *had* hired Ranja to track Elidyr. It just wasn't the whole truth.

"When you say your father is going to *interview* me . . ." Ranja trailed off.

"Don't worry. He's a member of the Order of Rekkenmark. The Academy teaches us to adhere to a strict code of honor. We don't use coercion tactics on prisoners." She paused. "Except in the most extreme circumstances, of course. And this isn't one of them."

Ranja sighed. "How reassuring."

Sure enough, just as Lirra had predicted, a pair of soldiers arrived to take Ranja away for questioning. As she left with them, she turned to give Lirra a parting wink, as if to say everything was going to be all right. With Ranja gone, Lirra was tempted to lie back on the bunk, uncomfortable though it was, and try to get some sleep. She'd been awake for over twenty-four hours, and while her symbiont granted her greater endurance, her supply of energy wasn't inexhaustible, and she was bone weary. But given the situation, she knew that she couldn't afford to waste time resting. Better to use it to gather some intelligence.

She rose from her bunk, walked over to the cell door, and leaned on the iron bars.

"So you're the two newest members of the Outguard. What are your stories?" Lirra had a good idea how the constructs had come to be under her father's command, but she wanted to get them talking to see what, if anything, she could learn from them.

"We're not supposed to talk to prisoners," the lean one said. Lirra had heard some of the human soldiers call him Longstrider, and given his legs, she could understand how he'd come to be called that. He didn't turn around to face her as he spoke.

"Though admittedly, you're not just *any* prisoner," the squat one, Shatterfist, said. He too didn't turn to face her. "We know you're General Vaddon's daughter, and that you used to be second in command of the Outguard."

"Technically, I still am second in command. That is, unless my father has gotten around to putting in the official paperwork to have me removed from the position."

"Please tell me you're not going to try to convince us to let you go because you still have your rank," Longstrider said. Though warforged didn't breathe and therefore couldn't sigh, somehow the construct managed to give that impression with his tone. "Just because we're not made of flesh doesn't mean we're stupid."

"Why would I think that?" Lirra asked. "I fought alongside many of your kind during the war, and on average, they seemed just as intelligent—if not more so—than flesh-and-blood soldiers." And they were a damn sight tougher too. Which was no doubt the main reason Vaddon had assigned them to guard her cell. Their stone and metal hides made them impervious to the tentacle whip's poison, and she couldn't use her symbiont coils to cut off their air supply and render them unconscious, for they had no need to breathe.

"Now you're attempting to flatter us in order to gain our trust," Shatterfist said.

"Not at all," Lirra said. "Besides, you're warforged. Flattery means nothing to you. That's a failing of us meat-and-bone types."

Shatterfist turned his head slightly so that one of his glowing crimson eyes could focus on her.

"Not necessarily. We are more alike than you might imagine."

Now Longstrider half turned to look at her. Lirra thought there was something strange about the construct's eyes. They still had the same glowing coal look common to warforged, but their color was slightly darker, and they were noticeably larger than normal.

"Please forgive my friend," Longstrider said. "He fancies himself something of an expert on human behavior. Especially humor."

"Would you like to hear a joke?" Shatterfist asked. "I know hundreds."

"Maybe later," Lirra said. "You never did tell me how you came to be in my father's command."

"Lord Bergerron sent us," Longstrider said, "as you doubtless have surmised by now."

"We're supposed to assist General Vaddon in whatever way we can," Shatterfist added.

"While at the same time still serving your real master, Bergerron," Lirra said. "I'd say you were nothing more than the warlord's spies, sent to keep a close eye on my father, but I know you're more than that. I saw you fight against Elidyr's creatures. You were most impressive."

Shatterfist did a passable imitation of a shrug, though he really wasn't built for it. "It's what we were made for. And of course we've been assigned to keep watch on your father. He's aware of our dual purpose—although he *does* resent us for it. He doesn't much like warforged, does he?"

"He's never been completely comfortable with your kind," Lirra admitted.

Now it was Longstrider's turn to shrug. Given his lean body, the gesture seemed more natural on him. "Many breathers don't like us. We're used to it."

"Breathers?" Lirra asked. "I've never heard that word before."

"It's a warforged word," Shatterfist said. "One we sometimes use for your kind. It's not very nice, though, and we're careful not to say it around others." He looked at Longstrider. "Although *some* of us are more careful than others."

Longstrider ignored his companion's jab and focused his attention on Lirra's left arm. She still wore her "borrowed" robe, but though her symbiont remained concealed, she had no doubt that's what had drawn Longstrider's interest.

"Your symbiont fascinates us," he said. "As does your people's attitude toward you for hosting it. It is common for our kind to have variations in our basic design, Shatterfist and I being obvious examples of this. I am built for speed, he for brute strength. But our forms can be altered if we so choose—and if we can afford it. Many of our kind seek to acquire attachments that are in many ways similar to your symbiont, weapons or tools that we can use to perform various tasks."

"It's one of the reasons we work," Shatterfist said. "That, and to afford basic maintenance on our bodies, much the same way your kind works to buy food and drink."

"Your people do not view your symbiont as an enhancement," Longstrider said. "Why is this?"

"Because it's not merely a tool that can be wielded with ease," Lirra said. "It's a living being with a mind of its own, and it fights me for control of my body. Not only that, but its constant psychic presence threatens to contaminate my own mind, endangering my sanity."

"Ah, I see!" Shatterfist said. "You're defective. No wonder your people wished to capture and imprison you. I assume they will attempt to make repairs on you, but if that proves impossible, they will most likely keep you locked away." He thought for a moment. "Unless they come to believe you're a total loss and simply decide to destroy you."

"You have an awfully bleak outlook for someone who's supposed to possess a sense of humor, you know that?" Lirra said.

"I'm not certain I would label you defective," Longstrider said. "After all, every weapon has its purpose. Some purposes are just easier to divine than others. I believe Lord Bergerron will be most interested to learn about you and your newfound abilities." The construct leaned closer until his face nearly touched the bars, the crimson light in his overlarge eyes seeming to glow more intensely. "Most interested indeed."

There was something disturbing in the warforged's tone, and Lirra decided she'd talked to the constructs enough. She turned away from them, walked back to the wooden bunk, lay down, and closed her eyes. She'd changed her mind about getting some sleep. It wouldn't be long before her father was ready to question her, and she'd prefer to be more rested when the time came for them to talk.

"Tell me if you've heard this one before," Shatterfist said. "Two halflings walk into a temple, and the first halfing says to the other . . ."

Lirra groaned and jammed her fists against her ears. Maybe her father had posted the warforged outside her cell not merely to guard her but to torture her as well. If so, it was working.

Close to two hours passed before her father summoned her. He sent a soldier to inform the warforged that they were to bring Lirra to him, and Longstrider unlocked the cell door and stepped aside so that she could exit. Her tentacle whip urged her to flee, and she half seriously considered an escape attempt, but she knew she'd never be able to get away from the two warforged in these close quarters. Besides, she wanted to talk with her father. The warforged marched her down the narrow corridor of the garrison barracks to Rol Amark's commandeered office.

"General Vaddon is waiting for you inside," Longstrider said. He then took up a position on the left side of the door, while Shatterfist stood on the right.

So the warforged were going to stay outside during their talk. She wondered if her father was trying to reassure her with a show of trust. It was something she might've tried if their positions had been reversed. She opened the wooden door and stepped into the office.

Once inside, she understood the reason why the warforged hadn't accompanied her. She'd forgotten that Rol Amark's office was simply too small to accommodate them. Geirrid wasn't exactly a thriving metropolis, and the garrison barracks, while serviceable, weren't lavish by any means. The office was plain as field rations: four stones walls, no windows, an oak desk with a single stool in front of it. Vaddon sat behind the desk, while Ksana stood behind him. The stool, obviously, was meant for Lirra. She elected to stand.

Lirra noted that Ksana held her halberd, while Vaddon's sword was drawn and laid out on the desk before him. His right hand rested on the table, in easy reach of his weapon. It hurt Lirra to see two of the people she loved most in the world prepared to defend themselves against her in case she decided to attack.

Vaddon must've noted the way her gaze took in their weapons, for he said, "Both Ksana and I apologize for bearing arms like this, but given the circumstances . . ." He trailed off, his eyes fixed on her left arm.

"No need to apologize," Lirra said. "I understand."

He nodded, clearly uncomfortable. He cleared his throat before speaking next. "Tell me about your association with the shifter." His tone was unemotional, the general questioning a soldier under his command. But Lirra was Vaddon's daughter, and she could hear the undercurrent of sadness in his voice, and she knew this was just as hard on him as it was her. She decided to follow his lead and respond to his question as unemotionally as she could.

"There's not much to tell. I tried to track down Elidyr on my own last night and failed." She chose to leave out the fact that she hadn't been in her right mind while scouring the countryside searching for her uncle. She didn't want her father worrying more about her sanity than he already was. "I hired Ranja to help me find him. We were on our way to buy supplies when Elidyr and his . . . creations attacked us." She shrugged. "Guess I didn't need to hire her after all."

Vaddon frowned, clearly unhappy with the brevity of Lirra's answers. "A number of farmers and their families went missing last night. What do you know about it?"

"Elidyr used them as raw material to fashion his monsters. At least, that's what he told us before he ordered them to attack."

Ksana interrupted. "What else did he you tell you?"

"He plans to reopen the portal to Xoriat and release the daelkyr lord that nearly came through last time. He believes by doing so he'll be able to transform our world into a paradise—or at least his twisted version of it. He also asked me to join him. I refused. That's when he set his white-eyes on me."

"White-eyes?" Ksana asked.

"Those monsters he made."

Ksana said nothing more, and for several moments both she and Vaddon just looked at Lirra. She looked back and waited for them to make the next move.

After a time, Vaddon said, "Elidyr's transformation drove him completely insane. How are we to know the same thing didn't happen to you?" Despite himself, his concern for her came through in his voice.

Lirra wanted to reassure him, but she felt she owed him the truth. "Oh, I'm not as mad as Elidyr. I don't think he could pretend to be sane if he wanted to. I don't think he even knows what sane is anymore. But I believe I'm sane. The problem is convincing you that I am."

Sadness crept into Vaddon's gaze. "Whatever the state of your mind, you're not the woman you were." He nodded toward Lirra's left arm.

"It's true that I've changed," she admitted. "It's a constant struggle for me to maintain control of my symbiont. But I *am* in control."

For the moment, the thought-voice said. Lirra ignored it and continued talking.

"Perhaps that's so," Vaddon said, a tinge of hope in his voice. "If it is, you'll let us help you."

Lirra didn't like the sound of that. "Help me how?"

"By removing your symbiont," Ksana said.

Lirra felt a surge of panic from the tentacle whip, and it began uncoiling from around her wrist, determined to defend itself. Vaddon reached for his sword, and Ksana moved her halberd into battle position.

Stop it! Lirra mentally shouted at the symbiont. *You go wild now, they'll be convinced I can't control you, and they'll remove you for certain! Calm down and let me play this my way, and there's a chance you and I will walk out of this room still bonded together!*

For an instant, she thought the tentacle whip was going to go ahead and attack anyway. But then it hesitated and slowly, reluctantly, coiled itself about her forearm once more and grew still. It remained on guard, however. If Vaddon and Ksana came to believe she couldn't control the symbiont, they'd attempt to remove it from her by force—and that would be bad for everyone concerned.

"It's all right," Lirra said. "I've got it calmed down."

Vaddon and Ksana looked at her, as if they were deciding whether or not to trust her. Finally, Ksana held her halberd at ease once more, and Vaddon removed his hand from his sword handle. Neither fully relaxed, though, and Lirra didn't blame them.

"As you can see," Lirra began, "the symbiont is a little touchy about any talk of our being separated."

"But the longer we wait—" Ksana said.

"The harder it will be to separate us," Lirra said. "I know." While the initial bonding between symbiont and host occurred rapidly, true fusion took time. The more time passed, the more intertwined Lirra and the tentacle whip became, not just physically, but mentally and spiritually as well. Eventually, it would be almost impossible to separate them without both suffering severe, perhaps even fatal, trauma. "But I don't want to be separated."

"How can you say that?' Vaddon asked in disbelief. "Don't you want to be free of the creature?"

"I'm being practical," Lirra said. "The whole point of the symbiont project was to create a new kind of warrior, one who could control an aberration and make use of it as a weapon. I am that warrior, Father."

"We thought Rhedyn was such a warrior," Vaddon said,

"but in the end he couldn't resist the corrupting influence of his symbiont and betrayed us all."

Lirra felt a hand of ice clench around her heart at the mention of Rhedyn's name, but she pressed on. "Just because he lost his battle against corruption doesn't mean I will lose mine. Besides, you need me, Father. Who among us is better equipped to face Elidyr than I am? He has to be stopped, and you both know it. The longer we talk, the more time he'll have to repair the Overmantle and reopen the portal to Xoriat. We need to mount up and ride after him!"

"In your position, I'd probably feel the same way," Vaddon admitted grudgingly. "But if you cannot fully control your symbiont, then you're a potential danger to your allies as well as your enemies. Not to mention a danger to yourself. Surely you can see that."

"Of course I do, Father. I also remember something the battlemasters at Rekkenmark taught us: 'Courage is risk.' Yes, there's a chance I will lose control of my symbiont and become a danger to those around me. There's also a chance that I'll be able to use the abilities granted to me by my symbiont to help stop Uncle from unleashing a terrible evil upon our world. I have to *try*, Father. It's my duty both as a soldier and as Elidyr's niece. I don't know if it's possible to restore him to sanity, but I do know this: The man he was before the daelkyr touched him would be horrified by what he's become, and he'd want us to do everything in our power to stop him. I intend to do that, Father, with or without your help." She smiled gently. "But it would be a whole lot easier with you."

Vaddon gave Lirra a long appraising look before turning and exchanging glances with Ksana. Then he turned back at Lirra and sighed.

"I never could win an argument with you, even when you were a child."

Ksana spoke then. "You realize that if we go in search of Elidyr, enough time will pass that there's a good chance you will become irrevocably bound to your symbiont."

"I do. The risk is worth it to me. When I became a soldier, I took an oath to defend Karrnath and its people with my life. 'We water the ground with our blood and our tears—for Karrnath.' Mother and Hallam took that oath, and they sacrificed their lives to uphold it. How can I shame their memories by turning away from using a weapon that fate has placed in my hands?" She glanced down at her symbiont. "Literally, in my case."

"Your mother and brother only lost their lives," Vaddon said. "You might end up sacrificing your mind and your soul."

Lirra shrugged. "It is a soldier's lot in life to do that which is required of us. You taught me that, Father."

"So I did." Vaddon sighed once more. "Very well. You can accompany us in search of Elidyr, but you must remain in my company, or that of another member of the Outguard, at all times. Is this clear?"

"Are you going to give me a curfew as well?" Lirra asked.

Vaddon scowled, though there was a hint of amusement in his eyes. "No joking. Do you agree to the terms or not?"

"I agree." The restriction chafed a bit, but she understood the reason for it. Then a thought occurred to her. "You won't be able to watch over me all the time, Father, so you might as well assign a baby-sitter to me. How about Osten? He's a good man, and he understands what its like to host a symbiont. He'll be less nervous around me than someone else." And he would be more sympathetic to her as well, something she might be able to use to her advantage later, if need be.

Vaddon thought about it for a moment. "All right. So . . . how do we go about finding Elidyr?"

"I don't know what you decided to do about Ranja," Lirra said, "but she's sensitive to the presence of symbionts and their hosts. That's why I hired her to help me track down Elidyr. She might still be willing to do the job for us."

"Oh, she's willing," Ksana said. "She made that very clear when we spoke to her."

"And for a hefty price," Vaddon added sourly. "A price that no doubt went up when she learned I was a general working for Lord Bergerron. Good thing the man has deep pockets."

Lirra smiled inwardly. Trust Ranja to find a way to turn the situation to her advantage.

"I've had time to think since you . . . invited me to accompany you to the garrison barracks," Lirra said. "Last night, I had no idea where Elidyr might go or what he might do. But now that he's reunited with Sinnoch and they have the Overmantle, I can think of only one place they would go. Do you remember how Elidyr first encountered Sinnoch?"

"Elidyr found the dolgaunt in a subterranean cave," Vaddon said. "In the Nightwood."

Lirra nodded. "I think that's where they'll go. They both know the place, it's hidden, and it can be easily defended. Elidyr may be mad, but he's not stupid. He'll recognize the strategic value of Sinnoch's cave."

"Makes sense," Vaddon said.

"The Nightwood is awfully big," Ksana pointed out. "We could search for years and never come close to finding the dolgaunt's cave."

"That's where Ranja comes in," Lirra said. "And me. I'm able to sense the presence of aberrations—assuming I'm close enough. Between the two of us, we should be able to lead the Outguard right to Sinnoch's hideaway."

"The question is, can you do so in time?" Vaddon said. "If Elidyr activates the Overmantle before we can reach him . . ."

"I don't know how badly the device was damaged, Father, but it will take Elidyr, Sinnoch, and Rhedyn some time to reach the cave, and then Elidyr will have to repair the Overmantle. I know he carries some of his artificer's tools with him, but not all. The lack of proper equipment should slow him down some. I'd say we have a good chance of getting to the cave before he can reopen the portal to Xoriat—provided we get moving soon."

"Very well." Vaddon smiled. "I never did much like sitting around and talking when there's work to be done." He stood and sheathed his sword. "I'll go inform the others. We'll leave within a half hour. Lirra, remain here with Ksana until I can find Osten and inform him of his new duty as your . . . liason."

Vaddon left the office without waiting for a reply from either woman.

"This is hard for him," the cleric said when they were alone. "He wants nothing more than to see you free of the symbiont."

"I know," Lirra said softly. "And if I could see any other course of action, I'd take it. But Elidyr must be stopped, regardless of the cost to me personally . . . or the cost to my father. Besides, isn't there a saying that the gods don't give us burdens heavier than we can bear?"

Ksana smiled. "Unfortunately, I've lived too long and seen too many good men and women fall in battle—or later collapse beneath the mental and emotional aftereffects—to believe it any longer." She came from around the desk and took Lirra's hand, both of them, in hers. "I pray to the goddess that you don't join the ranks of the lost, my dear."

Lirra squeezed Ksana's hands. "Me too," she whispered.

***

"Just like old times."

Elidyr didn't look up from his work as he responded to the dolgaunt's comment.

"Even better, my friend."

The artificer sat crosslegged on the rough stone surface of the cave floor, the pieces of the Overmantle spread out before him illuminated by a stolen everbright lantern.

Rhedyn stood off to the side, the shadowy aspect granted him by his symbiont causing him to be nearly invisible in the cave's gloom. "This is where you lived?" the young warrior said to Sinnoch. "It seems awfully . . . stark."

That was one word for it, Elidyr thought with amusement. Save for the three of them, the cave was completely empty, just as it had been all those years ago when Elidyr had first come here as a young scholar in search of aberrations to study, not knowing at the time that some decades hence, he'd become one himself. Life certainly took some strange turns, he thought.

Sinnoch laughed. "What can I say? I enjoy being alone with my thoughts."

The moment they'd entered the cave, Sinnoch had doffed the oversized robe he'd worn to conceal his body from mortal eyes and stood naked, shoulder tentacles undulating lazily in the dank air, the cilia that covered his body flowing like blades of discolored grass.

Rhedyn edged closer to Elidyr. "You haven't touched any of the pieces since you laid them out," he said. "Do you think you can fix it?"

The stormstalk draped around Elidyr's shoulders turned its milky eye toward Rhedyn, and Elidyr could feel the symbiont's irritation. It wanted nothing more than to unleash a bolt of lightning at the man, if for no other reason than to shut him up. Elidyr sympathized with his friend, but he told it to have patience.

We can always kill the fool later. Right now we have need of him.

The stormstalk relaxed, though Elidyr could sense it was only partially mollified. In some ways, having three symbionts was like having three children that needed to be placated and disciplined from time to time. But the power they granted made them worth the effort.

"I've been studying the remains of the Overmantle, getting a feel for what damage was done to the device and what I'll need to do to fix it. As I don't have proper replacement parts—let alone the right tools to do the job—I'm going to have to improvise. But improvisation is an artificer's stock in trade. I should be able to make do." He glanced up at Rhedyn. "That is, *if* I'm left alone to do my work."

It had taken them the better part of two days to travel from Geirrid to Sinnoch's hidden cave in the Nightwood. The horses had been near death by the time they'd reached their destination. Sinnoch had taken great delight in putting the beasts out of their misery in spectacularly gruesome fashion, though Rheydn had seemed a bit put off by the dolgaunt's actions—especially when he began jamming bloody chunks of horse meat and organs into his overlarge mouth. Elidyr wasn't entirely certain of the lad's dedication to their cause. His mental outlook seemed distressingly mundane, as if he hadn't allowed his symbiont to fully open his mind to the boundless possibilities of chaos yet. Hopefully, that would change in the days to come. If not . . . well, Sinnoch might get a chance to indulge himself with Rhedyn just as he had the horses.

During the trip from Geirrid, Elidyr had taken out the Overmantle a couple times and examined it, and the truth was, he was less than encouraged by its current state. Sinnoch had managed to gather all the main components of the device, and he'd had the foresight to bring along a set of Elidyr's tools from his workshop at the lodge. But despite all his months assisting in the construction of the Overmantle, Sinnoch was no artificer, and he'd only brought the most basic of tools with him. In order to effect the kind of repairs the Overmantle required, Elidyr was going to have to redesign certain aspects of the Overmantle.

And that would take time. At least most of the psi-crystals were intact and charged. They were highly expensive and difficult to come by, and without them, he'd have little chance of repairing the device. As it was, the task would take all his skill and knowledge to complete.

Too bad he couldn't reshape metal and crystal the same way he could rework flesh. Repairing the Overmantle would be a simple matter then. Ah well. Things would be different in the world to come. Once chaos ruled the land, anything would be possible. The landscape would change at the merest thought, and every desire would become an instant reality. But until that glorious day, he'd just have to work with what he had.

Glorious? Are you mad?

Strange. The thought wasn't his, and yet the voice was clear. *Chaos isn't freedom. It's slavery. The daelkyr use their abilities to enforce their whims upon others by reshaping reality as they wish it to be. People have a divine right to self-determination—a right the daelkyr would deny them. That's the glorious future you're trying to create, Elidyr. A future where the daelkyr rule and reality is nothing more than their toy.*

Elidyr frowned. He wasn't certain where this voice was coming from—it didn't belong to any of his symbionts—but it was familiar. As familiar as the sound of his own voice, in fact.

When reality responds to everyone's desires, then everyone shall be truly free, he thought back at the voice. *That is the great gift the daelkyr offer. Now be silent and let me think!*

Elidyr waited for the voice to say more, but it didn't, and he smiled in satisfaction. He returned his attention to the remains of the Overmantle and mulled over various redesigns in his mind.

Rhedyn, however, didn't stay silent for long.

"They'll be coming for us, you know. Vaddon and the rest of the Outguard. Lirra too. Whether separately or together, they won't stop until they've found us. Lirra especially will never give up."

"You almost sound as if you fear her," Sinnoch taunted.

"I respect her," Rhedyn said, perhaps a bit too quickly. "There's a difference. She's a dangerous opponent in her own right, but now that she has a symbiont *and* has experienced the power of the Overmantle, she's even more dangerous. It's a shame she wouldn't join us."

"Perhaps she will in the end," Elidyr said. "And if not, she will be one more casualty on the way toward creating a perfect world."

Sinnoch grinned with his mouthful of needle-teeth. "One among many."

Rhedyn scowled at the dolgaunt. "We need to be prepared in case they find us before the Overmantle is fixed. Together, the three of us are powerful, but I don't know if we can stop the entire Outguard. Especially if Lirra has rejoined them, which I think likely. Vaddon is a highly experienced commander who could've easily become a warlord if he had any patience for political intrigue. He's already added a pair of warforged to the Outguard's ranks, probably thanks to my uncle. He'll also recruit new members of the Outguard from the garrison at Geirrid to replace those who were killed. He might even convince Rol Amark to allow him to use the entire garrison. We could be facing a force of close to a hundred men and women. As I said, I fear the three of us will not be enough to stop them."

"Assuming they reach us," Sinnoch said. "This cave system is well hidden, and even if Vaddon and Lirra find it, locating us within its labyrinthine tunnels would be another matter entirely." The dolgaunt paused then, head tilted to one side as if he was listening to something Elidyr and Rhedyn couldn't hear. "But even so, your points are well taken, Rhedyn." He turned to the warrior and grinned. "So it's a good thing that I don't live alone here, isn't it?"

Elidyr felt the vibrations through the stone floor before he heard the rhythmic stomping of feet coming from somewhere deep within the cave system. He had no idea precisely how large the force was that approached, but he felt certain it was large enough to do the job. And whatever Sinnoch's friends were, Elidyr knew he could use his flesh-molding abilities to remake them however he saw fit. Now that he thought about it, why should he have them wait until Lirra and the others arrived? It would be so much more hospitable to send Sinnoch's friends out to greet them.

He refocused his attention on the Overmantle, and as the first of the dolgrim entered the cave, the artificer reached out and began reconnecting the broken pieces of the device.

CHAPTER FIFTEEN

A day and a half after leaving Geirrid, the Outguard entered the Nightwood. It was early morning, but the cloud cover was thick that day, and the forest interior was shrouded in gloom. The Nightwood lived up to its name, Lirra thought, for it always seemed to be dark within its confines. This wasn't her first time here. She'd led hunting parties into the forests in search of symbionts on numerous occasions. In fact, the tentacle whip had been captured here during one such hunt.

Welcome home, she thought to the symbiont. In reply, it gave her forearm a painful squeeze, as if to say, *Shut up.* She could sense the tentacle whip's foul mood. It hadn't seen any action since the battle against Elidyr's white-eyes a couple days ago, and she'd felt its frustration building ever since. The symbiont wanted to lash out, to strike at an opponent, to plunge its barb into soft flesh and fill it with poison. It wanted to wrap its coils around a tender neck and slowly squeeze. Tighter . . . tighter . . .

Lirra shook her head to clear her mind of the images. *Stop that!*

A starling perched on a nearby tree branch sang a few notes, and before Lirra could react, the tentacle whip unwrapped from around her wrist and lashed out at the bird. The symbiont's barbed tip speared the starling through the breast, and the animal was dead long before it hit the ground.

The whip retracted slowly and wrapped itself around her forearm with an insolent laziness. Lirra had to resist the urge to smack it, as if it were a dog that had just misbehaved.

"Target practice?" Ranja asked.

"Something like that," Lirra muttered.

The two women rode in the front of the Outguard, along with Osten, who had not left her side since Vaddon had appointed him to be her official watchdog. Longstrider and Shatterfist walked behind them, the indefatigable warforged needing no mounts upon which to travel—not that any horse could carry their weight. Vaddon and Ksana came after the constructs, with the rest of the Outguard following behind. Their ranks had expanded considerably in Geirrid, thanks to Rol Amark, who had allowed Vaddon to conscript half of his garrison soldiers. Vaddon had tried to persuade the man to allow him to have the entire garrison, but Rol had refused, saying he needed to keep some soldiers in town in case Elidyr and his monsters attacked Geirrid again.

Lirra didn't blame him, but it meant that the Outguard had only sixty or so members. A decent-sized force under other circumstances, perhaps, but Lirra feared it wouldn't be enough, not against Elidyr and the sort of creatures he could create. But it was all they had, so it would have to suffice.

One detriment to having such a large party was that it slowed their progress through the forest. The Nightwood was old, full of large, ancient trees growing close together, and while hunters and explorers had forged paths through the forest over the years, Ranja claimed this was the route that Elidyr, Sinnoch, and Rhedyn had taken, and so the sixty members of the Outguard made their way through the dense forest as best they could. One good thing about traveling with so many people was that it would discourage all but the largest and fiercest of predators, and so far their journey through the Nightwood had been without incident. But that didn't mean any of them were complacent. Every man and woman kept close watch on the surrounding woods as they passed, alert for the slightest hint of movement. A number of soldiers rode with crossbows resting on their laps, bolts loaded and ready to loose at the first sign of trouble. Others kept one hand on their horses' reins, the other never far from their swords. They all knew that Elidyr was far from the only monster inhabiting the forest that day.

Osten was one of those holding a crossbow, and he continually swept his gaze back and forth as they rode. Occasionally he'd give Ranja a sidelong glance, frowning slightly. He'd said less than a dozen words to the shifter since they'd left Geirrid, and it was clear to Lirra that he didn't approve of the woman. Lirra might almost have thought Osten was jealous, that he viewed Ranja as a rival of sorts as it was his assigned task to be Lirra's nursemaid. The thought was ridiculous, but she couldn't shake it. For her part, Ranja seemed to delight in talking as often as possible to irritate the young warrior, a result she accomplished all too easily.

Osten glanced at Ranja again, and this time the shifter flashed him a smile that was a touch more feral than usual.

"See something you like, big boy? You know what they say about shifter women . . ."

Osten's cheeks turned bright red. "No, I don't, and I'd prefer you don't enlighten me!" he snapped.

Ranja laughed and gave him a wink, but she said nothing more. Osten glared at her one more time before turning to Lirra.

"How are you doing?" he asked.

He didn't need to make the question more specific. Lirra knew what he meant. He'd seen the tentacle whip kill the starling.

"The symbiont is getting a bit restless, but it's nothing I can't handle." She kept her tone light, in hopes of reassuring

Osten, but in truth she was starting to become concerned. When the Outguard had first set out for the Nightwood, she'd thought the quiet routine of travel would relax her and help to keep her calm, which in turn would make it easier for her to control the tentacle whip. But instead the opposite had happened. The monotony of sitting in the saddle hour after hour had worn down her nerves to the point where she thought she might scream if something didn't happen soon. When Vaddon had talked with her at the garrison barracks in Geirrid, he'd wondered aloud how much she'd been changed by hosting a symbiont. It seemed she'd been changed in ways both great *and* small. It was important she came to understand those changes, for the symbiont would attempt to exploit any weakness to slip past her guard and wrest control from her. And that was something she couldn't let happen, not even for an instant. For if she did, there was a good chance her mind, her spirit, her very *self,* would be lost forever.

It hadn't helped any that her mount, a piebald mare, was skittish about having a rider with a symbiont sitting in the saddle. Elidyr, Sinnoch, and Rhedyn had taken the mounts that had been enchanted to tolerate the presence of aberrations when they'd fled from Geirrid, and Lirra had been forced to make due with one of the horses from the garrison stable. Since Geirrid was surrounded by farms, the town had a number of animal handlers who could lay spells on cattle and horses to make them more tractable, and the garrison stablemaster was skilled at such spellcraft. Unfortunately, he'd never had to enchant a horse to carry a rider fused with an aberration before, and while the mare tolerated Lirra's presence, Lirra had to constantly pay attention to her mount to make sure she didn't spook. Two days of babying her horse had worn Lirra down even further.

She sat up straight in the saddle and forced herself to take several deep, even breaths to calm herself before turning to Ranja.

"How are we faring?" she asked.

In response, Ranja raised her chin and sniffed the air. "Still on track. The scent's good and strong, as well it should be considering that the three we're tracking are all aberrations of one sort or another." She wrinkled her nose. "They reek. Even if a strong rain came along, I doubt it would be enough to dampen their scent trail. How about you? Sense anything yet?"

Lirra concentrated. She felt a slight tingle at the base of her skull, and a cold flutter deep in her stomach, but neither sensation lasted more than an instant. "I'm not certain. Right now, I'd say your nose is a lot more reliable."

Behind them, Shatterfist called out. "Speaking of noses, have you heard this one? One gnome walks up to another gnome and says, 'My dog has no nose.' The second gnome asks, 'Then how does he smell?' And the first gnome answers, 'Terrible!' "

Lirra groaned. She almost wished some unspeakable horror would come shrieking out of the woods and tear her to shreds. At least then she wouldn't have to listen to any more of Shatterfist's awful jokes. She wondered if she could convince her father that the warforged were still too close to Ranja and were interfering with her tracking. Perhaps then he'd move them farther back in the—

Tingling erupted at the base of her skull, and her gut twisted with sudden nausea as intense as when she'd sensed Elidyr's white-eyes in Geirrid. More so, in fact, and she knew that couldn't be good.

She raised her hand to call for a sudden halt. Vaddon saw her signal and commanded the Outguard to stop. He rode forward, Ksana riding at his side, until both of their mounts were at the front of the party with Lirra, Ranja, and Osten.

"What is it?" Vaddon asked without preamble.

"There's something ahead of us," Lirra said. "Something big. And it's coming toward us. I think it's an aberration of some sort . . . or maybe many aberrations massed together. I'm not sure. But whatever it is, it's approaching fast."

Vaddon looked at her skeptically for a moment, as if he didn't trust her perceptions. He turned to Ksana, and the half-elf cleric raised her right hand, closed her eyes, and whispered a quick prayer to her goddess.

She opened her eyes. "I think Lirra is right. Whatever's coming feels like those creatures of Elidyr's we fought in Geirrid. Not evil in the supernatural sense, but definitely unnatural."

Vaddon turned in his saddle to face the rest of the Outguard and made a series of silent hand gestures. The men and women under his command—including those who'd only just joined the Outguard—understood the code: *We're about to be attacked. Make ready.* Crossbows were raised and swords were quietly drawn from their sheaths. Without a word, the soldiers moved their horses into a circular battle formation so that they'd be prepared for the attack no matter which direction it came from. Lirra and the others did likewise, Longstrider and Shatterfist stepping forward to join them at the head of the circle.

Ranja sniffed the air and made a face. "They definitely stink like the white-eyes and that dolgaunt friend of your uncle's. Like rotten mushrooms covered in snail slime." The shifter shuddered in disgust. "I can hear them too. Dozens of them, approaching from all sides." She cocked her head as she listened more closely. "They aren't big, but there's a lot of them."

Lirra could hear them now as well. Thudding footfalls on the forest floor, harsh, labored breathing, and muttering voices. She felt the tentacle whip's coils slacken around her arm as the symbiont prepared for action, and the thought-voice whispered with glee: *Finally!*

Seconds later, the first wave of creatures came at them. Though she'd never seen them in the flesh before, Lirra recognized the things at once, thanks to the briefings Elidyr had given the Outguard on aberrations, the daelkyr, and their servants. These were dolgrims, creatures created by the daelkyr during their long-ago invasion of Khorvaire. To create a dolgrim, a daelkyr took two goblins and fused them into a single being using its flesh-molding powers. The resultant creature was a loathsome thing, three-and-a-half feet tall, squat and hunchbacked, with four spindly arms and no head. Its face was located on its chest, and it had a pair of toothsome mouths, one set atop the other. The skin was oily and white, though a number of these dolgrims bore garishly colored tattoos upon their flesh, as if to differentiate themselves from their brethren. They wore dark leather pants as their sole clothing, and carried four weapons, one for each hand: a morningstar, a spear, a light crossbow, and a shield, though some dolgrim wielded greatswords instead of spears. According to Elidyr, the creatures possessed two brains, though one personality was primarily dominant, and sometimes they held conversations with themselves, which explained the muttering Lirra had heard. While the creatures weren't particularly smart, their dual brains did allow them to wield all four of their weapons in a coordinated attack, which made them foes to be respected.

Many of these dolgrims were different from the standard breed, however, and Lirra knew that her uncle had added his own special touches to these before sending them out to attack. Some were covered with bony spikes, while others were encased in insect-like armor. Several possessed claws long and sharp as sabers, and a few had discolored foam—which Lirra had no doubt was poisonous—dripping from their twin mouths. As dangerous as the creatures had been before, they were doubly so now, thanks to Elidyr.

Vaddon shouted for the Outguard to attack, but he needn't have bothered. The dolgrims were upon the soldiers so swiftly that it was all they could do to defend themselves. The Outguard's horses had been trained for battle, and many held steady, but they hadn't been trained to deal with unnatural creatures like dolgrims, and some whinnied, bucked, and threw their riders. Those horses tried to flee in panic and were quickly dispatched by the dolgrims, though a few of the creatures fell beneath pounding hooves before all the terrified horses had been dealt with.

The creatures seemed reluctant to attack Lirra. She swiftly dismounted and smacked her horse on the rear to send her on her way. The mare had been a thorn in Lirra's side for the last two days, but she wished the horse good luck as she turned to face the nearest dolgrims, sword in hand, tentacle whip uncoiling of its own accord, eager to draw blood. Lirra didn't chastise her symbiont for acting on its own. Now was precisely the time to allow the whip the freedom to act on its own.

The whip lashed its barbed tip toward a dolgrim—this one covered with spikes—and struck the creature in the eye. The dolgrim howled as poison flooded its system, and it dropped all four of its weapons as it staggered backward, dying. Meanwhile, Lirra swung her sword at a different dolgrim, this one gnashing foam-flecked teeth. It swung its morningstar at her, but she batted it aside easily and dodged to the side as the dolgrim followed up with a spear thrust to her abdomen. Before she'd bonded with the tentacle whip, the strike might have hit home, but she was faster now and more agile, and while the spear tip tore the cloth of her tunic, it didn't draw blood. The dolgrim attempted to follow up its strike with a blow from its shield, but Lirra was ready for that. She commanded the tentacle whip to grab hold of the dolgrim's shield hand by the wrist, and then she took the opportunity to jam her sword into one of the creature's eyes.

The dolgrim shrieked in agony and fell away from her sword, blood spraying from the ruined socket where its eye had been. Lirra turned away from the creature before it could fall to the ground, selected another target, and set upon it.

Ranja assumed her full bestial aspect and leaped off her horse to engage the nearest dolgrim, while Osten remained on his mount, swinging his sword as the creatures came at him. But given the dolgrims' diminutive stature, his sword missed as often as it hit, and the creatures were able to come in close and attack his horse, using their weapons or even their teeth to wound the animal. The steed screamed in pain and started to go down under the assault. Osten vaulted out of the saddle in time and managed to land on his feet just as a pair of dolgrims rushed at him. His horse fell to the ground and was overrun and slain by dolgrims who then quickly moved on to other targets.

Longstrider and Shatterfist lost no time in engaging the enemy. It was, after all, what they'd been created for. The two warforged waded into the sea of dolgrims with devasting effect, Longstrider's spiked feet slashing flesh, snapping bones, and crushing bodies with his spinning kicks while Shatterfist's hands reduced dolgrims to so much oily white pulp with one blow after another. The creatures shrieked as they died, their cries high-pitched and grating, sounding more like yowling cats than unnatural aberrations.

Vaddon and Ksana dismounted and smacked their horses on the flank, sending them pounding into the ranks of the dolgrims, in hopes that the animals might escape or, failing that, at least kill some of the creatures before dying themselves. The two fought back to back, Vaddon's sword flashing almost faster than Lirra's eyes could track, Ksana's halberd matching him strike for strike. Despite Vaddon's age, he fought like a warrior in his prime, his blows precise and economical, guided by years of battlefield experience. Ksana fought with a fluid grace. The cleric's face was calm, almost beatific, as if she were praying instead of fighting for her life.

How long the Outguard fought against the dolgrims, Lirra couldn't have said. She fell into a state that she was well familiar with from her time on the battlefield, a state wherein she ceased thinking consciously and gave herself over to her training and experience, letting her body do what it needed to in order to survive. The state was quite peaceful in its own way, and since her symbiont was happily occupied with slaughtering dolgrims, the pressure she felt from the aberration's constant attempts to escape her control and subvert her mind had lessened. In many ways, this was the most relaxed she'd felt since bonding with the tentacle whip—and wasn't that a sad commentary on her current state of existence?

But Lirra had fought in too many campaigns not to recognize when her side was outnumbered, and before long she realized that the Outguard was losing this battle. A number of their people had fallen to the dolgrims, though thank the Host those closest to her remained alive, if not altogether unscathed. Still, if they didn't turn the tide soon, the dolgrims would overwhelm them and they would all perish here, their life's blood soaking the soil and feeding the Nightwood's trees.

Lirra heard the thought-voice whisper.

You know this is only a distraction, right?

The whip stabbed another dolgrim in the eye, and the creature screamed briefly before the symbiont's poison stole away its life. Lirra followed the whip's action by ramming her sword into a dolgrim's upper mouth, angling upward to pierce the creature's brain. As she yanked her blade free, she realized the tentacle whip was right. She'd been a fool. How many times on the battlefield had she commanded a squadron of soldiers to attack as a distraction or delaying tactic so that she could maneuver the main attack force into position? Elidyr might have trained as a scholar and artificer instead of a professional soldier, but he had a keen mind—albeit an insane one now—and would have had no trouble devloping the simple strategy of keeping his foes busy while he prepared to achieve his true aim: repairing the Overmantle and releasing the daelkyr lord from Xoriat. And Lirra and the others had fallen for his stratagem like green recruits fresh out of basic training.

Lirra continued killing dolgrims as she thought furiously. They couldn't continue fighting a losing battle against these creatures, not if they were to have any hope of reaching Elidyr in time. But given the dolgrims' superior numbers and their implacable savagery, there was no way the Outguard could prevail against them. Not unless something could be done to tip the scales in the Outguard's favor. But what?

You'd need a way to attack a number of dolgrims all at once, the thought-voice suggested.

Lirra continued hacking away at one dolgrim after another, the tentacle whip sometimes helping by keeping the creature's extra hands busy, other times simply by injecting poison into their bodies.

The thought-voice spoke again. *You don't just have my abilities to draw on. Remember what your uncle did back at the lodge.*

She remembered Elidyr holding forth a hand, the air distorting around them as he unleashed a newfound power, a wave of vertigo passing over her, accompanied by weakness and nausea. She recalled her uncle's words: Did you enjoy that? It's a little taste of Xoriat chaos energy.

Was the tentacle whip hinting that she had the same power? She hadn't been touched by the daelkyr as Elidyr had, but the power of Xoriat had been flowing through the portal while the Overmantle had been active. Perhaps the chaos energy had affected her more than she'd realized. Then again, perhaps her symbiont was toying with her, building up her hopes for its own amusement, just so it could see them dashed when she attempted to use a power she didn't possess.

Lirra didn't see what other option she had though. She swung her sword in a wide arc before her in order to push back the nearest dolgrims, and then she thrust out her free hand—the tentacle whip lashing the air to keep more dolgrims at bay—and, without a clue how she might release a power within her that she didn't know for certain she possessed, she concentrated. At first, nothing happened. But then she became aware of a stirring deep inside her, as if she was tapping into a vast reservoir of power that she hadn't known existed. The air around her hand began to waver, and then she felt a sudden surge of energy rush through her arm and blast forth from her hand.

A dozen dolgrims were caught in the line of fire, and Lirra could sense the chaos energy rolling over the creatures like a wall of flame. They staggered backward, swaying on legs suddenly grown too weak to support them, dropping their weapons and falling to the ground, where they lay twitching and mewling like newborn kittens. The Outguard defenders wasted no time wondering what had caused so many dolgrims to collapse all at once. They moved forward swiftly and killed the creatures while they were disabled. Not the most honorable of combat techniques, perhaps, but imminently practical given their current situation.

Lirra was able to release two more blasts of chaos energy, each less potent than the first, before she could do no more. The power simply wasn't there for her to draw on anymore. Still, it did its work. By the time she was finished, thirty or more dolgrims had been slain, and twice that number had fled in terror of the wild-eyed woman who commanded the power of Xoriat itself. Those few dolgrims who had the discipline—or perhaps simply the bad judgment—to stay and fight were easily dealt with by the Outguard.

One dolgrim remained alive, however. While the others were being killed by her companions, she selected one at random—one that had not been reshaped by Elidyr's flesh-molding power—and kneeled down next to it. The creature stank, just like Ranja had said earlier. Rotten mushrooms and snail slime. The dolgrim lay on the forest floor, arms and legs quivering as it struggled to overcome the debilitating effects of the chaos energy and get back on its feet, whether to fight or, more likely, to flee. Lirra sheathed her sword and kneeled by the dolgrim's side. She commanded the tentacle whip to lower its barbed tip to within an inch of the creature's right eye, and as an extra touch, she told the whip to allow a bead of poison to form on the tip. The dolgrim looked up at the barb with wide, terrified eyes, its breathing rapid and shallow.

Doing her best to ignore the creature's stench, Lirra leaned her head close to its ear.

"Can you talk?" she asked.

The dolgrim opened its upper mouth once, swallowed, and then tried again.

"Y-yessss . . ." it hissed.

"Good. Now listen to me very carefully. All of your friends are dead, dying, or gone. You are alone. The only chance you have of surviving is if you answer my questions quickly and completely. Do you understand?"

"Yes."

The creature's speech sounded clearer, and Lirra knew she had to hurry before the effects of the chaos energy wore off.

"A man named Elidyr sent you to kill us. Tell me how to find him and you get to live."

The creature opened its upper mouth to reply, but it lower one spoke first.

"Don't listen to her! She'll just kill us when we tell her what she wants!"

"If you don't answer, you will definitely die," she said, making sure to keep her tone icy cold. "Answering me is the only chance for survival you have. And the longer you take to start talking, the slimmer that chance gets."

The lips of both mouths moved silently then, and Lirra had the impression that an internal debate was taking place within the dolgrim's mind. She'd recently come to learn what that was like, and she waited for the two minds inside the creature to reach a decision.

"Two miles northwest is a clearing with a rocky hill in the center. At the base is an entrance to a series of caves. Elidyr is inside."

Lirra started to give the dolgrim her thanks, but before she could speak, the tentacle whip pulled back its barb to strike.

"No!"

Lirra reached out with her right hand and grabbed hold of the tentacle whip before it could sink its barb into the dolgrim's eye.

"I gave him my word that he could go free if he cooperated!"

So he can run and tell Elidyr that we're coming? the thought-voice asked.

Lirra hated to admit it, but the whip had a point. *Can you give him a low dose of poison? Enough to render him unconscious but leave him alive?*

The symbiont seemed to consider for a moment, and then Lirra felt its reluctant agreement.

She spoke aloud to the dolgrim.

"I'm going to put you to sleep for a time." She took in the surrounding area, noting all the dead, both dolgrims and soldiers. The bodies of those dolgrims who Elidyr had transformed were starting to liquefy, just as the creature formed from the combined white-eyes had back in Geirrid. The bodies of the normal dolgrims, however, remained intact. "I'll move you to a safer location so that any predators drawn to this place will not find you. With any luck, you'll awaken safe and sound."

The dolgrim's lower mouth said, "See? I told you she was going to kill us!"

Don't betray me on this, Lirra thought to the tentacle whip, *or I'll start keeping you on an even tighter leash! And don't sting him in the eye!*

The whip did as she ordered, injecting its poison into one of the dolgrim's spindly arms. The creature stiffened, then his eyes closed and he fell limp. Lirra placed her fingers on one of the dolgrim's wrists, and she felt a pulse. A strange pulse, actually, since it seemed to have dual beats. Then she remembered: two hearts. She released the dolgrim's wrist and stood.

Ranja, in human form once more, came over to stand beside her, and Osten hurried to join them. The shifter looked down at the unconscious dolgrim.

"Nicely handled," Ranja said. "You know, I think you'd do well in my profession."

Osten frowned. "What does questioning a dolgrim have to do with being a scout?"

Lirra fought to keep a smile from her face as Ranja sidled up next to the young warrior.

"If you're truly interested, perhaps the two of us can have a private conversation about it later," she suggested.

Osten's frown deepened into a scowl and he stepped away from the shifter. Ranja seemed amused, but she didn't tease Osten any further.

Vaddon and Ksana came over then, the two warforged following after. All of them were splattered with foul-smelling dolgrim blood—Longstrider and Shatterfist, especially—but none appeared to be seriously wounded.

"Did you learn anything useful?" Vaddon asked, and Lirra told him what the dolgrim had said. She also told him of her mounting suspicions about the creatures Elidyr reshaped for his own purposes.

"It's as if his power to rework flesh has its limits," she said. "I wonder if his creatures would decay on their own, given enough time."

"Let us hope that's the case," Vaddon said. "If the distorted monsters my brother can now create have a limited lifespan, that's a huge advantage in our favor. But enough talk. We need to get moving. Our horses are gone, so we'll have to proceed the rest of the way on foot."

"We can't leave yet!" Ksana protested. "I need to tend to our injured first, and we can't leave the dead unburied. Not only would it be dishonorable and an affront to the gods, our dead deserve better than for us to leave them for the scavengers to feast upon!"

"Honestly," Ranja said, "as bad as the dolgrims smell, I doubt even the hungriest of scavengers would come near this place."

Lirra gave the shifter a look that said, *you aren't helping.* Then she turned to the cleric. "I would never make light of your beliefs, Ksana. You know that. And I would never wish to dishonor fallen comrades, whether I served with them for years or, in the case of our new garrison recruits, only a short time. But even as we speak, Elidyr is working to repair the Overmantle. For all we know, he may have already finished. We have to reach him before he can activate it again and reopen the portal to Xoriat. And that means we can't afford to waste any more time."

Ksana's normally placid face clouded over with anger, and she gestured sharply toward a mass of dead soldiers. "You consider *them* a waste of time? Has your spirit become so poisoned by the corruption you carry with you that you've lost all common decency?"

Ksana's words stung, but Lirra did her best not to let her feelings show. She started to answer, but Vaddon put a hand on her shoulder—it was the first time he'd touched her since she'd joined with the tentacle whip—to gently silence her.

"Lirra's right," he said, "and you know it. Sometimes hard choices have to be made on the field of battle. This isn't the first time we've faced them. We'll leave the dead for now, and if possible, we shall return to give them a proper burial. As for the wounded, quickly tend to those who cannot travel. The rest you can heal as we march."

Ksana looked as if she might argue, but then she let out a sigh, nodded, and left to inspect the wounded. Vaddon raised his voice so that the rest of the surviving members of the Outguard could hear him.

"We march in five minutes, people! Make ready!"

Vaddon then turned back to Lirra. "Good enough?" he asked.

"I suppose it'll have to be."

He nodded then walked off to make sure his soldiers followed his orders. She turned to the two warforged and gestured to the dolgrim she'd questioned.

"Longstrider, carry him a safe distance away from this place and tuck him into a tree. Not too high, mind you. Shatterfist, you stay here and stand guard while we regroup and prepare to move out."

Longstrider nodded, scooped up the dolgrim as if he weighed nothing, and strode off into the forest. Shatterfirst looked around at the carnage that surrounded them.

"As I understand it, humans sometimes use humor to lighten the mood after a tragic event has occurred. Perhaps I could—"

Lirra, Ranja, and Osten turned to the construct and shouted in unison.

"No!"

The warforged crossed his stone and metal arms over his chest. "Fine," he huffed. "Look, this is me, standing guard."

A few moments later Longstrider returned, and the Outguard was ready to march. From a group of around sixty soldiers, they were down to just over twenty. A hard loss, especially after only a single encounter with Elidyr's forces. Lirra wondered what else her uncle had in store for them. She supposed they would soon find out.

Vaddon gave the command, and the Outguard started marching.

CHAPTER SIXTEEN

They found the cave entrance precisely where the dolgrim said they would. The hill was barren, rocky, and rather lopsided, as if somewhere in the distant past a mountain had tried to thrust its way up through the earth and had barely gotten started before giving up.

The entrance to the caves wasn't hard to spot. It lay at the southern base, and the opening was large enough for the soldiers to fit through one at a time, warforged included, though just barely in the constructs' case. Lirra assumed the tunnels would be narrow, though passable, since Elidyr, Sinnoch, and Rhedyn had been able to make their way through. Lirra felt a rush of anger at the thought of seeing Rhedyn again. Right then she wanted nothing more than to wrap her hands around his traitorous neck and—

That's right, get good and mad. We'll be able to use your anger when it's time to shed blood again . . .

Hearing the thought-voice's words, Lirra forced herself to calm down. The last thing she wanted to do right now was give her symbiont a stronger grip on her mind, and if she allowed herself to be carried away by anger, that's exactly what would happen.

"Here you go," Ranja said. "As promised. Now that I've led you to Elidyr's lair, my job's finished, and since there's an excellent chance that none of you will survive to leave the caves, I'd appreciate it if you could pay me my fee in full before you enter."

Osten took a step toward the shifter, his hand falling to the pommel of his sword.

"Why you mercenary little—"

Lirra shushed Osten and laid a hand on his arm to keep him from moving any closer to Ranja. But the shifter took a step toward Osten, her features becoming a touch more feral.

"I was hired to do a job and I did it," she said. "There's no shame in that, nor is there any in my wanting to be paid for my contribution."

Vaddon scowled, but he reached inside his uniform and withdrew a purse full of silver from a pocket. He tossed it to Ranja, and the shifter woman caught it easily and made it disappear into one of her own pockets. She then flashed Vaddon a smile.

"Pleasure doing business with you, General."

"So what will you do now?" Osten asked. "Head back to Geirrid while we risk our lives to stop Elidyr?"

"I think I'll stick around for a bit longer, just to see how things turn out," Ranja said. She turned to Vaddon. "I assume you're going to station some people outside the entrance to guard the backs of those going in. I'll remain out here with them, if you don't mind."

"Suit yourself," Vaddon said. "But don't think you're going to get paid any more for staying."

"Of course not, General. I'm well satisfied with what I've acquired." Ranja looked at Lirra and gave her a quick smile.

Lirra understood. The shifter spy had gained all the knowledge she needed, and if she couldn't find a way to blackmail Bergerron, she'd simply go ahead with her original plan and deliver the information to Raskogr. Either way, more silver lay in her future. Before she'd joined with her symbiont, Lirra would've reacted to the shifter's mercenary nature much the same way Osten had—with hostility and derision. After all, Lirra was a Karrnathi soldier, and she performed her duties out of loyalty to her country and a desire to serve its people, not in hopes of lining her own pockets. But now she couldn't find it in herself to think badly of Ranja. As much as Lirra had been raised by her father, and later trained at the Rekkenmark Academy, to view the world in simplistic black-and-white terms, in the last few days she'd come to realize that, in truth, existence all too often consisted of varying shades of gray. Lirra knew she and the others wouldn't have gotten this far without Ranja's help, and she was grateful for the shifter's aid. And if this was where they parted company, then so be it.

Lirra gave Ranja a nod before turning to her father.

"So what's the plan?" she asked.

Vaddon raised an eyebrow, and Lirra smiled. "You *are* in command of this mission," she reminded him.

Vaddon selected a half-dozen men and women to stand guard outside the cave. Lirra noted that he picked those who had been most seriously wounded during the battle with the dolgrims, and she could well guess why. While Ksana had used her healing powers to repair the soldiers' injuries, they were still somewhat weak. Better they guarded the others' rear flank than enter the caves to face whatever threats might lie within.

"The rest of us will go inside," Vaddon said. "Lirra, you will lead the way and Osten shall accompany you. Ksana and I will come next, and the warforged shall follow us." He turned to face the remainder of the Outguard. "The rest of you line up in pairs. If the tunnels are too narrow to permit us to walk two abreast, then we'll go single file. Lanterns out, and keep your swords in hand at all times unless there's not enough room to wield them efficiently, in which case, sheath them and switch to daggers. Any questions?"

"I know I'm not going with you," Ranja said, "but I have a question: What do you intend to do once you find Elidyr?"

Lirra responded to the shifter's query. "We'll destroy the Overmantle and attempt to take Elidyr, Sinnoch, and Rhedyn into custody."

"And in the extremely likely event that they resist?" Ranja asked.

Lirra's mouth was set in a grim line as she answered. "If it comes down to that . . . we'll do what has to be done." She turned to look at Vaddon, and though she saw the same conflict she felt mirrored in her father's eyes, the general nodded. Neither of them wanted to kill Elidyr, but if he gave them no choice . . .

There was nothing more to be said after that. The Outguard lined up as Vaddon had ordered, and—with Lirra leading the way—they entered the caves.

"They're here," Sinnoch said.

Elidyr hadn't moved from his sitting position since he'd begun work on the Overmantle. He hadn't slept, hadn't paused for food or drink. Now he looked up at the dolgaunt with tired eyes.

"So soon? Time truly does fly when you're enjoying yourself."

Rhedyn had been sitting with his back against the cave wall, dozing. But at the dolgaunt's words he leaped to his feet. "Could it be the dolgrims returning?"

"Doubtful," Elidyr said as he touched an etheric-balancing rod to several individual crystals on the reconstructed Overmantle. "I didn't expect the dolgrims to stop my brother and his soldiers, just slow them down a bit. It'll take more than a handful of dolgrims, even augmented as they were, to put my brother and my niece in the ground." He smiled to himself. "That's a pleasure I'm reserving for myself." Elidyr made one last adjustment with the rod, then leaned back to admire his work. "There! That should do it!" He paused. "I hope."

Rhedyn walked over to stand next to Elidyr, and Sinnoch glided over to join them.

"What do you mean?" the young warrior asked.

"I did the best I could, considering that I lacked the proper parts and equipment," Elidyr said, a trifle defensively. "Not only was I forced to redesign the device, I had to make certain . . . improvisations here and there."

"But it will work, yes?" Sinnoch asked.

"Oh, yes," Elidyr confirmed. "At least, it will activate. As to what it will precisely *do* . . ." Grinning, he touched a switch to bring the Overmantle to life.

Rippling waves of energy poured out of the device, its power filling the entirety of Sinnoch's cave.

~~~~~

Lirra held her sword in her right hand, and she kept her left free to wield the tentacle whip, so she carried no lantern to light the way. That duty fell to Osten, who stood on her left, an everbright lantern held in his left hand, sword in his right. The lantern's glow was eerie in the confined space of the tunnel, and the shadows it cast seemed to move with a life of their own. When they'd first entered the tunnel, it was so cramped they could barely walk in single file, but as the tunnel sloped downward, it opened up somewhat, and two people could walk side by side—though the squat, blocky Shatterfist still needed to walk by himself in order to fit. There was enough room for them to keep their swords out, though if it became necessary to fight, there'd be precious little maneuvering room. They moved in silence, no one speaking, everyone careful to keep from brushing up against the tunnel walls more than necessary, and they were especially careful to keep their weapons away from the walls, lest the sound of steel scraping against stone gave their presence away.

Not that Elidyr doesn't know we're coming, Lirra thought. One way or another, she was certain her uncle was aware that they were closing in. After all, hadn't he sent the dolgrims out to attack them? But she remembered something she'd learned at Rekkenmark: *Never give a foe an advantage you didn't need to.* If there was even the slightest chance Elidyr didn't know they were coming, the Outguard would remain silent.

The tunnel continued to slope downward as they progressed, and Lirra tried to use her new senses to feel the way ahead, casting about for any hint of symbionts or other aberrations. The base of her skull tingled and a familiar nausea roiled in her stomach. She could feel the presence of corruption somewhere out in front of them, and it was strong—far stronger than anything she'd ever felt before. It was repellant, but at the same time strangely alluring. Part of her wanted to turn back and flee in terror, while another part of her wanted to run forward to reach the foul presence as fast as she could.

What is it? she mentally asked the tentacle whip.

Chaos.

She leaned close to Osten and whispered in his ear.

"Do you feel that?"

"I feel *something,*" he whispered back. "Whatever it is, it's setting my teeth on edge. Too bad the shifter isn't here. Perhaps she could make something of it."

A second voice whispered in Lirra's other ear. "It's good to know I'm appreciated."

Lirra turned to her right, startled to hear Ranja speaking, but no one walked there. At first Lirra feared she'd only imagined the shifter's voice, that perhaps it was a new sort of mind trick the tentacle whip was playing on her. But then she realized what Ranja had done. The woman had used one of the magical toys she employed to render herself invisible, and then she'd sneaked past the other members of the Outguard until she'd reached the front of the line where Lirra and Osten were.

Lirra smiled. When going into battle, it was always good to have a surprise or two prepared for your enemy, and with any luck, Ranja would prove to be one hell of a surprise for Elidyr.

They continued onward, and the tingling in her skull and her nausea grew stronger as they walked, along with the strange compulsion to keep going forward. She raised her hand and made several gestures to let her father know they were getting close, even if she wasn't entirely certain close to what. Vaddon answered with a single gesture that meant Message received, before silently relaying Lirra's message to the warforged, who passed it back to the soldiers behind them, and so on. Within moments, everyone in the tunnel knew the time for battle was close at hand, and they did their best to mentally prepare themselves for whatever lay in wait ahead. Lirra had experienced the last few moments before battle more times than she could remember. Some soldiers became nervous and had to work hard to calm themselves. Others drew on their nervous energy to get their minds and bodies ready to fight. Still others attempted to visualize what the intitial encounter with the enemy might be like and what moves and countermoves they would make. Some simply emptied their mind of all extraneous thought, trusted in their training to carry them through the battle to come, and concentrated on simply putting one foot in front of the other.

Lirra became aware of a light not far ahead of them. At first, Lirra thought it was the glow from an everbright lantern, but the color was all wrong. Instead of a yellowish hue, this light was a shifting combination of colors, something like a kaleidoscope. She feared that they were too late, and Elidyr had activated the Overmantle, but then she remembered that the device's crystals had pulsed with blue-white energy. What they were seeing ahead of them looked very different.

Ranja's voice whispered once more in Lirra's ear.

"Want me to run ahead and take a look?"

Lirra was tempted. Intelligence-gathering was more often than not the key to victory. But she didn't fully understand the scope of Elidyr's new powers, and she didn't want to risk the shifter being detected by him. What good was a secret weapon if it was no longer secret? Better that Ranja approach Elidyr with the rest of them. That way, even if her uncle did possess some means of sensing the invisible shifter, there'd be a chance he'd be too distracted by the appearance of Lirra and the others to notice her.

Lirra shook her head once to let the shifter know she should stay close, and they continued cautiously moving down the tunnel toward the shifting lights. The tingling and nausea increased to the point of pain, and the feeling that she had to go forward and see what lay ahead became so strong it took all of her will not to break ranks and dash down the tunnel. It helped that she knew it would only be a matter of moments before she finally saw whatever it was that both repelled and attracted her so.

They reached a bend in the tunnel, and when they turned, they saw that the tunnel opened upon a large cave, roughly dome-shaped, with long stalactites hanging from the ceiling that reminded Lirra too much of teeth. In the center of the cave stood Elidyr, Sinnoch, and Rhedyn, the Overmantle lying on the floor next to them, its glowing crystals filling the cave with shifting, multicolored light. Lirra knew that the Overmantle was the source of the dueling impulses she felt, and she sensed that something was different about the device now. Different, and very, very wrong.

"Welcome everyone!" Elidyr called out. "You got here just in time! Come in, come in! You don't want to miss the show, do you? Not after you traveled all the way from Geirrid to get here."

Lirra and Osten stepped into the cave, and the moment they crossed the threshold, Lirra felt better. The tingling at the base of her skull and the nausea were still there, but they'd lessened. Lirra assumed Ranja accompanied Osten and her into the cave, though since she couldn't see the shifter, she didn't know for certain. Vaddon and Ksana came next, followed by Longstrider and Shatterfist. Vaddon ordered the warforged to remain with him, and he commanded the rest of the Outguard soldiers to spread out around the cave and surround Elidyr and his companions, and they hastened to do so.

Elidyr watched with amusement as the soldiers took up their positions, but he made no move to interfere.

Vaddon stepped forward, sword in hand, but held down at his side.

"I'm going to give you one chance to surrender, Brother. Shut down the Overmantle and come with us—please."

"Or what? You'll kill me?" Elidyr reached up with his crawling gauntlet to scratch the head of the stormstalk draped around his shoulders. "It's a little late for that, Vaddon."

Lirra felt the presence of new aberrations approaching, but she couldn't see any. There was something strange about the way the light given off by the Overmantle played upon the cave walls though. It made the stone seem hazy and indistinct, as if it were mist instead of solid rock, and she thought she could almost make out amorphous, shifting shapes within it. A strange mixture of scents filled the cave as well, the smells at once foul and sweet, stomach-turning and enticing.

"What's the Overmantle doing, Uncle?" she asked.

"I'm so glad you asked," Elidyr said, smiling. "It was too damaged for me to restore it to full functionality—not with the tools and equipment currently in my possession—so it's unable to open a portal to Xoriat. However, I was able to make some alterations so that it can do the next best thing. Here, in this cave, our plane of existence and Xoriat's intersect. A permanent crossing cannot take place, but within the confines of this cave denizens of both dimensions can coexist and interact, for as long as the Overmantle is active, that is. Not exactly what I'd hoped for, but then it should prove sufficient."

"Sufficient for what?" Lirra asked.

Elidyr's smile turned into a grin. "To see all of you dealt with. Then, with no one hounding me any longer, I'll have the time I need to completely repair the Overmantle so that it can open a true portal to Xoriat."

The sensation of approaching aberrations grew stronger, and Lirra looked about the cave, searching for any sign that something was coming. There could be other ways in and out the cave that were hidden from her eyes. With the strange visual effect caused by the Overmantle's light, it was so difficult to tell . . . Then she noticed a pair of large round shadows on the walls on opposite sides of the cave. Shadows that were cast by nothing she could see . . . shadows that grew larger with every passing second.

Lirra shouted a warning but it was too late. A pair of large floating orbs emerged from the walls as they crossed over from Xoriat to this in-between place that Elidyr had created, stone walls parting for them as if they were nothing more than curtains of cloth easily brushed aside. The creatures were eight feet wide, with a single central eye and a large tooth-filled maw. Ten stalks emerged from the top of the orb in a hideous parody of hair, and atop each of the stalks was a smaller eye. Lirra recognized the monsters from Elidyr's briefings in the early days of the symbiont project—beholders.

The creatures knocked down a handful of soldiers as they entered the cave, and they immediately spun around to begin attacking those members of the Outguard stationed around the cave's walls. Rays of energy lanced forth from the beholders' eyes, the beams striking a different soldier before they could mount a defense. Lirra remembered that each of a beholder's eyestalks was capable of casting a separate spell. One soldier fell to the cave floor, asleep, while another collapsed, dead. One turned to stone, while another disintegrated, leaving no trace that he had ever existed. To her left, a few doubled over, bleeding from wounds that magically appeared on their bodies, while beyond him, a woman suddenly turned on her comrades, plunging her sword into her companions' flesh before turning her blade against herself. Two were tossed high in the air by an unseen force to be impaled on the stalactites above, while others moved slowly, as if time had suddenly frozen to a near stop for them.

The beholders' attack took only seconds, but in that time they managed to take out almost every soldier that ringed the cave walls.

"Shatterfist, Longstrider!" Lirra shouted, and the warforged needed no more encouragement than that. Each of the constructs selected a beholder and charged forward to meet it.

"Stay out of their main line of sight!" Lirra called out. She remembered that the gaze of a beholder could create an antimagic effect if trained upon an enemy, and while she had no idea whether that could affect warforged, she didn't want to find out.

Shatterfist and Longstrider approached the aberrations from the side. The beholders began to swivel toward the attacking warforged, but they were too late. Longstrider leaped into the air and slammed a kick into the side of a beholder's head, sending it spinning. A second leap, and Longstrider landed atop the beholder, his weight dragging it toward the ground. Once on the floor, Longstrider began kicking the creature to death with his spiked feet. Shatterfist reached up to grab his beholder by the jaw, then slammed the aberration face first against the cave floor. He then started using his hammer-hands to pummel the creature to a pulp. Within seconds it was over. The beholders were dead, and the two warforged were covered with gore.

Elidyr clapped. "Well done! Though quite frankly, given how ugly the damned things are, it's not much of a loss."

"Enough talk," Vaddon growled. "Longstrider, Shatterfist, destroy the Overmantle!"

If Lirra understood what Elidyr had said, the Overmantle's power made this cave an in-between place where two dimensions overlapped. If the Overmantle was destroyed, the two dimensions would become separate once more, and no further aberrations would be able to cross over from Xoriat to attack them.

The warforged didn't hesitate. The two constructs turned toward Elidyr and charged. Elidyr watched them come, seemingly unconcerned. Lirra wondered if it was because her uncle was too mad to fear them, but an instant later she saw the true reason why he wasn't afraid. Another figure stepped through the cave wall, this one roughly the size and shape of a human, though its rubbery greenish-mauve flesh glistened with slime. The creature's head looked like a four-tentacled octopus that possessed a pair of bloated white eyes. It wore a black robe that was tattered in places, and it moved with sinuous, inhuman grace.

Fear gripped Lirra as she recognized this creature. It was an illithid, sometimes called a mind flayer. Its sobriquet was well-earned, for according to what Elidyr had told the members of the symbiont project, the creatures possessed highly developed psychic abilities and could shatter minds.

The illithid stretched out a four-clawed hand toward the warforged, and its eyes glowed bright as it unleashed its power at the charging constructs. Warforged might have been created magically, but they were still living beings with minds of their own—minds that were vulnerable to psychic attack. Realizing the illithid was a more immediate threat than Elidyr, Shatterfist and Longstrider turned toward the loathsome creature, but it was too late. The illithid's mind blast struck them full on, and the two constructs stumbled and crashed to the cave floor, stunned. With a single move, two of the Outguard's most powerful members had been neutralized.

Elidyr smiled and gestured toward the surviving members of the Outguard. "Feel free to attack whoever you like next."

But before the illithid could select another target, criss-crossing trails of long wounds appeared on its chest, running from shoulder to waist. Black blood gushed from the injuries, and the illithid let out an ear-splitting eerie screech, its mouth tentacles writhing in agony. Its eyes glowed once more before the creature turned and fled toward the cave wall, back the way it had come, and it passed through the stone as if it wasn't there, returning to Xoriat. An instant later, Ranja appeared on the floor, lying unconscious where she'd fallen after the illithid had managed to stun her.

Elidyr gazed upon the fallen shifter and shook his head in mock sympathy. "It must be so frustrating for you all, to come this far and to feel victory in your grasp, only to have it slip away in the end."

"Don't start celebrating your victory just yet, Uncle," Lirra said. She, Vaddon, Ksana, and Osten—the last of the Outguard—closed ranks and stood with weapons ready. Vaddon spun his sword into attack position, Ksana gripped her halberd with both hands, Osten held the handle of his sword in a white-knuckled grip, and Lirra grasped her own sword tight in one hand while she used the other to lash her tentacle whip in the air.

"Yes, yes, you are all impressive warriors," Elidyr said. "Especially you, my dear niece. But you don't seriously think you have a chance of winning, do you? From the moment I activated the Overmantle, you were defeated. All we've been doing here these last few moments is putting on a show for the amusement of my master."

At first Lirra didn't understand what Elidyr was talking about, but then she recalled what he'd told them when they'd first entered the cave.

"The Overmantle has turned this cave into a place where our world and Xoriat overlap," she said. "Here—and only here—creatures from both realms can meet. And that means the daelkyr lord you're trying to release . . ."

"Is on his way," Elidyr said, grinning.

CHAPTER SEVENTEEN

Lirra started to reply but stopped when a fresh wave of nausea gripped her, accompanied by tingling at the back of her skull so strong it felt as if her head might split open. She sensed the same malignant presence she'd experiencd at the lodge, when Elidyr had managed to temporarily open a portal to Xoriat, and she recognized it as that of a daelkyr lord. She sensed the presence originating from a spot on the cave wall behind Elidyr and trained her gaze upon it. Through the rippling gray stone that served as a demarcation line between the in-between zone and Xoriat, she saw a sour yellow-green light off in the distance. As she watched, the light slowly grew larger, and she knew that she was seeing the daelkyr approaching, striding through his dimension as he headed for the in-between zone. On one level, the light offended her senses. There was a wrongness to it, as if it weren't truly light at all but rather some corruption of it. But on another level, she felt an attraction to the foul light, as if part of her was being drawn to the daelkyr, and despite herself, she took a half step forward.

Elidyr saw and smiled.

"You have Xoriat in your soul now," her uncle said, "and that part of you recognizes the approach of your lord."

His words revolted Lirra, especially because she knew them to be true. She could feel the tentacle whip's growing eagerness as the daelkyr drew closer to the in-between zone, as if the symbiont were a dog awaiting the return of a beloved master.

"You said the Overmantle hasn't opened a true portal between dimensions this time," Lirra said to her uncle. "That means the daelkyr won't be able to permanently cross over to our world."

"True," Elidyr admitted. "But that's unimportant right now. Once Ysgithyrwyn has dealt with all of you, I'll be able to finish properly repairing the Overmantle. *Then* I can truly free him once and for all."

"So you plan to have the daelkyr kill us," Vaddon said.

Elidyr laughed. "Why would my master wish to kill you, when with a single touch he can open your eyes as he opened mine? I'll enjoy watching you experience a changed perspective, Brother!" He chuckled before turning his gaze on Lirra. "You mostly belong to Ysgithyrwyn as it is, my niece, but I'm looking forward to your transformation becoming complete."

Lirra would die before she allowed that to happen.

She leaned over and whispered in Vaddon's ear. "I'll take his left, you take his right."

"Agreed. Watch out for that crawling gauntlet of his. It's a weapon in and of itself."

Lirra nodded and then father and daughter rushed forward to attack the man that was brother to one, uncle to the other. Lirra felt a rush of excited bloodlust from her tentacle whip, and she fought to ignore it. With a foe as powerful and deadly as Elidyr, she'd need all of her training and battle experience along with a clear head to prevail.

At first it seemed as if Elidyr intended to do nothing as his brother and niece attacked, and given his insane state of mind, Lirra wouldn't have been entirely surprised if her uncle had simply stood there and let the two of them carve him up. But when Vaddon and Lirra came within five feet, Elidyr opened his mouth and extended his tongueworm toward Vaddon, while the stormstalk oriented its milky white orb on Lirra and unleashed a bolt of lightning.

Lirra dived to the side to avoid the blast of energy, did a shoulder roll, and came up on her feet running. Vaddon swung his sword at the tongueworm, but the rubbery hide of the aberration was tougher and more durable than normal flesh, and while the general's blade cut into the creature, the wound it inflicted wasn't very deep. Still, it hurt enough for the tongueworm to jerk back in pain, allowing Vaddon to get closer to his brother.

Lirra was within striking range of her sword, but as she raised it, the stormstalk's eye began to glow once more. She commanded her tentacle whip to reach up and grab hold of the aberration just below the eye and pull it sideways, spoiling its aim. Elidyr's symbiont unleashed its lightning, but the bolt flew well wide of its mark.

Lirra thrust her sword at Elidyr's unprotected abdomen, but before she could ram her blade home, Elidyr deflected it with a quick swipe of his crawling gauntlet, the chitinous claw scraping loudly against Lirra's steel. The blow was backed by more than human strength—another of Ysgithyrwyn's gifts to her uncle? she wondered—and Lirra was knocked backward. She stumbled and nearly fell, but managed to stay on her feet.

While Elidyr was busy dealing with Lirra, Vaddon moved in and thrust his sword into his brother's side. Blood gushed from the wound, but instead of crying out in pain, Elidyr laughed. He whirled to his brother and jammed his fingers into Vaddon's right cheek. Elidyr's fingertips sank into Vaddon's flesh as if it were made of putty, and then the artificer made a fist and yanked. Vaddon cried out in agony as his cheek was torn from his face and he drew away from Elidyr, blood pouring from his ruined face onto the cave floor. Elidyr tossed his brother's flesh aside, and then pressed his hand to his wound and massaged it with blood-slick fingers. Lirra understood what her uncle was doing—he was using his flesh-molding abilities to repair his injury—and she'd wager he was able to repair both the skin and the organs within. Was there no end to the man's unnatural powers?

She rushed to her father, tore a strip from her uniform sleeve and used it in a futile attempt to staunch his horrible facial wound. Elidyr broke off his attack and watched Lirra's inadequate ministrations with amusement, mad delight dancing in his eyes. Vaddon was breathing harshly and his wound was bleeding profusely, but his eyes were narrow and focused on Elidyr. She knew Vaddon was using every ounce of his ferocious will to concentrate past the pain, but she also knew that at the rate he was losing blood, he would rapidly weaken and lose consciousness. He needed Ksana's healing touch, and he needed it now. But though Elidyr seemed content for the moment to watch his brother bleed, Lirra knew the crazed artificer could resume attacking them any second. As much as she hated it, she had to face facts. She couldn't stand against Elidyr alone. She guided Vaddon's hand to the blood-soaked cloth so he could continue applying pressure on the wound himself. He pressed his hand against ragged, raw meat and exposed bone, and despite his years on the battlefield and the number of times he'd been wounded in combat, the old soldier shuddered. But he gave Lirra a nod to show that he'd manage, so she turned away and shot a quick glance to check on Ranja and the warforged.

Longstrider and Shatterfist had recovered from the illithid's mind blast enough to get on their knees, but it looked as if it was going to take several more minutes before the warforged were ready to rejoin the battle. By then, it would all be over, one way or another. Ranja was faring a bit better. She attempted to stand, wobbled, and then slumped into a sitting position. The shifter would recover before the war-forged, Lirra judged, but again, she feared it wouldn't be in time to help.

When Lirra's attention was on Ranja, the shifter flicked her hand outward, and a small object flew through the air toward Lirra. The shifter was still weak and her aim was off, but Lirra commanded her tentacle whip to intercept the object, and the symbiont snatched it out of the air with ease and dropped it into Lirra's open palm, the flesh wet with her father's blood. The object was a small copper ball the size of a child's marble. The metal felt warm against Lirra's flesh, but she had no idea what the object was or what it could do. She knew one thing though—this was one of Ranja's toys, and that meant whatever it was, it packed a punch.

Lirra turned toward Elidyr. She ordered the tentacle whip to sting his face, and as he blocked the strike with his crawling gauntlet, she hurled the copper ball at him.

The object hit Elidyr on the chest and flattened against his tunic as if it were made of copper-colored mud. He looked down at the splattered object on his chest quizzically, but before he could react, the copper began to spread like liquid, rapidly covering his torso, trunk, arms, legs, and finally his head. His entire body, symbionts included, was encased in the copperlike substance, rendering him immobile. Elidyr didn't seem particularly disturbed by his sudden confinement. He looked down upon his copper prison and murmured, "Interesting," as if his only concern was professional, an artificer admiring a work of thaumaturgical engineering.

Lirra grinned. Thanks, Ranja, she thought. With Elidyr incapacitated, she could get Vaddon to Ksana. But a quick glance showed Lirra that the cleric had problems of her own.

Sinnoch hissed like an angry reptile and charged Ksana, hands out and claws bared, shoulder tentacles whipping the air as he went, eager to grab hold of the half-elf and begin rending her flesh. The cleric stepped forward to meet the dolgaunt's attack, holding her halberd like a staff. When Sinnoch came within range, Ksana swept the butt of the halberd upward and connected solidly with the dolgaunt's chin. Sinnoch's head snapped back, but instead of grunting with pain, the aberration laughed maniacally as both of his shoulder tentacles wrapped around the halberd and yanked, tearing the weapon free from Ksana's hands. Sinnoch then swung the halberd around and smashed the flat of the axe head against the cleric's temple, knocking her to the cave floor. Ksana rolled as she hit the ground and came up on her feet, her hands blazing with orange-yellow light. She released twin blasts of sun energy at Sinnoch, and the dolgaunt staggered backward, his chest aflame. He shrieked in agony and dropped the halberd, and Ksana darted forward to snatch the weapon off the ground as Sinnoch frantically attempted to extinguish the flames by slapping his shoulder tentacles against his chest.

Up to this point, Osten had stood and watched the fighting, but he let out a war cry and charged Rhedyn, the latter so completely covered in shadow that it was difficult to determine exactly where he stood. Rhedyn raised his sword, the weapon also cloaked in shadow, and waited for Osten to come to him. Osten—no stranger to dealing with symbionts—made his best guess as to Rhedyn's location and swung his sword in a wide arc, the strike designed to hit Rhedyn regardless of where he was actually standing. Unfortunately, Rhedyn dodged at the last instant and Osten's strike missed. The shadow-shrouded warrior's return blow didn't miss, however. His black blade nicked Osten's forearm, and blood welled forth from the wound.

Meanwhile, Sinnoch had recovered from Ksana's strike and had managed to rake the half-elf with his claws several times, and she was bleeding from gashes on her arm, neck, and chest. The dolgaunt's hideous mouth was stretched in a bloodthirsty grin as he moved in on Ksana, claws outstretched, prepared to deliver a killing strike.

Blood loss had taken its toll on the cleric, but though she was weak, Ksana drew herself up to her full height, gripped her halberd tightly and shouted, "For Dol Arrah!" The axe head of her weapon flared with brilliant white light and as Sinnoch attacked, Ksana swung the halberd and buried the axe head in the dolgaunt's neck. Sinnoch stiffened as the holy light of Ksana's patron goddess flowed from the halberd and into his body. Beams of light shot forth from his eyeless sockets and poured out of his open mouth. His body began to shrivel up, as if it was being cooked from within. Lirra expected to hear the dolgaunt scream as he died, but instead he laughed uproariously, as if his death was the funniest thing he could imagine. Sinnoch's laughter cut off abruptly and then the dry, lifeless husk of his desiccated body fell to the cave floor.

Elidyr looked at the dolgaunt's corpse. "A pity that he won't get to witness Ysgithyrwyn's arrival, but at least he went out laughing. And speaking of Ysgithyrwyn . . ." Despite his imprisonment in the copper shell, Elidyr could still turn his head, and he glanced over his shoulder. The corrupt light that heralded the daelkyr's arrival was much larger, and its sour yellow-green color was beginning to overpower the multicolored light given off by the Overmantle.

Elidyr turned back around to face Lirra and smiled. "It won't be much longer now."

She glanced at her father. Seeing Elidyr defeated—or at least momentarily neutralized—he allowed his sword to slip from his fingers and nearly fell to his knees, weakened by blood loss. Ksana hurried forward to help her old friend, and she put an arm around Vaddon's shoulder to steady him.

"I've got him," Ksana said to Lirra, and Lirra nodded. Now that her father was in good hands, she turned to Osten and Rhedyn.

With everything that had been happening, she'd lost track of how their battle was going. She hoped to see that the young warrior was at least holding his own against her former lover. Instead, Osten had been disarmed and Rhedyn held him from behind, the edge of his sword pressed against the other man's neck.

"Surrender, all of you, or I'll slice his throat open!" Rhedyn warned.

Lirra calculated the odds of being able to reach the two men and disarm Rhedyn before he could make good on his threat. Even with the extra reach afforded by her tentacle whip, she knew there was no way she could prevent Rhedyn from killing Osten if he wanted to.

Elidyr spoke then. "While I applaud your efforts, Rhedyn, it's not necessary that they formally surrender. We need only keep them at bay a few more moments until Ysgithyrwyn arrives."

The foul illumination given off by the daelkyr had become so intense that it filled the cave. Lirra doubted they had moments left until Ysgithyrwyn appeared. More like seconds.

A slow, sly smile spread across Elidyr's face then. "Of course, my lord would prefer you to accept his touch willingly. Especially you, Lirra. Perhaps we can make a deal. If you go to greet Ysgithyrwyn, I'll guarantee that Rhedyn spares young Osten. If you resist, I'll order him to cut the boy's throat." He looked at the others. "And if the rest of you interfere in any way, I'll order the lad's death."

Vaddon stood with Ksana, and Ranja was with the two

slowly recovering warforged, and while none of them looked happy about it, they all kept their distance.

Rhedyn looked at Lirra. "Please do it. Everything will be so much more clear once you're touched by Ysgithyrwyn. Your thoughts will be sharper, more focused. Everything will make sense." He paused. "And then we will finally be able to be together."

Osten snarled and struggled briefly, but Rhedyn pressed the sword blade tighter against the man's neck. Beads of blood welled, and Osten forced himself to remain still, lest he cut his own throat.

"Not much time left, Lirra," Elidyr warned. "Decide now or it will be too late."

Lirra knew then what she had to do. "Very well. I will go to greet him." She sheathed her sword and started walking slowly toward the section of the cave wall where the sour yellow-green light was most intense, the spot where she knew Ysgithyrwyn would cross over from Xoriat into this place between dimensions that Elidyr had created.

"Lirra, no!" Vaddon cried out. Ksana was still in the process of healing him, and his words came out garbled, but they were clear enough. Lirra didn't look at her father. She couldn't bring herself to meet his eyes. When she reached the cave wall, she got down on one knee and lowered her head, as if she were a royal subject preparing to greet her liege, or a worshiper about to meet her god. But as she kneeled, she gave her tentacle whip a silent command.

No, the symbiont responded.

Do it! Lirra insisted.

Why should I?

Because if Ysgithyrwyn corrupts me, you can't.

The tentacle whip considered for a moment, and then it lashed out. Stretching backward behind Lirra, it wrapped around the Overmantle, picked it up, and dashed the mystical device against the stone floor. The metal casing broke apart, the crystals within shattered, and the multicolored lights the device had been generating winked out, leaving Ysgithyrwyn's foul light as the chamber's only illumination.

She looked up, squinting her eyes against the daelkyr's light and saw an otherworldly hand covered in a chitinous insect-like shell protrude through the cave wall. The hand reached down toward her head, but before Ysgithyrwyn could touch her, the daelkyr's yellow-green light began to dim. With the destruction of the Overmantle, there was nothing to maintain the intersection of the two dimensional planes, and they were beginning to pull apart.

As the daelkyr lord withdrew his hand, an alien voice echoed in her mind, one that didn't originate from her symbiont. It was male, the tone beautiful and ugly at the same time, as if she were listening to soothing music blended with hideous screams.

This was most amusing, Lirra. I hope we get to play again someday.

Then the voice faded, along with Ysgithyrwyn's light, and the cave walls resumed their solid appearance. Eberron and Xoriat were separate once more.

Lirra felt dirty inside, as if Ysgithyrwyn's mental voice had left a slimy residue on her brain. She shuddered once, and then did her best to forget about the daelkyr lord as she turned to face Rhedyn, determined to get him to release Osten. But Osten stood alone, bleeding slightly from the shallow wound in his throat, behind him only shadows—shadows which Rhedyn had used his symbiont's power to lose himself in. She started forward, intending to search for Rhedyn, but she stopped when she saw the puddle of coppery liquid where Elidyr had been standing. There was no sign of her uncle. Somehow, Elidyr had gotten free of his coppery prison and escaped, and Lirra had no doubt that wherever her uncle was headed, Rhedyn accompanied him.

Fury filled her at the thought that the two of them might get away, and she grabbed her sword handle, intending to draw her weapon and rush off into the darkness in pursuit.

Yes! the thought-voice said, the word accompanied by images of Elidyr and Rhedyn lying on the ground, covered in blood, begging for mercy as the whip lashed their bodies and Lirra plunged her blade into their flesh again and again.

Slowly, Lirra removed her hand from her sword. *There's been enough killing for one day. Now it's time to take care of my friends.*

Ignoring the symbiont's protests, she started toward Osten.

CHAPTER EIGHTEEN

They searched the caves for several hours afterward, but they found no sign of either Elidyr or Rhedyn, and it was late afternoon by the time they finally emerged. The clouds that had covered the sky earlier had parted, and the companions were greeted by bright sunshine, a rarity for Karrnath, even in summertime.

"A blessing from Dol Arrah," Ksana said, smiling, and Lirra couldn't say the cleric was wrong.

Ranja, Longstrider, and Shatterfist had long since fully recovered from the illithid's mind blast, and both Vaddon's and Osten's wounds had been healed, thanks to Ksana. Afterward, Ksana had examined the bodies of the Outguard soldiers that had fallen during the battle in the cave, and she'd found four who still lived, despite the severity of their wounds. She'd healed them, and they were standing guard over the others.

The warforged hadn't joined in the search for Elidyr and Rhedyn. Vaddon had ordered them to bring the Outguard dead out from the caves and bury them. Shatterfist and Longstrider had used their bare hands to dig the graves, and they had only just finished when the others broke off the search and exited the caves.

Vaddon glanced at the unmarked mounds where their dead were buried. "Sixty men and women rode with us when we left

Geirrid two days ago, and now only four remain. We might have won a victory here this day, but if so, it was a costly one."

"Was it a victory?" Lirra asked. "Both Elidyr and Rhedyn escaped."

"We destroyed the Overmantle," Osten pointed out.

"Elidyr's an artificer," Lirra countered. "He can build another."

"I don't think so," Ksana said. "The crystals he used to make the device were expensive and rare. He was able to afford them only because Lord Bergerron funded our experiments. I highly doubt he'll ever be able to acquire replacements on his own."

"So . . . what now?" Osten asked.

Lirra frowned. "What do you mean?"

"What are we going to do about Elidyr and Rhedyn? We have to hunt them down. Whether Elidyr makes another Overmantle or not, he's still extremely dangerous, and he's responsible for the deaths of those farmers he turned into the white-eyes, not to mention all the people in Geirrid the white-eyes killed, *and* he's responsible for the deaths of the soldiers who lost their lives trying to stop him—both in Geirrid and in the battle with the dolgrims. He has to be brought to justice." Osten scowled. "As does the traitor Rhedyn."

"Of that there is no question," Vaddon said. "But as to whether or not we'll be involved, that will be up to Lord Bergerron. I'll report to him as soon as I am able, and we'll see what, if anything, he'll want us to do." Vaddon paused. "Considering how this campaign turned out, Bergerron may well wish to place his trust in others to track down my brother."

Up to that point the two warforged had been silent, but suddenly Longstrider spoke up.

"You did the best you could given the circumstances, General Vaddon. I doubt anyone could've done better, and I'll make sure Lord Bergerron knows that."

Vaddon looked surprised, as if he'd never expected this sort of consideration from a being he viewed as nothing more than a mobile weapon. He inclined his head gratefully. "Thank you, Longstrider."

Osten turned to Lirra. "Sounds like we'll be on the hunt again soon."

"*We* may be," Vaddon said, "but my daughter won't." He turned to Lirra. "Your part in this is finished. I agreed that you could keep your symbiont temporarily only so you could use it to stop Elidyr. But my brother has escaped, and you must leave the search for him to others."

Lirra felt a surge of anger, and she struggled to contain it. "You saw what I can do with the tentacle whip, Father! If it hadn't been for my symbiont, I wouldn't have been able to destroy the Overmantle!"

"Please understand, Lirra. I am not denying your contributions, but you must give up your symbiont. For your own good, if for no other reason. Yes, you are strong-willed, and you will hold out against the aberration's influence as long as you can—longer, probably, than most people could—but inevitably it will corrupt your mind and spirit, just as it did to Rhedyn. You need to return with us to the garrison at Geirrid, and once there, Ksana can see to removing your symbiont." Vaddon paused. "I've lost my brother to the insanity of chaos and corruption. I don't want to lose you too."

Lirra felt her tentacle whip twitch, and she knew it wanted to bury its stinger into her father's throat and start pumping venom into his body and not stop until he was dead a dozen times over. But she understood how Vaddon felt, and though she didn't agree, she still loved him for it.

"What if I refuse?" she asked.

Sorrow filled Vaddon's eyes for a moment, but then his expression became impassive as he worked to constrain his emotions, just as Lirra had seen him do on the battlefield a hundred times before. When he next spoke, it wasn't as her father but as the general. "I'm afraid you don't have a choice in the matter."

"Really?" Despite her determination to keep her own emotions under control, she clenched her fists in anger.

Ksana stepped between them, and Lirra couldn't help thinking it was a place where the cleric had stood many times before. "Lirra, please—I understand how you feel, we both do, but you have to listen to reason . . ."

Lirra's anger built inside her, like a fire on the verge of blazing out of control, but she fought it. Part of her wanted nothing more than to strike out at Vaddon and Ksana, but these were two of the dearest people in the world to her and, however misguided their actions might be, she knew they did them out of love for her.

"I'm going to find Elidyr on my own," she said, voice tight with restrained anger. "I'm leaving now, Father, and if you want to prevent me from going, you'll have to kill me."

Shatterfirst turned to Longstrider. "She's joking, right?"

Longstrider shook his head. "I don't think so."

Ksana looked shocked by Lirra's words, but Vaddon—no longer able to hold back his feelings—regarded her with a sorrow-filled gaze.

"Very well, Lirra. You may go—for now," Vaddon said. "But this isn't the end of it. I intended to do everything I can to cure you. And if I can't . . ."

"What?" Lirra demanded. "You'll have me imprisoned for the rest of my life, where I can't be a danger to anyone? Or will you decide not to risk it and have me killed?"

Vaddon didn't reply, but he didn't need to. The sadness in his eyes spoke for him.

A storm of conflicting emotions raged through Lirra. Though she felt anger and frustration over her father's inability to see her point of view, she understood that he believed he was acting out of love for her. How could she fault him for that? He was a proud man, a strong warrior, and a capable leader—all in all, a noble son of Karrnath. But he was also a limited man in his way, unable to see beyond the world-view that had always shaped his life. Military discipline, rigid adherence to rules and regulations . . . Lirra had once been like that too, her father's daughter in every way. But the last few days had taught her that sometimes the rules changed on you, whether you liked it or not—and sometimes you had to make your own rules. Perhaps symbionts normally corrupted their hosts, but it didn't have to be that way for her. She would find a way to live with the aberration and make use of the abilities it granted her, whether or not her father believed it was possible. She wished Vaddon could understand, that they could somehow work together to track down Elidyr, but she knew it wasn't possible, and the realization filled her with heart-rending sadness.

Ksana must have realized much the same thing, for the cleric's gaze was sorrowful as she stretched out her hand and gently touched Lirra on the forehead. "May the blessings of Dol Arrah be upon you, my child."

Lirra felt a wave of warmth pass through her body, and when it was done, her anger was gone. She nodded her gratitude to the cleric, and then, without looking at her father, she turned to go.

"Hold up, Lirra," Ranja said. "You're not leaving without me!"

Lirra turned to the shifter. "I appreciate everything you did to help us, but the path I've chosen is one I must walk alone."

"Spare me the dramatics. You choose your path, I choose mine. It just so happens that they're the same." She grinned. "For the time being, at least."

Lirra was going to argue with the shifter, but then she decided not to bother. If the woman wanted to follow her, she would find a way to do so. It was simpler to let her come along openly if she wished. Besides, given the way Lirra felt right then, she figured she could use the company.

"Very well," Lirra said.

"I'm coming too," Osten said.

Lirra turned to him, surprised, but before she could say anything, Vaddon spoke.

"You are a Karrnathi soldier, boy! What you're talking about amounts to desertion!"

Osten glared at Vaddon defiantly. "I can't desert if I'm no longer a soldier. I resign my commission, General."

"Osten, please, think this through!" Lirra said. "I can't let you do this!"

"You're going to need allies to deal with Elidyr," the young warrior said. "You're also going to need someone who understands what it's like to carry a symbiont. Someone who can rein you in when it becomes necessary. Someone to be—"

"My conscience," Lirra said with a smile. "All right." She turned to the warforged and smiled. "Well, what about you two?"

The constructs' hands were still dirty from grave digging, and Longstrider rubbed his together, almost self-consciously. "Shatterfist and I admire you greatly," he said, "but we are loyal to Lord Bergerron, and as he assigned us to your father's command, that is where we shall remain until ordered otherwise."

"Too bad," Shatterfist said, giving the impression that he sighed without actually doing so. "I have so many more jokes that you haven't heard yet."

"Maybe Dol Arrah *is* looking out for me," Lirra murmured. She turned to Ranja and Osten. "All right then. Let's get going."

"Where are we headed?" Ranja asked.

Lirra felt an urge to glance back at her father one last time, but she couldn't bring herself to do so.

"Away from here," Lirra said. Then she turned forward and started walking, Osten and Ranja at her side.

＊＊＊

Many miles away, Veit Bergerron sat secure and comfortable in his study. The warlord wore a helmet that covered his entire head—a helmet that resembled the head of a warforged. And not just any warforged—Longstrider. The helmet's eyes glowed with mystical power, a sign of their link to Longstrider. Anything the construct saw, Bergerron saw. And the warlord had seen plenty over the course of the last couple days. Now he watched as Lirra and her two companions walked out of the clearing and into the woods.

Lirra Brochann was an intriguing woman. She had her father's spirit, but she was less rigid and more adaptable to changing circumstances than Vaddon. Plus, she'd shown herself adept at handling the symbiont she'd become bonded to. Bergerron could make use of someone with her special capabilities. In fact, he could think of several ongoing projects that she'd be perfect for . . . projects that required a specific combination of finesse, discretion, and brutality.

A shame about Rhedyn turning traitor though. Bergerron would've thought a member of his bloodline would've been stronger than that, but then again, Rhedyn *was* his youngest sister's child, and she'd always been the weakest of his siblings. It was like they said, the apple never falls far from the tree. Ah well, he decided. Nothing to be done about it.

All things considered, it looked like the symbiont project had turned out to be a success in the end. He smiled. For him, at least.

Bergerron removed the helmet and placed it on the small table beside his chair. Then he sat back, interlocked his hands over his stomach, and began making plans.

━━━━━◆━━━━━

"Aren't you the least bit upset that the Overmantle was destroyed?"

Elidyr gave Rhedyn a sideways glance. "There's no point in dwelling on the past. What's done is done."

The two men had been walking through the Nightwood ever since leaving the caves. After escaping his coppery prison—a simple matter, really, given the number of magic devices he carried on his person—and slipping away while everyone's eyes had been on Lirra and Ysgithyrwyn, Elidyr had led Rhedyn down a hidden passage that Sinnoch had showed him when the artificer had first visited the dolgaunt decades ago. The passage had led to a long winding tunnel that eventually let them out in a different section of the forest from the main cave entrance, far enough away that Elidyr was confident Vaddon and the others wouldn't be able to find them—especially since Elidyr was using a concealer, one of his most useful artificer's toys, to mask both his presence and Rhedyn's. Too bad about Sinnoch though. The dolgaunt had been a good assistant, and Elidyr could truthfully say he wouldn't be the man he was now if not for Sinnoch's help.

Rhedyn went on. "But we failed! Ysgithyrwyn remains in Xoriat, and . . ." The warrior trailed off and directed his gaze to the ground. His shadowy aspect was drawn around him like a dark cloak, as if to mirror his mood.

"Go ahead and say it," Elidyr prompted.

Rhedyn looked up. "And Lirra didn't join us."

"Perhaps not this time. But you know as well as I that she can only hold out so long against the corrupting influence of her symbiont. Eventually she will come to see things our way. It's inevitable."

"So you say. But Lirra isn't just anyone. She's stronger than I am." He paused. "Stronger than you, in many ways."

Elidyr bristled at the warrior's words, but he chose not to remark upon them.

"Do you know what your trouble is, my boy? You're still in love with my niece. Love is an emotion for lesser minds. It's childish and limited, and it impedes clear thinking. In time your symbiont would've helped you realize this. But as your emotional state is obviously causing you a certain amount of discomfort, I'll be happy to speed up the process for you."

Before Rhedyn could react, Elidyr spun around and jammed his fingers into the warrior's forehead, sinking through flesh and bone to penetrate the brain matter beneath. Grinning, Elidyr went to work on tidying up Rhedyn's messy mind, and the warrior's screams filled the Nightwood.

ABOUT THE AUTHOR

Tim Waggoner has published over seventy stories of fantasy and horror as well as hundreds of nonfiction articles. He currently teaches creative writing at Sinclair Community College in Dayton, Ohio, and in the MA in Writing Popular Fiction program at Seton Hill University.

JAMES
WYATT

THE GATES OF
MADNESS

PART
FIVE

An exclusive five-part prequel to the worlds-spanning
DUNGEONS & DRAGONS® event

THE ABYSSAL PLAGUE

VOIDHARROW

What has happened?" The Chained God's form became a dark whirlwind of fury, scattering the Progenitor into crystalline mist. "You betrayed me!"

"Betrayed," the Progenitor whispered, its echoes surrounding him.

"They would have freed me!"

"They freed us," the whispers replied. "Now we spread, your will and my substance. The Voidharrow."

The Chained God began to see. "Like a plague," he said.

"Plague . . . A plague . . ."

"Your substance and my will."

"Our will."

The Chained God's fury diminished, and he reached his thoughts to his old dominion where the Voidharrow had taken root. Yes, his will was present there—the merest echo of his thoughts and desires. It was more of a foothold in the universe he'd left behind than he'd ever had, though.

"It is enough," he said.

"Like a plague."

~~~~~~

"I hate to interrupt this touching reunion," Sherinna's cold voice said, "but you agreed to help me find my companions once we'd found yours."

Miri released her hold on Demas, and his hands dropped

from her back. Miri's eyes stung as she realized that his half-hearted embrace was the most demonstrative expression of his care for her that he'd ever given. And she'd had warmer embraces from innkeepers. Something in Sherinna's tone irritated her just enough that she turned her frustration to the eladrin wizard.

"Is that all it is to you?" she said. "An exchange of services?"

"Of course," Sherinna said. "What else would it be?"

"Aren't you worried about them?"

"They can take care of themselves."

Miri couldn't be sure, but she thought that Sherinna put the slightest emphasis on the word "they"—as if to suggest a contrast between her competent companions and Miri, who had reacted to being separated from her companions by cowering in a temple.

"Don't you care about them?" she asked. "Don't you think they might be worried about you?"

"As my original statement conveyed, I am eager to find them. Brendis and Nowhere are my associates, and very valuable ones. However, I assure you I won't greet them with a tearful embrace when we find them."

"Your associates?" Miri could hardly believe what she was hearing.

"Of course. We cooperate together to accomplish specific tasks for which our particular skills are well suited. Each of us brings different strengths to the group, and we cover each other's weaknesses. It's a lucrative line of work, and we divide the profits equally. It's not so different from a trading venture. I can't imagine what else I would call them."

"Friends? You trust your life to them."

Sherinna shrugged. "The same is true of partners in any sort of high-risk venture."

"And what would they call you?"

"The same thing, I imagine."

"Even Nowhere?"

For the first time, Sherinna's perfect composure slipped, just a fraction. "What do you mean?"

Miri smiled. "The look in his eyes when you're around doesn't say 'associate' to me."

Sherinna's face froze, and Miri felt the temperature in the temple drop. "Enough," she said, and Miri could see the eladrin's breath in the suddenly frosty air. "I have no need to be chided by a half-elf child with stars in her teary eyes. Demascus promised to help me find my *associates,* so they and I can continue the task set before us. As soon as he has fulfilled his end of the bargain, I shall take my leave and hope that our paths never cross again."

A sudden flare of light and warmth drove away Sherinna's chill as Demas stepped between the two women, his face stern. "That's enough, wizard. Miri may be young, but I have seen more proof of her valor and strength than I have yet seen from you. I am proud to call her a dear friend, and I can't stand by and let you insult her."

Miri's heart sang as the wizard's frosty glare softened. "I am sorry," Sherinna said. "Perhaps I am more concerned about my associates than I was willing to admit, and my concern has shortened my temper."

"Let us find them, then," Demas said, "if only that we may part ways sooner."

***

Nowhere stepped out of the rowdy tavern, and a bottle smashed on the cobblestones by his feet. Without a glance back, he hurried out of the alley, smiling broadly. When he reached the thoroughfare where he was to meet Brendis, his eyes lit on the Sword of the

Gods first. Even in the cosmopolitan streets of the City of Doors, Demascus stood out like a troll at a banquet. Sherinna and Miri walked beside him, one on each side.

"Sherinna!" he called, and changed course to meet them. He saw Sherinna's face brighten, then she brought it under control and shot Miri a dark glance. What was that about? Brendis emerged from an alley across the street, and Nowhere waved to catch his eye.

"You found us," he said as he drew near enough to be heard. The group met in front of a potter's shop, but Miri stood a few paces away from the others, her gaze fixed on Demascus. "What happened?" he asked.

"The portal was unstable," Sherinna said. "As soon as the cultists had passed, it started to close. Before it did, though, the far end of the portal—the one in this city—started to slip. For each of you that went through, your destination fell back a significant distance. I suspect even Brendis never saw the cultists."

"That's right," the paladin said.

"Sherinna and I used our magic to stabilize the portal and hold it open," Demascus said. "Then we set about collecting our . . . *associates*."

"The Sword of the Gods drew on Ioun's wisdom to lead us, first to Miri and then here," Sherinna said. "His abilities really are uncanny."

"We could use those abilities," Brendis said. "Are you still interested in chasing those cultists?"

Demascus glanced at Miri. "Our mission has failed," he said. "Ioun sent us to Bael Turath to destroy the Staff of Opening before it fell into evil hands, but we were too late. I would like to correct that failure."

Miri scowled and looked away from the group. For that matter, Sherinna didn't look too pleased at his words.

Brendis smiled, apparently oblivious to the two women. "We believe they're on their way to put that staff to use. If Sherinna's right, and I have no doubt that she is, the staff you seek incorporates a shard of the Living Gate. They plan to use that shard to open a doorway into the prison of the Chained God."

"They seek to free the Undoer," Demascus said.

Nowhere shuddered as a chill shot through him. He hadn't heard that title before, but it brought to mind the sense of a dark god unraveling everything, reversing mortal achievements and bringing plans to ruin. He glanced at Sherinna and found her eyes on him. She looked distracted, and he gave her a quizzical smile. She looked away.

"We believe they're heading for Pandemonium to perform their ritual. So Nowhere has been asking around, trying to find out where you go if you want to get from the City of Doors here to the howling wastes there."

"Ioun will lead us," Demascus said.

Nowhere bit his tongue, fighting down the urge to say something pointed—or draw his dagger. He couldn't deny that Demascus's gifts were useful, but did he have to be so sanctimonious about them?

The Sword of the Gods struck him as the worst kind of zealot—the kind of follower who never learned to stand on his own feet because he trusted the gods to hold him upright. And then had the gall to reproach others for not living as he did. He thought he understood why Sherinna didn't look pleased that Demascus wanted to tag along on their adventure.

Miri turned to Sherinna, though her eyes were fixed on the ground. "I—I'm sorry," she said. "I didn't mean to chide."

So they had fought—that explained the tension in the air and the angry glances. Sherinna looked taken aback, but quickly regained her composure. "No, I'm sorry if I insulted you," she said.

"Together, then," Brendis said, beaming around at his companions. "Demascus, lead on."

The Sword of the Gods closed his eyes and took one firm step. Then his eyes opened wide in shock. He clutched his hands to his ears and fell to his knees,

"Demas!" Miri cried, rushing to his side. "What is it?"

The Sword of the Gods stared blankly as if he hadn't heard. Nowhere searched the street and what he could see of adjoining buildings, looking for a fleeing assassin or some other explanation for Demascus's sudden collapse.

"Demas!"

"I'm all right," he said at last. "I saw the doorway we seek, but I cannot lead us there."

"Why not?" Brendis demanded.

"I . . . There was a scream, and . . ."

Nowhere gaped at Demascus. He'd never seen the Sword of the Gods at a loss for words or appearing anything but supremely confident, but something had shaken him.

"It's all right," Nowhere said. "I can get us to the portal." He drew a silver charm from his pouch, a depiction of a bent spiral—the Elder Elemental Eye. "I even got us a key."

Pain convulsed Albric's body, shattering his focus and making the image within the gate shift more rapidly. He looked down and saw the Progenitor completely covering his lower body, and he could feel it starting up his spine. He couldn't feel his legs at all, and he realized that his left leg was liquified—a column of the silver-scarlet liquid supported his body.

"Albric!"

Jaeran's voice jolted him out of his shock, and he forced his attention back to the gate. The image stabilized again, showing the gleaming streets of a celestial city. A moment later it shifted to a range of brooding mountains, then a castle with soaring spires, its walls fluttering with blue pennants.

"Tharizdun!" he muttered through his pain. "Ender and Anathema. Eater of Worlds."

With each second, the gate revealed a new world to his eyes. The Chained God, once free, would tear through them all like a bulette scattering anthills when it burrowed up from the earth. He would consume them, and each life he extinguished would feed the furnace of his power.

"Undoer," he grunted. "Come and wreak destruction."

"Wreak destruction," Jaeran echoed, shouting through his own agony.

"Destruction," whispered a third voice. It was all around, and in Albric's mind. It might have been his own voice. He recognized it as the voice of the Voidharrow—*That's its name, what Tharizdun called the Progenitor. Tharizdun doesn't know.*

Doesn't know? Tharizdun knows all!

Jaeran screamed and staggered away from the gate, clutching his face. He dug his fingertips into his empty eye socket, trying in vain to pull the Voidharrow out.

The gate flickered again, showing him a dozen worlds in the span of his glance. A dozen worlds that would all be destroyed by the coming of the Chained God.

"Let them burn," he growled, and he bent his will to steady the gate once more.

Nowhere stepped through the arch first, the spiral symbol glowing slightly as it activated the portal's magic. An oblivion of darkness and silence seized him, and he felt nothing—no wall within his reach, no ground beneath his feet, no breath of air on his skin.

A presence appeared at his shoulder, invisible in the darkness, and a voice croaked in his ear, "You proceed to your doom."

Nowhere's body went cold with terror as he recognized the voice of Tavet the Heartless, the night hag of Nera's undercity. *What is she doing here?* he thought.

"Have you tired of hunting this hydra yet, tiefling?" Tavet asked. Her voice set him on edge, reminding him of every unexplained noise that ever frightened him in the night.

"The profit's been small the last few days, I must admit." Nowhere tried to sound more cavalier than he felt, but his voice sounded small and fragile in his own ears. *Where are the others?* he thought. *They were right behind me.*

"And you're about to lose it all. What a pity."

A hot flare of anger started to thaw his terror. "What are you doing here, Tavet? Aren't you a long way from home?"

"Not as far as you are, tiefling. I'm here to save you."

"Save me? Why?"

"Silly child. You bring meat and blood—you're one of my best customers. I'd be heartbroken if anything happened to you." Her croaking laugh came from all around him.

"I have no cow's heart to pay you with now, Tavet. What price would you ask for saving me?" He knew the answer, but he had to hear her say it.

"I told you before. I want Sherinna."

Nowhere thrust his dagger backward into the empty air where he'd thought the night hag stood. Her laugh grew louder and sharper, until it felt like a harsh winter wind buffeting him on all sides.

"I told you before," he said through clenched teeth, "I won't hand her over to you. Not even to save my own life."

"Suit yourself. Perhaps I won't be so heartbroken after all."

Tavet's laughter became a howling wind and a stone floor beneath his feet, and his shoulder slammed into a rough wall. The faintest glimmer of light filtered up from somewhere below, just barely enough to trace the outline of a tunnel to his infernally enhanced senses.

An instant later, bright light stabbed at his eyes, and he saw Demascus standing like a beacon, divine radiance shining from his staff and enveloping his body without casting a shadow. Miri appeared in the tunnel next, then Sherinna, and finally Brendis, in quick succession.

"What took you all so long?" Nowhere whispered.

Looks of confusion flitted across every face, then Brendis laughed, dismissing the question as a joke.

Nowhere swallowed hard. Tavet must have snared him somewhere in between the portal in Sigil and its destination, turning an instantaneous journey into an opportunity for that disturbing conversation. To his companions, no time had passed.

A long, wordless howl echoed up the tunnel from somewhere below, carried on the rushing wind. It sounded like a tormented beast, and it did nothing to soothe Nowhere's nerves.

What am I doing here? he thought. This isn't worth dying for.

He let Brendis and the glowing Torch of the Gods lead the way down the tunnel, staying back near the edge of Demascus's circle of light so he could duck into shadow at the first sign of trouble. The two of them set a pace that was more eager than safe as more howls, screams, and shouts filtered up the tunnel.

"Albric!" someone cried. A bestial squeal answered the cry.

Whatever the cultists were doing, it didn't sound good. Nowhere wondered if their ritual had gone awry, or if it had succeeded in summoning a powerful being that failed to show the proper gratitude for its liberation. He realized he was clutching his dagger too tightly to use it, and he tried to relax his grip.

Brendis and Demascus paused as they reached the end of the tunnel, and Nowhere tried to peer around them to get a clear view of the vaulted chamber beyond. An archway formed of scarlet crystal stood in the center of the room, shedding a dim red light around it. Through the arch, Nowhere could just make out an unfamiliar city with a tall black tower rising above it. One man stood beside the arch, gripping the crystal with two hands while wailing in evident pain. His lower body was covered with a substance that looked like a liquid version of the crystal that formed the arch, shot through with flecks of gold and veins of silver. One tendril of the liquid stretched up his spine.

Seven other figures were spread across the large chamber, none of them fully human. One was a six-armed hulk with red crystal formations jutting from its back and shoulders. Another was a pain-wracked elf face at the center of a teeming mass of crystalline spiders. A dragonborn man clutched his own wrist and, as Nowhere watched, exhaled a cloud of fire to engulf his crystal-covered hand. The fire clung to his hand, drawing a scream of pain and fear from the dragonborn's mouth.

"Minions of the Chained God!" Demascus shouted. His voice filled the huge chamber and echoed through it, silencing even the wind for an instant. "You stand under the judgment of all the gods, and the Sword of the Gods has come to execute that judgment."

"And I didn't think he could get any more arrogant and self-righteous," Nowhere muttered.

Sherinna heard him and smiled. "Shall we?" she said.

Nowhere frowned. No pile of gold waited to be claimed in the chamber—in fact, what gold he could see, gleaming around the neck of the man by the arch, was in imminent danger of being swallowed by the liquid crystal. Nowhere was pretty sure he didn't want to touch that stuff. Tavet's warning stuck in his mind: *You proceed to your doom.*

Why? he wondered. Why should I die here?

Sherinna didn't wait for his answer. Stepping into the mouth of the tunnel, she stretched out her hands and hurled waves of fire into the chamber ahead of Brendis's charge.

That's why, he thought. Damn it.

He drew a deep breath to steady his nerves. As he slipped past Sherinna and into the chamber, he rested his hand on her shoulder for a moment. She shot him a puzzled smile even as gleaming bolts of magical energy shot from her fingertips to plunge into the six-armed monster that was lumbering toward her.

The cultists and monsters were in confused disarray, especially the ones who were still caught in the transformation from one to the other. Brendis intercepted the hulking thing, ensuring that it kept its distance from Sherinna, while Miri charged around to the left and attacked a creature with human legs, plated in armor, and the forequarters of a pantherlike monster, sleek and predatory. Demascus drew the sword from his back as he rushed straight toward the arch. As he moved, a column of divine fire roared down over the archway and the three nearest cultists.

Nowhere scowled. Brendis and Miri wore heavy armor, and each of them had picked out one foe to deal with. Demascus wore chainmail beneath his ornate robes, but he was heading for the thickest concentration of foes and seemed most likely to need Nowhere's help. Keeping to the shadows, he circled slowly around the outside of the chamber, his eyes fixed on the nearest cultists.

A cultist whose left hand was covered with the scarlet liquid moved to intercept Demascus. He held a sword and swung it wildly at the cleric, who blocked it with an easy parry.

"You," Demascus said. "I saved your life in Bael Turath."

The cultist didn't answer, but his left hand moved to his throat as if of its own volition.

"And this is how you respond to the grace of the gods, freely given to you?" Demascus said.

The liquid crystal that swathed the man's hand extended a snaky tendril and found his mouth. He started to scream, but the liquid choked the sound off. His lips twisted in disgust, Demascus cut the man's head from his neck with one clean stroke of his sword. A spray of blood and droplets of red crystalline liquid trailed from the edge of his sword.

Across the room, Miri killed the pantherlike creature before it fully completed its transformation. An orb of greenish goo hurtled from Sherinna's hand and splashed into the six-armed hulk as Brendis's glowing sword whirled around it in a deadly dance, wearing down its defenses.

Demascus advanced on the next cultist, but he hesitated as he realized that the man was too wracked with agony to even acknowledge his presence. Nowhere stalked out of the shadows to approach the cultist from the other side, and saw that the man was clawing at an eye socket that was filled with the liquid substance. The Sword of the Gods was reluctant to kill a man who posed no immediate threat, but Nowhere felt no such compunctions.

As the tiefling thrust his dagger forward, the man's body jerked out of the way as if yanked away by some unseen hand. His good eye, wide with fright, focused on Nowhere as he stumbled through the arch. With a flash of crimson light, the man disappeared into a desert landscape under a dark red sun.

Nowhere paused, not sure whether he should try to follow. He glanced at Demascus, who seemed uncharacteristically hesitant. As he looked back to the archway, though, he realized that his decision had been made for him. In place of the desert landscape, he now saw a dark forest, with a wooded island of earth and stone floating in the air above it.

Another creature swept in, this one no longer recognizable as the cultist it had been. Its body was formed of shadow, though crystalline structures extended from its back like wings and swirled around its legs in long, twisting tendrils that lifted it off the ground. As it moved closer, Nowhere felt a pressure on his mind, as if the monster were sifting through his thoughts. He threw a dagger at the creature, but the blade flew wide and clattered on the stone. Then he heard the croaking cackle of Tavet the Heartless, and turned to see the night hag standing right behind him, tearing her claws into Sherinna's lifeless corpse.

"No!" he screamed, recoiling from the hag's bloody grin.

Then he heard a grunt of pain from the direction of the shadow creature, and Tavet seemed to flicker. For a moment, in place of Tavet he saw a smear of darkness in the air, and he glanced around to see Sherinna standing several paces behind Demascus, launching another arcane barrage at the creature. Demascus, too, looked like he was pulling himself out of his own nightmarish vision, and he was visibly shaken.

Nowhere growled his rage. The creature had dredged his mind and woven his worst nightmares into a weapon to use against him. Even as he rushed toward the monster, he felt the pressure on his mind again, but he honed his fury to drive the nightmare weaver's tendrils out of his thoughts, and the pressure faded completely as his dagger slashed into the creature's shadowy substance. A blast of fire from Sherinna's fingers engulfed the creature, stopping inches from Nowhere's face and bathing him in waves of heat as it roared over the nightmare creature's body. With a shout and a flash of light, Demascus drove his sword deep into its shoulder.

With the last of his anger, Nowhere pushed the smoldering body as it fell, sending it tumbling through the arch and into the dark forest of another world.

He looked around to get a sense of the tide of battle. It seemed to be going in their favor: Brendis had toppled the four-armed hulk, and he and Miri were locked in battle with a creature formed of fire, with a pulsing core of liquid crystal at its heart. The dragonborn cultist whose fiery breath had given birth to the creature was dead on the floor nearby. Near the archway, only one cultist remained—the human with crystalline legs, who looked like he was still trying to manipulate the portal. As Nowhere looked at the gate, though, he saw the cultist-monster he'd forgotten: the chittering swarm of spiders was in the process of forming itself into a single creature, forming a sheath of black chitin around itself and shaping it into spindly legs and a bulbous body.

While the swarm-creature was still gathering its strength, Nowhere stepped forward to deal with the cultist at the arch. He moved up behind the man, who had somehow remained completely focused on the arch as battle erupted around him. He saw the liquid crystal pulsing on the man's spine and undulating where his legs had once been. He struck out with his dagger in hatred and revulsion, driving the blade up beneath the man's ribs. The man's head and shoulders slumped, but the quivering column of liquid crystal kept the corpse upright. Nowhere stepped back, but the liquid lashed out at him.

<hr />

The pain had all but stopped as the Voidharrow fused with Albric's spine. He was so intent on tuning the portal to free the

Chained God that even the destruction of half his body failed to deter him, and though there was a brief battle of wills, he had bent the Voidharrow to his own purpose.

Then the dagger slipped into his side, piercing a lung and his heart, and Albric's mortal body died in the span of three heartbeats.

He was not Albric any longer, but neither was he only the Voidharrow. He saw, though not with Albric's eyes any longer. He saw the corpses of the others—the other exarchs of the Voidharrow, the former acolytes of Albric—strewn here and there on the floor of the chamber, clots and puddles of liquid crystal flowing back from the bodies to pool in the center of the room. Albric's plans, the Chained God's plans, and even the Voidharrow's plans all lay in ruin, thanks to the interference of these five mortals. He saw the one who had stabbed him, recoiling in fear and disgust, and reached his substance to seize that body.

The scream pleased him, the terror and pain given voice as he found his way into the body and made it his. It was different than Albric's form, stronger and faster. The mind was quicker, too, and he could make use of it as he crushed its will with his own.

"Nowhere?" The female, the wizard, was bending over him, concern on her face. The dagger had fallen from his grip, so he used his bare hand, focusing all his strength into one blow that drove her off him and slammed her against the wall.

He got to his feet and surveyed the wreckage of the chamber.

The man's name had been Nowhere, and now he was nothing. He shaped the muscles of the face into something like a smile.

"I am Nu Alin," he declared.

Miri shot Brendis a smile. She liked fighting alongside the paladin—they were coordinating well together, even without speaking. More importantly, she realized, Brendis was relying on her. He trusted her to keep up her end of the partnership, which she could never really say about Demas. The Sword of the Gods was nothing if not confident, and while he certainly deserved to feel sure of himself, it often left her feeling like an unnecessary appendage. A child, tagging along at the whim of the champion.

Together, they easily defeated the strange elemental creature formed of the dragonborn's fiery breath. Brendis loaned her some of his own divine power, making her axe shine like a shard of the sun, which seemed to make the creature and its pulsating liquid heart more susceptible to her attacks. Brendis drew it out so she could strike the killing blow, slicing cleanly through its heart and scattering the glowing embers of its substance.

She wanted to say something to Brendis, to communicate her appreciation, but as she sought for the right words his gaze drew her eyes to the others, across the room. Only one monster remained, an enormous spiderlike creature of glossy black chitin with scarlet crystal visible in the spaces between plates. As she stared, it clambered on top of the arch and crouched, ready to pounce down on Demas. At the same moment, Sherinna flew backward from Nowhere's prone body, as if hurled by some enormous strength.

Brendis and Miri broke into a run at the same moment. All Miri could think of was what Brendis had said to Demas when they met: "You are chasing your doom." As they ran, the spider-thing leaped, crashing into Demas and knocking him to the ground. Crystals flew from its body with the impact, then skittered around to swarm over Demas's body.

"Ioun protect me!" he shouted, and he erupted with a burning light as bright as the sun. The larger creature staggered back as the crystal spiders crawling over Demas melted into tiny puddles of scarlet liquid.

Nowhere, who had found his feet, also recoiled from the light. His movements seemed stiff and awkward, and the snarl that twisted his face looked like nothing she'd seen from the tiefling before. He strode toward Demas, and Miri quickened her run to intercept him.

He met her charge with a backhanded swing that knocked her off her feet and sent her crashing into the arch. She felt the energies of the arch crackling around her and a gentle pull starting to draw her through, into the dark forest on the other side. Her head was swimming from the force of Nowhere's blow, but she kept enough presence of mind to drag herself away from the arch before it could pull her through to whatever world lay beyond.

Brendis and Demas assaulted the spider-creature from opposite sides, but it didn't seem the least bit troubled to fight on two fronts at once. Spindly, chitinous legs slashed at Demas as more crystalline spiders swarmed over Brendis, keeping clear of the deadly divine nimbus that surrounded the Sword of the Gods. Both men seemed oblivious to Nowhere and the threat he presented.

Sherinna was not. She'd been hit even harder than Miri was, and her face showed the mark of it as she pulled herself to her feet again. She met Miri's eyes and nodded.

Gripping her axe, she rushed at Nowhere again, more cautiously this time. He ignored her, stooping to retrieve a dagger from the floor as he continued walking toward Demas. "Nowhere!" she shouted.

He spared her little more than a glance. "Nowhere is gone," he said, his voice strange, the words stilted.

Sherinna used the brief distraction to utter a brief incantation that sent bolts of lightning cascading from her fingertips to engulf Nowhere's form. His body arched with pain and his eyes met Miri's for an instant. In that moment, she thought she saw Nowhere again, not whatever force was controlling his body, a look of sadness replacing the twisted fury on his face.

"Nowhere!" she called again. "Fight it! You can do it!"

"No, he cannot," Nowhere's body said.

Miri's voice drew Demas's attention, and he shifted so he could see both the spider-thing and Nowhere, finally recognizing the tiefling as an enemy. Brendis struck a mighty blow that flared with divine radiance, and the chitin shell shattered under the force of it. Tiny red spiders scattered in a wave that washed over Demas, sending him staggering backward.

"No!" Miri screamed.

Demas stumbled back and hit the arch, sparking a flare of crimson light as the image inside the arch flickered. Hundreds of the crystal spiders vanished through the archway as Demas fought to regain his balance. Terror distorted his normally serene countenance, a fear like Miri had never seen on his face. Brendis dropped his sword and grabbed Demas's arm, then Nowhere leaped.

He covered five yards as easily as a single step, slamming into Demas's body when he landed. He pushed the Sword of the Gods out of Brendis's grip and through the arch, sending Brendis sprawling on the floor with one mighty kick, then swept his arm through both supports of the arch.

Miri dove for the arch, too late. The forest scene winked out as the arch collapsed, sealing Demas in whatever world lay beyond. Cold fear and despair gripped her heart. How did everything go wrong so quickly? she thought. We were doing so well.

Scarlet light blazed from the wrecked arch to cast Nowhere's huge shadow across the vault as he faced the wizard. "Sherinna," he said. "He had such strong feelings for you."

Nowhere's hand twitched sharply, and he looked sharply down at it. "Once I kill you, his resolve will be shattered."

So he's still fighting, Miri thought. Fighting against this thing's control, whatever it is.

"How do we fight this thing?" she asked aloud. "Can we get it out of Nowhere without killing him?"

Brendis got slowly to his feet, obviously in a lot of pain. He looked to Sherinna.

"I have an idea," Sherinna said. "But it's not a very good idea."

"Right now, it's all we have," Miri said.

The tiefling was fighting hard for control of his body—much harder than Nu Alin had expected. He struggled to keep the body under control, and to make sure that no sign of the struggle was visible to the three enemies he faced. He could not display his weakness.

Nowhere felt like he was deep underwater, struggling to reach the surface as his lungs burned for air. The thing, whatever it was that had seized his body, was getting ready to kill Sherinna. Using his body. He couldn't let that happen.

A spasm went through the body as Nu Alin's control wavered. He saw the wizard, Sherinna, raise her hands and chant the syllables of a spell. He tried to leap at her, to strike her and disrupt the energies of her spell before she could cast it, but the body would not respond. He took a few staggering steps forward, then Sherinna's spell took effect.

Motes of gray-blue light danced around Nowhere's body, and Nu Alin felt it stiffen. The magic hindered his control and seemed to help the tiefling exert his own will. Nu Alin began gathering his energy and his essence, preparing to leave this body and claim another if the battle took a turn for the worse.

"Sherinna . . ." Without Nu Alin's consent, the lips formed her name and the breath gave it voice.

Nu Alin could no longer collect sense information from the lower part of the body, nor could he move the legs to walk. Sherinna stepped close. He tried to strike her, to drive her away, but the arms would not respond to his commands.

Water streaked Sherinna's face. Nu Alin didn't understand it—he tried to probe the tiefling's thoughts but found them closed to him. He pooled his substance in the tiefling's throat, but he found his own form congealing, thickening, growing slower and less responsive to his will.

What has she done?

Her lips brushed the tiefling's mouth, and the last bit of sensation he experienced from the body was the softness of them as they touched his. Nowhere's flesh was hard, unyielding, dead— it was stone, and his own substance was crystallizing as well. Too late, he tried to expel himself from the tiefling's mouth, but the stone mouth was closed, no exit remained to him, and then he too was stone.

I have failed, he thought. But someday, somehow, I will finish what we have begun. I swear it by the Chained God and the Voidharrow.

Then he thought no more.

The Beginning

To chart the progress of the Abyssal Plague pick up a copy of the prologue novel, The Mark of Nerath *by Bill Slavicsek. And read on as the Voidharrow takes root in the world with* The Temple of Yellow Skulls *by Don Bassingthwaite.*

THE ABYSSAL PLAGUE

Continues in

DUNGEONS & DRAGONS®

THE TEMPLE OF
YELLOW
SKULLS

DON
BASSINGTHWAITE

MARCH 2011

DUNGEONS & DRAGONS®

FROM THE RUINS OF FALLEN EMPIRES, A NEW AGE OF HEROES ARISES

It is a time of magic and monsters, a time when the world struggles against a rising tide of shadow. Only a few scattered points of light glow with stubborn determination in the deepening darkness.

It is a time where everything is new in an ancient and mysterious world.

BE THERE AS THE FIRST ADVENTURES UNFOLD.

THE MARK OF NERATH
Bill Slavicsek
August 2010

THE SEAL OF KARGA KUL
Alex Irvine
December 2010

The first two novels in a new line set in the evolving world of the DUNGEONS & DRAGONS® game setting. If you haven't played . . . or read D&D® in a while, your reintroduction starts in August!

ALSO AVAILABLE AS E-BOOKS!
Follow us on Twitter @WotC_Novels

WELCOME TO THE DESERT WORLD
OF ATHAS, A LAND RULED BY A HARSH
AND UNFORGIVING CLIMATE, A LAND
GOVERNED BY THE ANCIENT AND
TYRANNICAL SORCERER KINGS.
THIS IS THE LAND OF

CITY UNDER THE SAND
Jeff Mariotte
OCTOBER 2010

*Sometimes lost knowledge is
knowledge best left unknown.*

FIND OUT WHAT YOU'RE MISSING IN THIS
BRAND NEW DARK SUN® ADVENTURE BY
THE AUTHOR OF *COLD BLACK HEARTS.*

ALSO AVAILABLE AS AN E-BOOK!
THE PRISM PENTAD
Troy Denning's classic DARK SUN
series revisited! Check out the great new editions of
*The Verdant Passage, The Crimson Legion,
The Amber Enchantress, The Obsidian Oracle,*
and *The Cerulean Storm.*

Want to Know Everything About Dragons?
Immerse yourself in these stories inspired by
The New York Times best-selling

A PRACTICAL GUIDE TO

DRAGONS

RED
Dragon Codex
978-0-7869-4925-0

BRONZE
Dragon Codex
978-0-7869-4930-4

BLACK
Dragon Codex
978-0-7869-4972-4

BRASS
Dragon Codex
978-0-7869-5108-6

GREEN
Dragon Codex
978-0-7869-5145-1

SILVER
Dragon Codex
978-0-7869-5253-3

GOLD
Dragon Codex
978-0-7869-5348-6

Experience the

power and magic

of dragonkind!

Follow us on Twitter @WotC_Novels

Books for
Young Readers

Enjoy these fantasy adventures inspired by
The New York Times best-selling
Practical Guide series!

MONSTER SLAYERS

A Companion Novel to *A Practical Guide to Monsters*
Lukas Ritter
.978-0-7869-5484-1
Battle one menacing monster after another!

NOCTURNE

A Companion Novel to *A Practical Guide to Vampires*
L.D. Harkrader
978-0-7869-5502-2
Join a vampire hunter on a heart-stopping quest!

Aldwyns Academy

A Companion Novel to *A Practical Guide to Wizardry*
Nathan Meyer
978-0-7869-5504-6
**Enter a school for magic where even the first day
can be (un)deadly!**

Follow us on Twitter @WotC_Novels

Don't wait until you're accepted into wizardry school to begin your career of adventure.

This go-to guide is filled with essential activities for wannabe wizards who want to start

RIGHT NOW!
Ever wonder how to:

Make a monster-catching net?
Improvise a wand?
Capture a werewolf?
Escape a griffon?
Check a room for traps?

Find step-by-step answers to these questions and many more in:

Young Wizards Handbook:

HOW TO TRAP
A ZOMBIE,
TRACK
A VAMPIRE,
AND OTHER HANDS-ON ACTIVITIES
FOR MONSTER HUNTERS

by A.R. Rotruck

Follow us on Twitter @WotC_Novels